Quest For The Crescent Moon
Book 1
Healer

Michelle L. Levigne

www.YeOldeDragonBooks.com

Ye Olde Dragon Books
P.O. Box 30802
Middleburg Hts., OH 44130

www.YeOldeDragonBooks.com

2OldeDragons@gmail.com

Chapter One

Sholeh woke from hazy dreams of fire falling from the sky and the songs of the sea holders shredding into screams. She lay still, sweat soaking her thin sleeping shift despite the breeze off the water. Her heart raced loudly enough to drown the song drifting up from the shore.

"Please, Verdidan, blessed Unseen …" she whispered, her throat dry and tight enough to make her prayer feel like sand in her mouth.

The songs whispering across the water faded the visions of death and destruction. She opened her eyes and turned over, searching for the sunrise in her window.

Her mother Adastra's house sat on the highest ridge of land on the northern tip of Isle of the Moon. The ridge divided the island, with most homes on the western side, and the archives, scholars' buildings, healer halls and all the crafting halls and docks on the eastern side. The sunrise always touched Sholeh's home first, and the long columned porches where the worship singers practiced. As she grew, she had learned that with high position came heavy responsibility.

That responsibility included dealing with threats to the safety and sanctity of Isle of the Moon. Sholeh's father and six brothers led in the defense of their island, the sacred texts, and the hidden springs of healing water, serving Adastra, Keeper of Songs and chief healer.

Sitting up and rubbing at her eyes, Sholeh blamed her dreams on the discussions she and her brothers had listened to, between their parents, aunts and uncles, and others on the island's Council. For the past two years, increasingly grim tales had come across the water with the tribes that ventured over the waves to trade with the islanders. Tylanok, a despot and despoiler of many lands, was working his way south and east. First he had to overcome the small nations that lived along the deep curve of the coast to the west, before he could make the leap of six days of sailing to reach Isle of the Moon. Adastra regularly led the islanders in prayers for the strength and protection of the people of the coast, who stood between Isle of the Moon and those who would despoil the treasures Verdidan had put into their guardianship.

Tylanok approached, even if his pace was slowed. Just last night Adastra and Ilward and the Council had discussed the news that his weapons included flaming vats of pitch that he flung through the air from massive catapults. Whatever those vats hit burned long and hot, and the flames were nearly impossible to drown with water.

Sholeh shuddered now, remembering tiny fragments of her dreams. Enormous globs of flames, as big as her home, fell into the sea. The sea holders screamed as they boiled to death.

"It will not happen," Sholeh muttered as she rolled out of her bed. Her bare feet hit the chilly tiles and she shivered harder as she peeled off her sleeping shift and reached for her binders. Then she pulled on the short, sturdy tunic she had worn yesterday to walk the warm sands of the shore, looking for debris washed up by the last storm, raking up the debris and smoothing the sand to prepare for a day of song and worship. She would have to hurry home to bathe, change her clothes, and join her family on the porch overlooking the shore for worship.

First, she needed to check the sea holders. Their song continued despite the warm sunlight spilling across the water, and that was unusual. For them to sing beyond the silver-light at dawn and dusk hinted at things Sholeh had never experienced in her fourteen years of life, but had only read about. All her lessons filled her head with a sense of dread, so she no longer noticed the chill of the tiles under her bare feet. She slipped over the low sill of her window and careened down the eastern slope, out of the formal gardens surrounding the house, heading for the shore.

A woman in a blue robe walked down the long, pink marble steps to the water gate. Sholeh stumbled when she saw her, then she sped up. She looked up the smooth pathway to the house and saw her mother, Adastra, standing at the edge of the porch. Her white sleeping shift rippled in the morning breeze and her white hair hung unbound past her knees, glistening contrast to the warm, breadcrust tones of her skin. Sholeh turned her path to the tall arch of pink marble embedded with seashells that marked the dividing line between land and sea. She silently chanted, *Please, please, please*, in time with the slapping of her bare feet on the wet sand. With a flying leap, she vaulted up onto the platform just before the arch, a few heartbeats after the woman with her silver-toned skin and short-cropped silver hair vanished into the shade of the arch.

She fully expected to find nothing but a blue robe lying on the bench that curved along the inside of the arch room, and dying ripples in the water. Perhaps she might glimpse a sleek body vanishing into the shadows of the green marble shelter that extended under the water. A yelp escaped her throat as she came face-to-face with the woman, nearly colliding with her as her feet slipped on the wet marble.

"Sholeh," the woman whispered. "How lovely. I feared I would never see you again, and yet here you are. Verdidan blesses me."

"Great-grandmother." The girl swallowed hard and went down on one knee, bowing her head for the blessing touch.

Shyreen laughed and bent to press her cheek to the girl's, and hugged her as she drew Sholeh back to her feet. The touch of her skin, sleek and damp, as if the transformation would occur right that moment, wrung another shiver from the girl. She clung to the elderly woman when Shyreen gripped her shoulders to move her back to arm's length.

"No need to fear or weep, child," she whispered, the pitch of her voice rising as her neck thickened.

"I dreamed—"

"Yes, as did we all. I was chosen to speak our water visions to your mother. You are to go on a quest, dear one." Her silver-hued eyes darkened. "We shall not speak again before I am called home to Verdidan's Rest. It shall be many years, I think, before you return to our home, and even then … I cannot see clearly. You must be strong. You must beware and be ready. Remember my love goes with you always."

"Great-grand—" Sholeh choked as the woman kissed her on both cheeks and then her forehead and stepped away, turning as she slid out of her robe. The girl took the robe, clutching it to her chest as Shyreen bent and slid headfirst into the water, arms melting into her sides and her legs joining together. The silver tones of her skin deepened before she vanished into the shadows and the green marble tunnel filled with water.

Swallowing hard, Sholeh stayed there on the edge of the water, waiting, praying for one last glimpse, though she knew her great-grandmother would not speak or look back once she had finished her transformation into the graceful sea holder. Closing her eyes, she was surprised to feel two hot tears trickle down and catch in the corners of her mouth. After a few moments, the girl hung up the robe with all the others, in soft shades of blue and green and pink, waiting for the next sea holder who returned from the water with messages from Verdidan.

Her breath came hard, ragged, for a few steps, as she turned and walked out of the arched shelter. Her legs inexplicably ached as she followed the marble path up to the platform where Adastra waited, arms clutching her waist and tears drying on her cheeks. As Sholeh neared the top, her mother held out her arms and tried to smile. They clung to each other as the song of the sea holders faded. When the cries of shore birds took over, Sholeh turned to look out over the water. White speckled the silver-shimmering surface of the water where the sea holders leaped and dove down, swimming back out to the open sea, beyond the invisible line where the two peninsulas, north and south, reached out to each other from many days of sailing away.

"She feared she would not be able to say goodbye," Adastra murmured. She smoothed Sholeh's long, straight white hair back from her face. "You are nearly as tall as I am, and yet I didn't notice until now."

"Where am I going?"

"Many places, my darling. You and your cousins. The hope of our people and our guardianship goes with you." She looked down at herself and seemed to find something amusing in the nearly sheer white cloth fluttering around her knees.

"Then I won't go alone. Good." Sholeh managed a smile and followed her mother up the marble path, back to the house. She stumbled slightly as she crossed from pink marble to silver-white, feeling as if she had made some irrevocable change.

"Yes … and no." Adastra shook her head, raising a hand for silence when Sholeh opened her mouth to ask what she meant. "Dress quickly and go fetch your cousins, everyone who has passed into womanhood. Have them gather in the Painted Hall."

Sholeh murmured acquiescence and followed her mother into the shadows of the columned breezeway that divided their home into two parts. To the left were the living quarters, to the right the archives and the council chambers and the audience chambers. Separate buildings going down the slopes on both sides housed officials and the classrooms where healers and singers learned their duties and craft, and historians worked. Beyond that were the workrooms where healers compounded and brewed and stored the medicines that made Isle of the Moon revered. Beyond them were the rooms where worshippers joined to lift their voices to Verdidan, and the ill came to be healed.

In the breezeway, Adastra turned left for her quarters, likely to dress for the day. Sholeh turned left also, but took stairs on the outside of the building, climbing to the second level. The daughters of their family lived there when they were old enough to leave their mothers and begin their training and discover their gifts, as singers, scholars, or healers. The instruction to fetch all her cousins who had passed into womanhood was clear enough, meaning only the female cousins. She wondered about the male cousins, and her brothers. Would they have other tasks, when the daughters of the family went out on the journey decreed by the visions of the sea holders? She couldn't imagine leaving Isle of the Moon without one of her brothers or cousins as a guard and guide. The men of their family line usually chose among three vocations in life: scholar, healer, or warrior. All her brothers and most of her mother's brothers were warriors, explorers, or tasked with dealing with the world that lay beyond the protective barrier of the sea.

~~~~~

Sholeh had time between giving her cousins the instructions to gather in the Painted Hall and arriving there herself. She bathed quickly, braided her hair and put on her best dress and sandals. On the way to the hall, she took the time to hurry through the kitchens in the lower level of the residence portion of the house. She went in through the door that gave outside access to the chill-room, down the stairs into the gloom and damp,
~~~~~

to get a skin of milk. Chances were good no one else had time to eat. She took the door on the other side of the chill-room, to go through the kitchen for a stack of wooden cups.

"Ah, good girl," Aunt Rayeen called, when Sholeh stepped through the door into the kitchen with a skin hanging over her shoulder. She gestured with her elbow at a long serving tray of wooden cups and a stack of biscuits. Her hands were busy, cutting up apples. Two more aunts stood on the other side of the long wooden preparation table, cutting up peaches and pitting cherries. "That's three crescents you two both owe me."

"Auntie!" Sholeh tried to look scandalized as she stepped over to the end of the table to pick up the tray. "You didn't bet on which of us would come first to find something to eat, did you?"

"Guilty," Aunt Noor said, with a toss of her shaggy head of fiery curls. "I'm a terrible influence on all of you."

"Addie said you spoke with Great-grand," Aunt Sireena said. "What did she tell you?"

Sholeh shrugged as she picked up the tray. "Traveling."

"And?" Rayeen stopped the girl with a touch on her shoulder.

"She said goodbye." Her voice threatened to break on the last word.

"That could mean a dozen different things," Noor said. She reached out, her milk-pale hand damp with peach juice, and cupped Sholeh's warm brown cheek. "Don't take up the weight of the world any sooner than Verdidan tells you to, understand?"

The other two aunts murmured agreement. Sholeh tried to smile and hurried out of the kitchen. Backing through the doorway to push the door open with her backside, she paused just a heartbeat to capture the image in her memory. Rayeen and Sireena were her mother's sisters, cut from the same cloth with the same wheat bread complexions and moon-white hair, pointed chins and wide cheekbones, tall and elegantly strong in all their movements. Noor had married into their family, tiny and pale-skinned with amazing green-blue eyes and hair that her husband, Syrus, teased her could be seen glowing like a torch on a moonless night. She belonged as if she had grown up with them, even though she came from one of the mystical mountain tribes from lands far north of Isle of the Moon. The three aunts were royalty in their own right, priestesses in the service of Verdidan, yet just as comfortable in stained aprons and roughspun clothes working in the vast kitchen, as they were sitting around the council table or leading worship through song and dance.

Sholeh loved them dearly. She shuddered hard enough she nearly dropped the tray, when it struck her that she would be leaving them behind just as surely as she would leave her mother and father and brothers. If Great-grandmother Shyreen felt the need to say goodbye, what were the chances Sholeh would be gone so long she might never speak with her aunts again? Granted, they would join the sea holders if they were blessed with the gift, but not everyone in their family line made the transformation. Even if they did join the visionaries and seers, they might never come out of the water to speak with their descendants.

"Please, Verdidan ..." Sholeh's throat felt sticky-dry so she could hardly swallow. Her mind felt just as sticky, refusing to form a prayer. She trusted the holy writings that said Verdidan knew the unspoken prayers of his servants, and the flamewings carried their concerns and joys, thanks and petitions upward, day and night.

Despite her delay in the kitchen, she was still the first to arrive in the Painted Hall. She put the tray down on the long table that ran down the center of the room, careful to nudge aside the stacks of wax tablets and styluses, bound parchment bundles, inkwells and metal-tipped pens. She filled ten of the wooden cups and carefully tied up the spout of the skin of milk before laying it down on the tray. Not everyone would want milk, and those who came later could serve themselves. No sounds of approaching feet came through the door she had left open, so she picked up a cup and sipped as she walked over to the closest mural. Since she had left training and took up her duties in the healing hall with Myxell, her grandmother Arryen's cousin, she hadn't had an opportunity to study the murals that gave the Painted Hall its name.

The history of her family and its stewardship and the history of their people were recorded in images here, and in writing in the archives. As a child, Sholeh had loved coming to the Painted Hall for lessons. The storytellers made history sound exciting and as recent as her grandparents' youth, not several centuries ago. And certainly not as dry as the minutiae of details stored in the archival records.

A shiver brushed across her scalp, making her feel as if a distant wind tried to lift her hair. She studied the mural showing sea holders defending Isle of the Moon by overturning the longboats of invaders, then pulling them down to the sea floor to drown. The images reminded her of her dreams, of fire burning the sea holders beneath the waves. She moved on to the next mural, depicting the artisans harvesting gold from the tunnels under the island. Refined, it was formed into thin sheets to hold the sacred writings, the prophecies and holy words, preserving them for the ages.

Voices echoed down the interior stairs into the hall as she stopped at the mural that was the shortest of all, a simple square, as wide and as high as her spread arms. Men and wolves stood in silhouette against different phases of the moon. No details, just black silhouettes. She stretched out one finger to touch the muzzle of a wolf raised up on its hind legs, head tilted up and back, mouth open in a howl she could hear in her spirit. When she was a child, she had stayed up on the nights of the full moon, straining her ears to hear the howls, praying for Verdidan to send the guardian wolves back to the Isle of the Moon. They never came.

Her cousins spilled into the room in a straggly line, two and three at a time until all eighteen were there. They weren't all the daughters of her mother's siblings. Some were the daughters of cousins and granddaughters of her grandmother's cousins. It didn't matter how far the girls stood from the direct line of descent: if they had a gift, a talent useful in service to the Unseen, they were trained.

Their chatter slowed and quieted as they came into the room and gathered around the table and snatched up cups and biscuits.

"Do you know anything?" Elli asked, joining Sholeh in front of the mural of the guardian wolves. She offered half of her biscuit.

Sholeh hesitated, then reasoned that her mother hadn't told her *not* to tell anyone what she knew. One more glance at the wolves that had filled her imagination as a child and launched dreams of adventure and travel, then she turned back to the table. The other girls seemed to be watching her and gathered around as she stepped up to the far end.

"Does this have anything to do with the holders singing longer than usual this morning?" Careena said.

"Great-grandmother Shyreen came to speak with Mother about a vision. I think we are being sent on a quest." Sholeh turned her empty cup between her hands, studying the thin film of milk clinging to the sides.

"You always wanted to go looking for the guardians," Thalia said with a smile. "Wouldn't it be lovely if that was the end of our quest?"

"When you return," Adastra said, coming into the hall, with the members of the Council walking behind her, "perhaps we should send you for training with the seers." Her smile was weary, but it broadened when excited whispers spun out among the young women and girls.

"Have the guardians been found?" Sholeh said. "Is that what Great-grandmother told you? The seers know where they went?"

"No, only that the guardians do still live. You all are being sent, throughout the entire world, even to the far eastern lands." She turned and gestured for Great-uncle Harron.

"Prophecy has been given," he said in his whispery, sand-in-the-wind voice that still had the power to penetrate to the far reaches of the long room.

> *"Flee!*
> *Stolen fire and poisoned flame fall from the skies*
> *Blood guardians must return*
> *The waters of life shall be death*
> *The enemy cannot cross until he holds the holy blood*
> *He will move the shore*
> *And hold the shore*

> *And the holy line will dwindle to dust and darkness*
> *Joined and ever parted*
> *Two bodies and one soul, one mind*
> *The holy line will find the blood guardians*
> *The two will be one -- flesh and soul*
> *Together, to swim the waters of death, to regain the moon*
> *Beware the deceived do not mirror darkly, merging blood*
> *and death and life and moon, or all shall be lost and the hidden*
> *wisdom shall be dust upon the storm*
> *The splintered line will be rewoven*
> *The guardians will return*
> *Land and sea will be pure*
> *The air will again fill with wings and fire will cleanse."*

Sholeh held her breath and tried not to hear all the questions rising up in her mind. All that mattered was holding onto every word of the prophecy. Common sense said that most of it would not be understood until the time of fulfillment had come, or even passed. Those words would guide her actions and were the reason why the daughters of the family were being sent on this quest.

The moon and guardians and blood were linked in her mind, making her heart leap against her ribs. This was her childhood dream, darkened with urgency and misty with questions. Was it wrong of her to think she and her cousins were being sent at long last to find the guardians and bring them back to the Isle of the Moon?

Chapter Two

"Tylanok approaches," Adastra said, after a long silence as the ripples from the words of prophecy faded away. "He attacks with words, with lies, with gifts. He never outright defies Verdidan's teachings, but always asks questions, planting seeds of doubt that sprout into tangling, choking vines of disobedience. He fills the air with a poisoned fog that dulls the mind and blinds the eyes, only resorting to his clinging fire, to brute force, when those who trust to Verdidan continue to hold fast in the face of man's false, blind wisdom." She turned and held out her hand to Ilward, who came up from the back of the long line of council members.

Sholeh caught her breath, stunned to see her father wearing his sword, his battered leather breastplate and greaves, with his quiver full of brass-tipped, black-feathered arrows hanging off one shoulder, and his unstrung bow off the other. His ebony skin and blue-black hair had never before made him seem so much a fierce, deadly shadow. Ilward had earned his position as Captain of the Guard for Isle of the Moon long ago. It was no honorary position because he was the husband of the Singer.

"Tylanok has conquered the far northern kingdoms." His gaze swept the cluster of young women and girls as he spoke, his voice rough, thanks to an enemy who had tried to slit his throat when he was young, serving as bodyguard for one of the island's ambassadors. "We can thank Verdidan that those northerners are as cold in their minds and blood as the snow on their mountains. They resist, despite the devastation they have suffered. If we are blessed, it will take Tylanok years to secure his control over those territories. More time for us to prepare. Our island is the prize he seeks. Only a fool would think Tylanok will be happy with land and riches and slaves. He wants the collected wisdom and healing powers of our island and the holy waters, and the prophetic gifts of the sea holders. Word has come that he has promised his allies they will be free to cross the waters and step on our shore and go into the caverns to drink of the healing waters whenever they choose. He has vowed he will melt the golden sheets holding Verdidan's teachings, to make ornaments for his concubines."

His gaze caught on Sholeh and she trembled, seeing the fire in his crystalline gray eyes, which only she had inherited.

"He has vowed he will geld the sons of our island and he will give our daughters as gifts to his generals and his allies."

"They will not cross the water and they will not take our shores," Elli said, stepping out in front of all the cousins. She was the oldest of all the unmarried girls. She stood tall, her voice strong with determination. "Our warriors are strong and our allies are loyal, and even if they come in ships as large as the island, the sea holders will let no one pass the reef and cross the water to us."

"True. Yet we are not so foolish as to believe that we cannot be betrayed or make fatal errors. We must be prepared for every ending to our tale, even if that is disaster. Failure. What will happen to us if the enemy sets foot on Isle of the Moon?" He waited, sweeping the young women with his gaze again.

"They will forbid Verdidan's people to worship and to sing and to learn." Sholeh kept her voice steady and clear, despite the shuddering deep inside. "They will try to starve us. We are to be sent on a quest. Where? To find what?"

"Not what," Adastra said. She and Ilward clasped hands. "Who. The guardians were lost to us. Legend disagrees on how they were lost. The full moon burned too hot in their blood, and they succumbed. That much is clear, but only that much. Perhaps they were lost to us or stolen away or sent away or they fled. Perhaps the separation came through treachery or arrogance or impurity. Some fault of ours or some fault of theirs. The why and how no longer matter. We believe the prophecy given this morning by the sea holders directs us to seek out the guardians. Purity of blood and heart will succeed when all the wisdom and skill of mere mortals fail." She blinked rapidly several times, hinting that she fought tears. "As well, we were advised to send you away to keep you free of Tylanok's grasp, if we should somehow fail in our guardianship."

Aunt Noor stepped forward and gestured at the panel depicting the men and wolves. "What do legends tell us of the guardians?"

"Our island was their home first, and Verdidan sent them to find our ancestors when they were few in numbers," Elli said. "This was their sanctuary. They found healing here, cooling for the fire in their blood. The crescent moon grants peace and control, countering the fire of the full moon. They brought our ancestors here to become stewards of the holy writings and the healing waters. They vowed their lives and their souls to serve us and guard us, and went away when they could no longer keep that vow."

"What else do the legends say?" Her lips twisted, fighting a mischievous smile when many of the girls glanced at each other. She sighed. "Sholeh, certainly you know?"

"Aunt?" Sholeh's face warmed when she caught whispers among her younger cousins. When she had shared a dormitory room with some of them, she earned some teasing for learning everything she could about the guardians. "I know that they are more than just wolves, but there are too many conflicting reports and stories in the archives to know what is truth and what is a wish-tale."

"True, the guardians are above wolves much like the sea holders are above dolphins, which you will surely encounter as you cross the sea. What do the wish-tales say, then?"

Sholeh glanced at her parents. Adastra nodded slowly, her smile conveying that it was not just permitted to speak the speculations, no matter how unbelievable, but necessary. She licked her lips. "Many stories claim the guardians are two bodies, but one soul. So many stories say the guardians have the souls and minds of men and can travel back and forth between man and wolf. They are not like the sea holders, who only return to their Human form when they are tasked to speak wisdom from Verdidan. They can change their form at will." She spread her hands, surrendering to what she sensed her aunt, one of the highest-ranking scholars on the island, wanted her to say. "There are so many stories, if it were not so strange, if it did not smack of evil magic, of things that come from the Flaming Deep … I would believe it could be true."

~~~~~

"Are you afraid you'll find out you're seasick?" The male voice coming from the doorway startled Sholeh out of her thoughts.

"Are you?" Sholeh laughed and darted across her room to hug her oldest brother, Indago.

She shrieked when he picked her up and spun her around, fast enough her feet swung out, threatening to knock the stack of parchment sheets and wax tablets off her low study table. Then the import of his words struck her. She barely waited for him to put her feet back on the floor before she pushed herself away to arm's length. His grin had faded into that grim, stoic control that always made her feel safe and protected.

"I did not get sick on the voyage to the northern horn. Am I going on one of the ships heading across the open sea, then?"

The cousins had been dispersed to their quarters to pack for long journeys, then to report to their duty or study assignments, to gather up the supplies they would all need. Those assigned to assist scholars and work in the archives were to gather up and copy all the information on the guardians that the searchers would need to know. Those working in the healer halls, such as Sholeh, were to assemble all the herbs and ointments and other healing supplies they might need to deal with illness and injuries. The ability to offer healing should help them find acceptance and hospitality in the foreign lands where they journeyed. Their brothers and cousins and uncles were to receive their assignments as guards, and the destinations for each of the girls. Sholeh prayed Indago had been given the duty of protecting her.
~~~~~

"Through the horns, across the open sea, straight east." He bent down enough their foreheads touched and lowered his voice. "To the coast of Nedaia, and then inland."

"Nedaia!" She jerked back, stepping away from him, half-hoping he would burst out laughing and tell her he was joking. "Nedaia is a land of brutes. Not even their kings learn to read. They leave it to their scribes and then mock them for it. They enslave each other. Their women and children are property."

"Olee, you know that isn't true."

"Close enough to the truth." She fought the urge to stick her tongue out at him for using that pet name she insisted she had outgrown. "Why Nedaia, when there are so many other lands we could go to, closer lands? Wouldn't it make more sense that the guardians went to the horns and traveled either north or south to the mountains, where wolves can vanish and hunt?"

"Nedaia has legends of wolves who walk in the light of day in the skins of men. Among all their tales of multiple gods and goddesses, many of their gods take on the forms of animals. Including wolves."

"Multiple gods." She dropped down onto the edge of her bed. "Fools. Lawless, selfish, foolish people. There is no god but Verdidan, creator. Anyone who claims to be a god is a servant of Biss."

"The tales say these gods have powers that prove they are gods."

"*We* have powers. That does not make us equal with Verdidan." She shuddered, fighting down the surge of anger that she suspected had its roots in the sharp-edged, sour taste of fear in her mouth.

"That is the difference between them and us." He sighed loudly and leaned back against the wall next to her door. "You didn't expect to go so far away, did you?"

"Far enough for an adventure." She echoed his sigh. "I think I am a silly little girl. You will be there with me, won't you?"

"If Father hadn't assigned me, I would have insisted."

"This is wrong." Everything went still inside her as understanding crept through her mind like a bee crawling through frozen honey.

"What—"

"They are stripping our island of the best warriors. They are sending us as far away as possible. Does Father fear the shore will indeed be lost?"

"Perhaps, and perhaps not. We have time to build up the numbers of our warriors before Tylanok gets here. But here is what frightens Father, and everyone on the Council. Tylanok's brutes are said to march in a river of blood." Indago's face seemed to age ten years in as many seconds. He closed his eyes and slid down a few hands against the wall. "The power that resides in pure blood, pure bodies, pure hearts ... even if so much of it is a false belief, *our enemies believe in it*. They wish to take that power away from us. They believe if they capture all the virgins of our family and enslave them, overpower them, brutalize them, and father children on them, they will overpower us and capture the island. What they believe has power, even if it is a false belief."

"So we must flee."

"So we must hide the treasure and take the power from our enemy's hands."

~~~~~

Two Moons Later...

The dolphins along the far eastern shore of the sea, as Sholeh learned to her delight, were not entirely without intelligence. They reacted with pleasure when she and her cousins touched their minds, and they could carry on simple conversations in images, carrying an impression of the squeaks and clicks and squeals of their vocal language. When she thought of the sea holders who inhabited the sea far to the west and guarded the waters around Isle of the Moon, she shuddered at the difference between them and dolphins. There was an essential something lacking in dolphins, despite her growing understanding and appreciation of their wit and culture. Did she dare call it a missing soul?

She thought of her great-grandmother and other sea holders who had re-taken their Human form to walk on dry land and communicate with those left behind. Sholeh suspected they would laugh at her and gently scold her for daring to make such a judgment. Who could truly define what a soul was? Who could designate the worthiness of a being to possess a soul? Who was she, Sholeh, to presume to make such a determination or assumption? That would be like assuming that just because she was her mother's only daughter, that automatically made her heir to the leadership of the island. The most worthy of her generation would be chosen, by the Council and by the searching and weighing of the sea holders, and by the choice of the flamewings. In essence, chosen by Verdidan. Leadership as the Singer was a gift and a grave duty, not a privilege and not an inheritance to be expected or taken lightly.

If she found the guardians and persuaded them to return to Isle of the Moon, would that mark her as worthy?

If another of her cousins found the guardians, would that make her the heir?

If she didn't carry all that responsibility, would she feel sad, or relieved?

If there was an island to return to, someday...

"Stop thinking such sad thoughts all the time," Indago scolded, coming up behind her perch in the prow of their ship. She sat with her skirts pulled up to her knees and her legs dangling so the spray from the
~~~~~

prow slamming into the waves wet her toes.

"Aren't you worried?" she countered, still facing forward, where the coast of Nedaia hovered like a dark smudge of smoke on the horizon.

"About home?" He stepped up next to her, so his leg, wrapped in the light-woven shipboard leggings, brushed against her bare shoulder. "If we can't trust our father and uncles and all Verdidan's dedicated warriors to hold the shore, even in the face of Tylanok's oily fire … I think we must trust Verdidan even if everyone else fails us."

"I know home is still there, but I fear." She leaned back to look up at him, grateful once again their parents had sent him as leader of the expedition force on her ship. To have a bit of home steadied her against the feeling of creeping unreality, after two moons of travel to the other side of the sea. Sometimes she feared that Isle of the Moon was nothing but a dream, or a wish-tale she had created to fight the sense she belonged nowhere, and to no one.

The bundle of gold leaves engraved with Verdidan's teachings, part of the essential supplies for each hunting party, should have been assurance enough that she had come from a real place. Where, in this barbaric land they had crossed the sea to explore, could she have found such delicately made, wondrous things? The gold-masters of the Isle of the Moon held the secret of pounding gold as thin and light as thistledown, so that one hundred sheets were barely as thick as her thumb, yet stiff and as impervious to breaking and bending as Indago's sword. She unwrapped the bound stack of sheets to read from them and lead in the morning worship and singing. Kept in her pack of waterproof cloth with other essential items, the bound leaves were her personal, sacred responsibility to protect. If the ship were rammed by marauders or sank in a storm, Sholeh would strap it to her back to keep it secure as she swam to shore. She sometimes feared the pack would drag her to the murky bottom of the sea with its weight.

Her responsibility to find the guardians, or at least determine if the tales of wolves that spoke with men's tongues were false or true, rested on her shoulders with an even heavier weight.

"The captain says we are safest here, ready to slip out of sight of the sentinels on land." Indago gestured at the smudge of land on the horizon. "The people of these lands believe that just beyond the horizon, the world ends like a tabletop and everything falls off. If anyone chases us, even the most desperate marauders won't follow, for fear they'll die."

"Safe doesn't fulfill our quest," she murmured.

"No, it doesn't." He bent down and brushed his arm against her shoulder, turning to hold his closed fist in front of her face.

Sholeh sighed and smiled and stuck her forefinger in the small gap where thumb and forefinger curled together. When she was small, it was a game for them. He would hold out both hands and she had to dig to find the treat he had hidden in one fist or the other. Indago's fist opened to reveal a thin square of folded reedsheet, startling a happy gasp from her. He chuckled as she snatched it and unfolded the sheet.

"Just shows how busy you've been, brooding over Nedaia, that you didn't see the messenger hawk from Cleita's ship arrive."

"Brooding." Sholeh stuck her tongue out at him, then reached up to catch hold of the railing over her head to pull herself to her feet. She leaned against him, holding out the sheet with the tiny, neat handwriting of their cousin, so they both could read it together.

The message was short enough, merely giving the star chart coordinates of their ship and proposing that they meet. A storm three days ago had forced the captain of Cleita's ship to turn south in crossing the sea. He calculated the ship was close enough to the northern reaches of Nedaia that they could meet and confer before Cleita's ship headed north for her assigned hunting territory.

Indago and Sholeh headed to the back of the ship and the high platform where the captain stood watch and controlled rudders and sails. They had barely finished climbing to the top of the platform, three man-heights above the main deck, when another messenger hawk winged in over the water from the south. Captain Wylles raised one eyebrow in silent question and waited while Indago convinced the small, fierce bird to land on his forearm and let him remove the tiny leather case from its leg.

"Loree," Sholeh announced, recognizing the emblem on the case that protected the piece of reedsheet from the elements. Her brother nodded as he unfolded it. He grinned after glancing over it, then handed it and the message from Cleita to the captain.

From the brief, half-sighed chuckle that escaped Captain Wylles, Sholeh easily guessed that their other cousin was proposing almost the same thing: meet up and confer before separating to go to their assigned hunting territories. This entire continent seemed to be filled with small countries where brutal people foolishly worshipped many gods and followed barbaric worship customs. She didn't blame her cousins for wanting a taste of home before diving into their duties.

Within half an hour, the messenger hawks were on their way back to their home ships. Captain Wylles kept their ship where it was, waiting for Loree's ship to meet up with them, then they would continue north together to meet with Cleita's ship, which was much farther away.

~~~~~

Cleita and Loree were both older than Sholeh. She found it discouraging and disappointing that both her cousins were so fearful of this far-off continent that they wanted to stay together. Cleita proposed that they combine forces, present an image of strength with three ships
~~~~~

and three crews, and go inland together, helping each other in their quest. Loree only hesitated for a moment before agreeing, looking both ashamed and hopeful. Sholeh wanted so strongly to agree with the plan, she almost felt seasick. That startled her, so she hesitated.

"The Council said we were to go small and quiet, to travel swiftly, and not to alarm anyone in any of the lands where we hunt," she said instead, after swallowing the sour taste of fear in her mouth.

"We can stay safe by convincing strangers that we are no threat, yes." Cleita glanced over her shoulder at the coastline, a little darker, a little closer, with some barely visible ridges. Then she shuddered and turned her back on the land and settled more firmly on the cushion set on the deck. "Wouldn't it be wiser to convince them that we are strong, that we have allies and numbers enough to defend ourselves?"

"You mean present a challenge for the idiots and brutes?" Garyon, third-oldest of Sholeh and Indago's brothers, nodded, his lip curling up on one side. "Oh, yes, let's offer them a target. Let's make them think we're rich, that we have something to defend—"

"We do," Loree said.

"What we consider valuable, these brutes would just melt down and use it to decorate their temples or their temple harlots." He stepped up a little closer to her and bent down to squeeze her shoulder. "The council had good reason for every instruction they gave us for carrying out our quest." He looked around the small circle they made on the forward deck, with the three girls sitting on cushions and the brothers and cousins and other blood-related warriors assigned to them standing behind them.

Their small group did make a fine show of force, with all the men in light armor and their swords strapped to their thighs. Still, her brother was right. They were more likely to escape notice if they presented an image finely balanced between being able to defend themselves and not being worth the trouble of chasing and attacking. Why stir up enough interest to wonder what they defended or present a challenge?

The Isle of the Moon protected its sacred treasures and kept its shores safe by having visible defenders, but in small enough numbers that no one wondered what those warriors protected. The sea holders and flamewings were ready to defend the island, but according to all the archives Sholeh had read, that hadn't been necessary in nearly a century. The guardians had patrolled the shore of the island, making the night and moonlight their domain. Of course, that had been centuries ago, before they succumbed to the allure of the full moon and bloodlust and the trap of the flesh.

Chapter Three

As she tried to gather her thoughts to persuade her cousins to obey the Council's instructions, Sholeh understood even more clearly why the guardians had to be found and returned to Isle of the Moon. Evil had come against them, against the sacred treasures and the holy knowledge stored there. Creatures of claw and fang and brute strength were needed to counter the strength and cruelty of Tylanok, the servant of Biss.

"Still ..." A smile caught up one corner of Garyon's mouth. "I wouldn't mind spending a little time together before we separate."

Loree blushed and looked down at her clasped hands. Cleita let out a gasping chuckle and reached across the circle to grasp Loree's elbows and shake her. Sholeh hated feeling as if she had missed something simple and obvious. It didn't help that both her cousins were older than her and she always felt as if she were several steps behind them.

Caron, Cleita's brother, shook his head. His mouth twitched as he visibly fought to scowl, but a grin took over. "I don't know if I should congratulate you two fools or not."

Sholeh caught her breath, seeing the momentary glance that Loree and Garyon exchanged. She felt as if the deck tilted on its side for just a moment, and everything shifted position in her perceptions. Loree and Garyon? She was the granddaughter of a cousin of Sholeh, Indago and Garyon's grandmother. The bloodlines had split far enough to permit marriage. She should be happy for them. And sad. They would have to wait until they returned home to perform the ceremony of binding. They certainly couldn't ask one of the unholy priests in this foreign land to officiate over their ceremony. While their bodies might be joined, how could their souls and minds begin the merging that would take the rest of their physical lives to complete?

Did they truly need a Singer to stand between them and Verdidan? If their hearts were pure and firmly decided, and they willingly gave themselves to each other, and asked Verdidan's blessing, why wouldn't they be truly and fully wed, their souls bound for eternity? Was a marriage only real if they stood before the leaders of the island to make their promises and drink from the binding cup?

"We need to hurry, then," she said, sliding forward onto her knees to reach out to hug Loree. "Let us find the guardians and hurry home, so we can celebrate."

The leaders of the three ships agreed they had to obey the Council's instructions and separate, each ship and hunting team to its assigned lands. However, just like the cousins, they found excuses for staying together for the next several days as they delayed approaching the nearest port to land. Sholeh sometimes woke in the morning from fragments of dreams that made her shudder, so she wondered if she was displaying the first vestiges of a prophetic gift. She said nothing about it, because it was very nice to have her cousins nearby, to step out onto the deck in the silvery light before dawn, raise her voice in worship singing, and hear voices join with hers from the ships to the right and left of her.

And yes, the longer they delayed, the more reluctant she grew to leave the ship, go inland, and begin her quest.

~~~~~

Four mornings after the three ships met, they tied up at Teviss, a large port where rocky promontories stretched out jagged arms like claw pincers, offering a deep harbor and high walls to shelter against storm winds. Cleita and Loree insisted that Sholeh had to come with them to find the marketplace in this busy, sprawling, smelly, loud city. She would be their interpreter when their limited vocabularies failed them. The sounds of hammers and people's voices raised in talk and laughter and argument reached the ships, soon after the sun appeared over the tops of buildings that stood an amazing six and seven stories tall. Each ship had been provided with two or three people who had learned the language of each land where their hunting teams had been assigned. The teams had spent the voyage across the open sea learning those tongues. The tongue of Nedaia served as a trade language for most of the kingdoms and countries that touched the great sea. While they knew the essential words in Nedaian, her cousins insisted Sholeh was better suited to helping them obtain fresh food and other supplies for their journeys inland.

Captain Wylles sent his two sons as assistants and guards for the three cousins. Even if the girls knew the local language and customs perfectly, it wouldn't be safe for three strangers, especially females, to wander the port city by themselves. Someone could assume they were escaped slaves or brothel girls looking for customers, or some other excuse to take them prisoner. The two boys in their early teens were the right escort: enough to protect them, enough to give them a sense of modesty and propriety, but not wealthy targets for kidnappers or thieves. Neither would they look so defenseless that slavers would try to take them.

Just the thought of all the precautions they had to follow in the marketplace made Sholeh weary. She agreed with the Council's instructions that each team hunting the man-wolf guardians should be small, to avoid notice. If she had gone by herself into the city to buy supplies, accompanied by the two boys but not her cousins, she suspected
~~~~~

she would have encountered far less notice. She could have covered her shining white hair with a veil.

Captain Wylles was wise to be reluctant to let them leave the ship. Their coloring was unusual enough to attract attention immediately. After the third stall, where they bought loaves of fresh, warm, fragrant bread as long as their forearms, the chorus of whispers that seemed to follow them through the marketplace had grown large enough to be annoying. How soon until annoyance turned to threat?

"Such rude folk," Cleita said in their own tongue, affecting the obnoxious, superior drawl of a woman who had come to the Isle of the Moon to study singing for a year.

She had assumed that claiming to be someone of importance in her far southern nation would grant her a place of prominence and apprenticeship with the highest ranked singer. When she got over her injured pride, she tried to buy that position. Her haughty manners had been a source of amusement for many of the cousins, and her humiliation served as an object lesson for those who were tempted to believe their bloodlines made them superior.

"Why is it so astounding to have white hair, but no lines on our faces?" Loree said. "Maybe we could find some face paints and make ourselves look old, the next time we visit a port town for supplies?"

"I think there should not be a next time," Sholeh said. She knew how her brothers would react when they returned to the ships. Which she hoped would occur as soon as possible.

As if thinking of Indago or Garyon was like shouting for them, she felt their presence. Trying not to seem obvious, she turned and looked around the marketplace. It took only a matter of seconds to find her brothers, and a handful of other men from the three ships. They wandered through the marketplace alone or in pairs, making purchases of their own, but always keeping their gazes on the women.

The next stop in the marketplace was a large stall down another street, where they bought skeins of thread and needles and lengths of cloth. The woman who took Sholeh's silver bits caught hold of the girl's hand in both of hers and rubbed it, front and back and leaned closer, studying her face and hair. Sholeh froze, then a quiet voice at the back of her mind laughed when she decided the woman wanted to see if her coloring rubbed off. Maybe people stared because they thought the cousins painted themselves? She was proven right a moment later by the woman's comment.

"What do you use to make your hair that color?" The merchant glanced over her shoulder, as if she wasn't supposed to talk to people outside of selling.

"Verdidan gave me my coloring."

"Who is she? Where is her stall?" A mischievous smile twisted her lips for a moment. "My man would stop breathing if I had hair your color."

"Verdidan is the one true god, the only god," Cleita said. "This is the hair and eyes and skin we were born with."

The woman took a step back, eyes widening as she looked back and forth between the cousins. She muttered, "Barbarians," and then tipped her head back and laughed.

"Who does she call barbarian?" Loree said in their own tongue. She turned to walk away with a sniff and her head tilted back in pique.

Cleita and Sholeh exchanged grins, gathered their purchases into their baskets, and hurried to follow.

The other end of the street emptied into an open, cobblestone-paved area with a tall fountain in the middle and multiple spigots for water to spill out. Women took turns filling tall pottery jars at the spigots. Stone troughs extended out from the fountain in a starburst pattern. Wooden panels near the center of the fountain were raised to fill the troughs with water. The women then scrubbed their clothes right there in public. Sholeh stared for a few seconds in fascination. Nedaians definitely had different standards for propriety and modesty. The three cousins and their escorts walked around the perimeter of the open space, where seven streets converged. They passed two offshoot streets and were aiming for the third, where a sign indicated they could find leather goods. They would need materials to repair boots and sandals if they were going to go inland for any length of time.

Shouts and clattering sounds erupted from the next street. A horse burst out of the end of the street, dragging a two-wheeled cart, tipped onto its side with its wheels in the air. The contents of the cart spilled out as it bumped over the uneven ground. People shouted and leaped out of the way. The horse snorted and screamed and jerked, darting one way and then the other.

"Sholeh." Loree dropped her basket to snatch at her cousin's arm. "Stop that horse—a child!" She pointed.

A child hung onto the inside of the cart, legs dragging on the rough ground, bouncing with every jerk and jolt. Sholeh hesitated. She had only a small gift for touching the minds of dogs and the ponies on Isle of the Moon. What made Loree think she could stop a frightened horse?

For half a heartbeat, Adastra's serene face filled Sholeh's mind. She shook her head slowly, her expression softly disappointed.

Sholeh closed her eyes and reached out with her spirit and her fleshly hands for the frightened horse.

No, not frightened. Angry. Hurting. Something had jabbed its backside. It was bleeding. Through the horse's nose, she smelled its blood.

The scent was maddening, hot, frightening. Sholeh blocked the smell from the horse's mind and soothed the sharp, hot sensation in its rump. She enfolded the horse with her thoughts, trying to calm the massive, sweating, unhappy beast.

Her head hurt and she felt slightly queasy. Loree wrapped an arm around her waist and whispered, "Well done," as the shouts around them changed pitch. Sholeh opened her eyes to see the horse standing still, snorting and breathing heavily, only a few paces away from them. Cleita hurried to the cart. The amazed, alarmed people stayed back. She knelt and caught hold of the wrists of the child, who still clung to the inside of the cart. As people calmed and turned away, back to their own business, now Sholeh heard the whimpering cries like the bleating of sheep from the boy, clothed in little more than a loincloth.

Cleita murmured to the child, struggling to get him to let go of his death-grip on the straps inside the cart. Loree gathered up their dropped baskets with the help of the two sailor boys, while Sholeh crossed the last few steps to the horse. It stared at her, nostrils flaring, foam streaking its long, grizzled brown muzzle. Trying to call up soothing thoughts, Sholeh reached for the frayed rope still hanging from the worn leather straps of the bridle.

More shouts cut through the calming, dispersing crowd. The horse snorted and tried to tug its head free. Sholeh whispered to it and held on. Two men approached. Their draping, purple-edged white cloaks, indicating they were men of rank and power, trailed behind them in the breeze. A handful of men followed them, wearing leather breastplates, high boots with metal straps, shields on their backs, and simple bucket helmets, with short swords strapped to their sides. Two men dragged a ragged man behind them, his hands bound with rope. His nose dripped blood and one eye looked puffy and he sneered as his gaze fell on the cart. The horse snorted and tried to tug its head free again. Sholeh guessed this was the man who had stabbed the horse.

Cleita stretched the injured boy out on the ground, turning enough to reveal him to the onlookers. Both noblemen let out cries of alarm and pushed through the last few people between them and the boy. The younger-looking one shoved Cleita aside and bent to scoop up the boy, who lay limp, his leg oddly twisted.

"Don't move him!" Cleita shouted, and shoved the man just as hard, before he could take the boy in his arms. "His leg is broken."

The other nobleman shouted words Sholeh didn't know, but she understood their meaning from the fury twisting his face. He gestured, and the two soldiers dragged their prisoner forward. The nobleman swung hard with his fist, knocking the prisoner off his feet.

"My son," the first man moaned, and went to his knees next to the boy. "Please, Pallon—someone—I will not lose him, too!"

"Lose him?" Loree stepped up next to Sholeh, with the two sailor boys from their ships behind her. "It's only a broken leg."

"Only?" he snarled, leaping to his feet. Then he seemed to see them for the first time. "What manner of women are you?"

"Sir." Wyllan, the older of the two boys stepped up to put himself between Loree and the stranger. "These ladies are from a far distant kingdom."

"I dare you to show me any kingdom where a broken leg is a small thing. He will lose his leg—he could die—he will not be able to ride or lead our household soldiers. How can he inherit if he is a useless cripple?"

"There are many things a man can do and not be considered useless." Loree shook her head and stared at him. Her voice strained, caught between pity and disbelief. "Cleita?"

"Yes, I can help him. The young heal easily," their cousin said.

During the few moments the man had been distracted, she had stretched out the boy's leg and now knelt over him, both hands gripping the slim lower leg bone. Cleita tipped her head back and closed her eyes, and liquid vowels spilled from her mouth, starting low as she sang the healing petition to Verdidan. Sholeh and Loree moved around to stand behind her, joining hands and resting their free hands on her shoulders, to share their life force. They raised their voices in the healing song, creating harmony. Sholeh closed her eyes just as the soft, pearly glow of healing power spilled from Cleita's fingertips to wrap around the leg.

She felt the spreading pool of silence through the fountain area. Soon the only sounds were of water spilling from the spigots, the soft flapping of banners in the gentle breeze, and the babbling of a few babies and smaller children many steps away. The horse no longer snorted and heaved, and the shuffling of booted feet on the hard-packed ground sounded loud the few times it occurred.

"All thanks to Verdidan, who gives us life and heals all our wounds and illnesses," Cleita whispered after they stopped singing. The music of the power they had called up lingered a few heartbeats longer, fading slowly to a soft chiming in the air. Then that too ended.

Sholeh opened her eyes and wasn't surprised to see the two noblemen and their soldiers and even the prisoner staring at them, their long, sharp-boned features softened with wonder and a slight touch of fear. That last made her shudder. Her father had warned her before she set sail that when men of power felt fear, it made them angry. They often needed to punish someone or something for what they saw as weakness in themselves. How could men who didn't know of Verdidan understand that holy fear was a good thing? Cleita had been the vessel of Verdidan's power and blessing, but how could these people who worshipped many gods understand that?

The little boy coughed and struggled to sit up. His father pounced, snatching him up and holding him tight to his chest. He turned him roughly in his arms, cradling him so the other man could examine his leg. From his apparent age and the similarity in their features, most likely he was the boy's grandfather. They talked so rapidly, Sholeh couldn't make out the words.

"Leave." Indago appeared as if out of the ground behind the three cousins. He gestured to the sailor boys, who hurried to gather up the dropped baskets and bundles. Several more men from the three ships emerged from the crowd and gathered around the cousins, as the two noblemen stopped exclaiming over the injured boy.

"You are from Pallon's temple, yes?" the older nobleman said. "We can find you there, to bring our thank offerings and gifts?"

"I serve Verdidan," Cleita said. "If you want to give thanks to your — if you want to thank whatever god you worship, you may." She swayed a little, and Sholeh nearly dropped her basket, hurrying to support her.

Indago gestured for silence when the nobleman opened his mouth, most likely either to protest or ask more questions. He scooped up Cleita, cradling her, though she was probably still able to walk. His expression stony and imposing, he led the way out of the fountain square. People whispered and then murmured and then called to each other, growing louder as they followed the travelers back through the marketplace, then to the docks, then to their ships. Sholeh wanted to stay on the docks and wait until Cleita had been carried onto her ship. Indago gestured at their ship with a jerk of his chin and a stern look. Captain Wylles' sons stepped up closer to her. Sholeh knew better than to argue.

~~~~~

"Did we do wrong?" Sholeh confronted her brother, as soon as Indago stepped onto their ship. She stood on the high platform with Captain Wylles, studying the crowds of people milling around the docks. The crowds watched their ships just as intently as the warriors standing sentinel on the docks, blocking access to the ships, watched them.

"It is never wrong to heal the injured and especially the innocent." Indago sounded as weary as Sholeh felt. He stretched out his arm and she gladly stepped into his embrace. "You all three did well. Cleita told me how you calmed the horse." His loud, deep sigh shook Sholeh, pressed hard against his side. "I am afraid, though, we have attracted the wrong kind of attention."

"We should have separated before we came within sight of land. Too many of us together, we are too easy to see. We are attracting Biss's fury. If we need the guardians to withstand Tylanok, if there is a chance we will succeed in this quest, then the evil one needs to stop us."
~~~~~

"True … but there is no unraveling the past. We can only go forward and change the pattern already established."

"We are leaving?" She caught her breath. He sounded much like their father, and some of their philosophical great-uncles and great-aunts. Sholeh feared she might burst into tears and homesickness would pounce on her if she told him that.

"As soon as the tide turns." Her brother sighed. "If we can without looking like we are running away. The surest way to make people chase you, make them think you have something to hide or something worth stealing, is to flee."

Yes, but every moment we delay gives someone more time to think of a reason to stop us. Sholeh knew better than to speak aloud what she was thinking. Her brother was likely thinking the same thing. *Any fool can see those people aren't curious. They want the power Verdidan gave us to use. The only question is when their fear will fade enough to allow them to do something about it.*

The shadow on the sun dial embedded in the stern of the ship had moved two notches before a crowd approached the docks where the crews of the three Isle ships prepared to cast off. Sholeh sat in the shadow of the hatch leading below decks, where she could see everything, but no one on the docks a man-height below could see her. Three men and six women, all robed in white, all with shaved heads, led the crowd. The men carried tall staffs with the symbol of Pallon, a harp framing a sun symbol, in gold on top. Healer priests. The women carried golden censors on long chains, and swung them in time with their slow, stately steps, so green-tinted clouds of smoke spread out from them to right and left. The healer temples were constantly filled with smoke to let petitioners inhale the healing powers of Pallon. Sholeh wrinkled up her nose when the breeze off the shore brought her the scent. She recognized some of the healing herbs, charred and rendered useless by burning. Her already low opinion of the followers of Pallon dropped even further. Infusions were better, especially the ones made by cold-soaking in wine or water, to let the properties of the herbs fill the liquid without damaging the essences of the plants.

She supposed Great-Uncle Harron would say this was further proof that all the false gods were merely masks of Biss. The Destroyer amused himself by fooling people into thinking they were being helped as they misused the many gifts of Verdidan.

Chapter Four

Captain Wylles stepped down from the prow and walked along the deck to the one remaining gangplank that connected their ship to the dock. The other two Isle ships had done the same as soon as the three captains and hunting team leaders had conferred on their plan of action. The mooring ropes could be sacrificed, cut with swords if need be, and the sails had been prepared, ready to loose into the stiff breeze coming from the land like a gift from Verdidan.

The shortest man of the three priests stepped forward and thumped his staff twice when he reached the bottom of the gangplank. The murmuring crowds behind him silenced immediately. Sholeh was impressed. She leaned forward, trying to hear better. The old priest had a creaky, sour voice, and slurred his words. He sounded like some of the old folk who sat by the docks where visitors were allowed to tie up their ships at the Isle and told stories to entertain travelers. She could never understand why the ones who had lost most of their teeth insisted on being storytellers. Between his unpleasant voice and the slurring and the foreign language, Sholeh could only make out maybe half the words. "Pallon's temple" was the clearest phrase, because the old priest said it over and over, like a magic spell. Chills crept up her back when the old man gestured at the ship, then to the right and left, taking in the other two ships, declaring them Pallon's property.

"I'd like to see what the other gods of this land say about that," Indago muttered, stepping up next to the hatch where Sholeh crouched.

"He is claiming our ships as Pallon's property? How can he?"

"Not the ships. You and Cleita and Loree. Especially Cleita. He's being generous and offering to hand you over to Remdos, since you hold power over horses, and horses belong to the war god." Indago spat, the sound muted as Captain Wylles finally responded to the old priest.

Sholeh shuddered, wishing the captain sounded more defiant. He stood with his fists on his hips, legs spread to block the entire width of the gangplank and responded in a calm voice. He could have been discussing the timetables for the tide, or the weather.

"He doesn't have to obey them, does he?" Her face warmed when her brother glanced down at her and his fierce expression softened into something like pity. What had she been thinking, even doubting for a minute that Captain Wylles would defend them?

"Captains have some power, some freedom, because their services are so vital to trade. Sailors belong to Agantes, and the sea god hereabouts is the highest ranked. Even the priests of Pallon don't dare order sailors about, for fear of insulting Agantes. A ship could refuse them when they need to travel to consult with the high priests or import exotic animals for sacrifice." He stepped forward, blocking her, and for a moment Sholeh feared the priest, whose voice was rising, had urged the crowd to storm their ship.

If only there were some horses on the docks. She would touch them with her thoughts and turn them wild, to disperse the crowd. If these fool priests thought she was better placed at Remdos's temple, maybe they would fear her anger, displayed through the horses? Earlier that morning, when she could stand on the deck and look out across the docks without people staring and pointing, no dogs or horses had been visible. Despite that, Sholeh now reached out for them with her mind. Any distraction would be helpful, wouldn't it? Especially with the priest getting louder, his voice shriller and words faster. Captain Wylles sounded angry now, and he raised his voice, no longer polite and reasonable.

The sleek, cool feeling of a dolphin's mind brushed up against her seeking thoughts. Sholeh nearly laughed aloud. What was a dolphin doing so close to port? She asked the creature, trying to frame her query in images. She received images of the deep waters of the harbor and especially tasty little fish and bottom-crawling shelled creatures that thrived here. Sholeh asked if the dolphin and his friends would like to come dance around their ships. She promised a song on her quartz flute if they would come splash water on the nasty old men in their white robes.

Peels of dolphin laughter erupted across the docks. Sholeh laughed, infected by the images in their minds and their eager compliance. This was a game for them.

Indago jerked backward a step, his eyes widening and his mouth open as if he would scold her. He paused, then grinned, and tipped his head back to laugh a few loud bursts, before reaching down to help her to her feet. Sholeh stuck her tongue out at him. Fortunately, she carried her flute carved of blue and green-veined quartz attached to her belt. She ignored the increased shouts of all nine priests and felt them watching her, gesturing at her, as she walked to the other end of the ship, farthest from the docks, and hitched herself up on the railing. The dolphins screeled and dove and danced on their tails, drawing cries and shouts from the crowds on the docks. Sholeh pulled out her flute, then swung her legs over the railing so she sat facing the water, her back to the docks. The priests fell silent as she played and more dolphins appeared, leaping and laughing and bobbing their heads in time with the lively dance tune.

"Verdidan is gracious," Indago murmured when she finished the tune and paused to catch her breath. He rested a hand on her shoulder. "How much can you make them do?"

"You don't *make* dolphins do anything, you can only ask." She glanced up at him, relieved to see laughter sparkling in his big, dark eyes. "I can't see. Are they doing the same around the other ships?"

"And our cousins are smart enough to mirror you. I suspect when we ask the captain, he will tell us these folk are afraid of the dolphins. Maybe they consider them the messengers of Agantes."

"Likely Agantes and his children and concubines turn into dolphins whenever they please." She nodded and brought the flute back to her lips when he opened his mouth, probably to tell her to keep playing.

Sholeh continued playing, stopping only briefly between songs to hear whatever news or ideas her brother or the captain had. The sun reached zenith and started to descend. At one point, Indago informed her that the brief shouting she heard came from the king's soldiers coming onto the docks and chasing everyone away. Except the priests. The captain stepped down onto the docks to talk with them. The king didn't want to get involved in a pending dispute between several temples, and only cared about maintaining order.

"What temples?" Sholeh asked. The flute slipped in her grasp.

"Agantes' priests have heard about the dolphins dancing for you, and Remdos's priests insist you have to be handed over to be sacrificed in the war god's service."

"*We're* the barbarians?" she blurted, remembering the woman in the marketplace. Her headache from sitting in the sun and playing for so long turned into a churning in her stomach as her brother's expression hardened. "What other kind of sacrifice is there?"

"Remdos's priests are warriors who don't like to waste women flesh. Very civilized, they are," Captain Wylles said, joining them at the railing. He leaned against it, looking across the ship toward the docks and not at them as he spoke. "They share their women. Makes for less baggage when they're on a campaign."

Sholeh looked down into the water. Three dolphins popped up from the shadows cast by the ship and chattered at her, asking for more music to accompany their games. She thought about diving in and asking her friends to take her out far from shore. She wouldn't know until she was very old if she had the gift of becoming a sea holder, but perhaps Verdidan would be merciful and allow her to shift shape now? To save her life?

"So when they say 'sacrifice,' they mean ..."

"You'll be the property of the most important priests, who will keep you pregnant and producing babies with the power over horses that belongs only to Remdos." Indago spat.

"Thank Verdidan, Agantes' priests are fighting with them, and the lesser priests of both their temples have been quarreling with the healer priests' underlings." Captain Wylles met her gaze just for a moment. "If we're lucky, they'll batter each other until there's no one who can force their way onto the ship to take possession of you and your cousins."

"No one has that much luck," she whispered. The dolphins chattered, making her flinch. Indago caught hold of her arm. Did he think she would slide into the water?

"The problem is that if we're not careful how we make our escape, one of the gods' followers will claim it's a sign that their god is most powerful. My men have been spying, listening to the people who didn't move off very far. You should hear the wagers being placed on what we're going to do, when we'll make our escape, and which god will win."

"How soon until we can't escape?" Indago said. "It only makes sense that Agantes' priests have ships, and they'll be able to block us in."

"How much power does Agantes have over storms at sea?" Sholeh asked. "If Verdidan blesses us, how much of that blessing will be attributed to Agantes?"

"Ah, all the weather belongs to a group of nasty half-breed gods." Captain Wylles stood up, no longer lounging against the railing, with that thoughtful look in his eyes that gave Sholeh some hope.

"Half-breeds?" Indago said.

"From the stories I've heard ..." He shrugged and gave Sholeh an apologetic look. "The gods of Nedaia take whatever they want. If the women aren't willing, and they don't feel like wasting time on seduction, they masquerade as the husbands. When a woman gives birth during a brutal storm and there's some question of who the father is, the belief is that the child is a half-breed god, expressing his fury at being born."

"So we should pray for a storm, and pray we don't founder at sea?"

~~~~~

The storm did not come, though Sholeh prayed multiple times. There was precious little for her to do, hidden below decks to keep the curious and the spying eyes from finding her. Night came, and a wall of the king's soldiers stood on the docks with their backs to the ships, to keep everyone from approaching. The only light came from the pair of torches in front of the mooring post for each ship. The usual watchfires along the shore weren't lit, and Sholeh imagined every thud against the hull was an attacker climbing out of the dark water, having approached in the thick cover of shadows.

In the gray light between twilight and moonrise, the crews of the three ships loosed the mooring ropes, to allow the retreating tide to pull them away from the docks toward the mouth of the port. The sailors worked in silence, with reed pipes trilling soft over the water to signal locations and when to loosen the sails to let them unfurl.
~~~~~

Sholeh spent the waiting time in prayer, whispering songs of petition for safety and speed, and for a strong wind at the precise time they needed it. She felt the sudden leap in tension throughout the body of the ship when the sails fell down into place and sailors moved to catch hold of the bottom edges, to slide the weight bar into the bottom loops. The ship jolted softly. She laughed as she heard several sailors cry out in hushed voices, and a moment later felt a gush of cooler air. The wind had come, the timing too perfect to be anything but an answer to prayer.

Soon the ship approached the crab claw pincers of rock at the mouth of the harbor. Sholeh braced, praying not to feel the jolt-and-tip and the explosive burst of sound that meant they had run aground on the rocks. Not until the ship had passed out of the mouth of the harbor did she dare go above decks. When she climbed out into the fresh air and let the breeze tug at her hair, she turned, seeking torchlight from shore. There was nothing but rough black shadows in front of her. She shuddered and wrapped her arms around herself, then a moment later reached for the rail of the ship. Though she strained her ears, she heard no sounds over the water, no signs of pursuit. No shouts, no war drums.

Until day came and she could look behind them and make sure no one chased them, the quiet of the night meant nothing.

Perhaps the priests of the various gods making claims on her and her cousins had decided to give up their arguments. Perhaps whoever was posted to keep watch on the ships had fallen asleep or abandoned their posts. Perhaps the rival gods would be blamed for the escape of the ships and the cargo that so many coveted.

No … Sholeh didn't think so. Until she and her cousins separated to finally go to their destinations and begin their hunt on dry land, they would not be safe.

Whoever found the man-wolf guardians and convinced them to come back to Isle of the Moon to fulfill their duty would likely draw the attention of similar people. Anyone who saw someone with unusual gifts automatically believed those gifts belonged in the service of whichever god was preeminent in that place. While Sholeh could admire such devotion, she shuddered to think that such service focused ultimately on Biss.

~~~~~

When she finally slept, Sholeh dreamed of a mountain that grew higher with every step she took. *As she walked, heading east and searching for the sun, the mountain turned west under her, presenting more of its face. A vast, hooked shadow spread over her and she looked up, tipping her head back and back, more with each step. A ridge curved up and out over her head, looking like a wave of stone arrested in that terrifying second before it crashed down on her.*

Multiple sets of eyes appeared in the black shadows oozing out of the base of
~~~~~

the stone wave. The dream carried her forward. She tried to turn, change direction, but the mountain continued turning, like a massive claw reaching for her.

"Please, Verdidan ..." Sholeh muffled a sob when the eyes merged into just one pair of red-tinted eyes and a shape coalesced around them. A whimper broke out of her throat as the shape stepped out of the darkness.

The sound shattered in her throat. The shape was a wolf.

Wonder pushed away terror. Her feet stopped moving against her will now that she no longer fought them. Sholeh took a deep breath. Everything went still inside her and outside her.

Except the wolf. It took one step closer to her. Pause. Another step.

From far away, the wolf was just one solid black shadow with red eyes, towering over her so she felt like a mouse before it. After four steps, the eyes changed to soft green. The blackness gave way to details and the massive shape diminished with every step. The fur was still black, but it looked soft and warm, and she saw rolling muscle and elegant, sleek lines under the fur.

The wolf came close enough, Sholeh should have felt his breath on her skin, but this was a dream and she felt nothing. No sound. No smells. Nothing but the images before her, the sense of motion, and cold.

"Please ... where are you?" she whispered. Her voice seemed to clog in her throat, so she could barely force out sound.

The wolf's ears twitched in reaction. He came close, so she thought he would touch her cheek with his nose in another moment.

"What is this place? Is it a real place? Please, Verdidan, is this you leading me?"

"Who is Verdidan?" a man whispered, his voice swirling around her so she couldn't tell where he stood, where the voice came from.

"Verdidan is the All Above, the One, the Eternal, the Maker of Life."

"Another useless god." He snorted, and the sound echoed through the darkness that enfolded her.

Sholeh woke with a soft cry, reaching out as if she could find the speaker and pull him closer. For a few moments she shivered in the darkness, and her sling bed swayed with her abrupt movements, so she thought she might feel seasick for the first time in the voyage.

Her hands still shook a little as she dug in one of the baskets hanging from the ceiling of her tiny nook below decks, to bring out wax tablet and stylus. She chose not to light a lamp she would have to shield so the light didn't spill out into the larger sleeping area. Indago would wake, and he hovered so close to her lately she thought she would smother. Instead, Sholeh took herself up onto the deck. The moon at three-quarters was halfway down the night sky. It spilled plenty of light across the deck for her to sketch the mountain from her dream into the soft wax. She smoothed out the thin grooves multiple times, changing and fixing and revising her sketch until the moon touched the horizon and the light dimmed to silver shadows as dawn approached, and she no longer had light enough to draw by.

After breakfast and morning prayer songs, she showed her drawing of the mountain from her dream to Captain Wylles and other members of the crew, who had visited Nedaia before this voyage. None of them recognized the mountain, but she wasn't disappointed because they all admitted they hadn't gone more than two days' journey away from the coast. Captain Wylles promised her he knew of several old sailors at the next port who had journeyed from western to eastern shore of this continent. Maybe one of them had seen the mountain with that distinctive feature. Certainly, it had to be one of the mountains far inland, rising up high enough to catch the clouds on their peaks.

"Whatever we do," Indago told her, as she settled down with reedsheets and ink to make copies of her drawing for their cousins and their hunting teams to use, "we need to travel separately now. Maybe you should dye your hair. All of you. There is no telling how far the tale will spread, of the three of you singing healing into the boy's leg, and then the dolphins dancing and singing around our ships. It might be the safest thing to do, getting away from our ships."

As they neared the next port, Captain Wylles signaled the other two ships to stay far out at sea, out of sight of the land, while his ship went into the shallow harbor. The captains of the other two ships wanted to know what he was doing, why he was going in to port when the initial plan of escape had been to sail north three days and outrun anyone trying to chase them on land. There was only so much that could be communicated with the flags and drumbeats. The messenger hawks were fidgety and reluctant to fly in the stiffening breezes that seemed to swirl around the ships from all directions. Sending the drawings of the mountain and a brief recounting of her dream to the other two boats didn't solve anything, and more time was lost to delay.

Sholeh chafed against the time lost in dropping anchor and waiting for the crewboats from the other two ships to come alongside with the captains and her cousins, to confer. Cleita and Loree were excited about Sholeh's dream, Garyon and Caron not so much. They agreed with Indago's suggestion that they make small changes in their appearance, such as dying their hair and adopting the hair styles of the women of Nedaia. Unmarried girls wore their hair in long braids, or simply bound back in a horse's tail, while married women pinned their hair up on the backs of their heads. On the Isle, unmarried girls let their hair hang loose down their backs, taming it with combs and pins, or braiding on the sides to keep it out of their faces. Sholeh found the whole idea of pinning up her hair, spending time on elaborate braids, disturbing. She wasn't a married woman, she wasn't even betrothed, and though she knew it was necessary to make potential enemies think she was something she was not, she disliked it. Still, it was a wise plan, and she was grateful her brother was here to look out for her.

As their ship headed in toward port, Sholeh stood in the prow, straining her eyes for the coastline rising above the water. When they drew close enough she could make out the colors of people's clothes and hair on the long docks, Indago made her go below decks. He would look for dye for her hair on the first foray into the marketplace, but he would not let her leave the ship without some disguise. Wearing a veil was too risky. They were far enough to the north of Nedaia that the practices of several smaller, northern kingdoms interwove with the Nedaians' practices. Some cultures in the north made harlots wear veils, while others veiled priestesses or royal women. Only a few days earlier, someone mistaking Sholeh for a priestess or a princess would have been amusing, but now Indago would not allow her to take the risk that the wrong man would assume the wrong thing about her and cause them trouble.

"No matter what these foreigners think a veil signifies, to me it means you are trying to hide something. More than just little boys want to know what is being kept hidden from them." Indago tucked four small sketches of the dream mountain into his belt pouch, to use when he went around the marketplace. "Say prayers and sing petitions for our success while we are away, little sister."

"I already am." She embraced him and tried to smile.

Her longing to get off the ship and walk through the marketplace battled with the growing fear that Indago would meet the one man in the entire port city who would recognize him from Teviss and stir up trouble against them. She followed him to the steps leading up to the deck and stood in the shaft of sunlight falling down on her, listening to his booted feet cross the deck and go down the gangplank to the docks. Captain Wylles and an escort of four sailors waited for him.

"Please, Blessed All-Maker, keep them safe. Give them success. Give them the answers we need. Let this mountain like a cresting wave be close. Please, let us find the guardians live in its shadow."

Chapter Five

Sholeh settled on the bottom step belowdecks, where the sunlight could touch and warm her, and tried to compose a tune on her flute that matched the feeling from her dream. By the time the sun had dropped far enough that the stairwell filled with shadows, she was ready to admit defeat. The more she tried to call up the feeling of eyes appearing from the darkness, and the chiming in her soul reacting to the man's voice, the more the feelings and sounds faded and warped in her memory. Soon she doubted what she had heard altogether.

The mountain was still clear in her memory, however. Sholeh made herself another copy of the drawing and waited until the ink was thoroughly dry, then she tucked it between the thin golden leaves of the sacred words and wrapped everything up snug and safe again in layers of waxed cloth and leather, for safekeeping.

When she turned around from resealing her waterproof pack, Sholeh glanced out the side slit in the belowdecks cabin. At first she thought another ship had pulled up alongside them, blocking the sunset gleam on the water. She stepped to the slit to look out. The sun had vanished behind clouds, pushed in by the sporadic gusts that had teased their sails all day. A chilly breeze slipped through the opening and seemed to curve an even chillier hand around her chin and cheek.

"Of course, now it comes." She hunched her shoulders at the thought of a storm hitting them at sea. They could have used it yesterday to escape the port city. "Please, Indago, finish and come back."

Wyllan came down below with news that his father had found the old man he was looking for, but it might be another hour before he and Indago and their escort returned to the ship. Old sailors liked to talk and took advantage of every chance to ramble and boast, especially when they had a captive audience. He assured her before she could ask, yes, the crew was preparing to leave the docks. Right now, the wind of the coming storm blew off the land, so that was in their favor. This harbor was shallower than at Teviss, and more open to the sea. They could move faster without fear of other ships coming into port blocking their way. Sholeh thanked him and settled down to add more prayer songs to the ones that had hummed at the back of her mind ever since her brother left, just after noon.

She had barely finished the first song and lowered her quartz flute to her lap, trying to think of another, when she heard the thudding of bare feet running up the gangplank. A familiar voice called out. The light, young voice belonged to a man in their crew. She was ashamed now to recall his face, but not the name. Something in the young man's hail, asking if the captain had returned yet, sent a cold touch up her back. Sholeh tucked her flute back into her pack and moved over to the bottom of the steps to try to hear what was going on. She didn't dare show her face above decks while they were in port.

"Lady Sholeh." Wyllan slid on the top step and nearly fell down the next one, catching the edge of the hatch to stop himself. "Another ship is here, from Teviss." His eyes widened, and he swallowed loudly.

She understood. If the sailor had recognized the ship as being in Teviss when they were there, then chances were good someone on that ship recognized their ship.

"Send someone for the captain. Have you?" she hurried to add, instantly knowing how she would feel if someone in her care gave her orders to do something that was only common sense. "Thank you," she hurried to say when the boy nodded.

"Should I—do you want someone to stand guard with you?" He reached back with one foot, poised to turn and run to the next task.

"Thank you, but I am able to fight." A bubbling urge to laugh rose in her throat. Hadn't Wyllan seen her sparring with Indago on the deck during the voyage? Her father had always insisted that the women of their family be as skilled in defending themselves with their hands and feet, swords and spears, as any man.

Wyllan nodded and dashed away. Sholeh returned to the thin cushion on the floor in front of her sleeping nook, but the thought of sitting and praying itched in her soul, even knowing it was just as important as preparing to leave port. She set about sealing the view slits in preparation for the oncoming storm, and raised her voice in song, more a taunt thrown at Biss and his followers than strictly a prayer. As she slid blocks of wood into place and pressed strips of wax into the gaps, she declared to the enemy that Verdidan the Unseen stood as a wall between his followers and all evil.

She paused in her song to light a lamp. Between the oncoming storm and the blocked view slits, the cabin was almost too full of shadows to see what she was doing. When she bent to pick up the next block, she heard a step creak behind her. Sholeh turned, hefting the block.

"I thought we should be prepared in case—"

The man facing her was a stranger. He was also dripping wet. Sholeh knew as if he had boasted aloud that he had swum from the ship that had arrived from Teviss. The man's face split into a grin full of broken teeth and malice. He reached for the long knife in the sheath at his waist. The wet leather refused to release the blade.

Sholeh flung the block at his face and lunged at him, leading with both fists. She caught him right in the gap between the ribs. He went down with a shattered curse and a gust of foul breath. She leaped over him to fly up the steps. He snagged her skirt and yanked while both her feet were in the air. Sholeh shrieked with all the power of her lungs as she went down and twisted herself in mid-air, to land directly on top of him.

Fury and terror gave strength to her fists and knees and feet. Sholeh kicked and punched and shouted. She shrieked louder when arms wrapped around her and lifted her up, out of the stairwell, onto the deck. Wind heavy with threatening rain slashed at her and the sky was black with scudding clouds. She went limp as she realized Wyllan held her. Her face heated as her feet finally touched the deck and she stood on her own. The crew gathered around. Those not hauling the whimpering, bloody intruder onto the deck grinned at her.

"I think we have proof the other ship's crew recognized us," she offered, when she couldn't think of anything else to say.

"They'll come investigate soon enough," the second mate said, nodding, as he tossed some rope to the men restraining the intruder. "If he doesn't come back. But we have time. You near as killed him, I think." He winked at her, tricky, with only one eye.

"Here they come, now." Wyllan grasped her arm, turning her to look out across the docks. Sholeh couldn't make out the returning party, through the people running about the docks as ships and crews prepared for the incoming storm. She had to take the boy's word for it.

The crew were still discussing what to do with the intruder as Indago and Captain Wylles hurried up the gangplank. Her brother opened his mouth, the scolding visible in his expression. Sholeh pointed at the bound man lying on the deck behind her. She didn't resist as her brother escorted her back below decks. The second mate and Wyllan hurried to explain to Captain Wylles what had happened.

Indago gathered her into his arms, holding her tight against him. Sholeh was startled to realize how much she needed that. A tight trembling filled her that she didn't detect until it died. She sat down on a bench with him and grudgingly explained what had happened, when she would much rather have heard first what the old sailor had to say. Still, it was pleasant to see her brother's scowl turn into a grin.

"Now, tell me," she demanded, after he kissed her forehead and declared she was better suited for the Isle's guards than as a healer.

"You saw Mount Aerno. There is no other mountain in all the known world, according to old Bagras, with that outcropping that looks like a cresting wave. Legend says the gods of this land made the mountain out of the tallest wave of the sea, when they pulled the land out of the water centuries ago."

"You can tell me the stories later, when we're on our way. Where is it? How far a journey? Do you know the way?"

"Little one ..." Indago's face seemed to glow in the lantern light. He gripped her shoulders. "Mount Aerno is called the home of the gods ... and it is said that wolves with the voices of men prowl its slopes, keeping intruders off the sacred land."

"Wolves ..." She trembled, a few quick shudders. "So the guardians who served Verdidan now serve false gods?"

"The truth could be very different. These gods could be people with gifts from Verdidan who live apart, in fear of being forced to serve the false gods, just like the priests tried to do to you."

"You try too hard to be reasonable." She wagged her finger in her brother's face, earning a snort of laughter. "How do we get there, and how long of a journey is it?"

"We could have headed inland from this port, but now ...? First, we will meet with the others, tell them our news, and find another port where we can obtain horses —"

"That long a journey?"

"Six days by mounted courier to Mount Aerno. It takes twice as long for ordinary travelers, three or four times longer for merchant companies with wagons. We were discussing what was safer for us, to avoid notice, on our way back to the ship. It might be wiser to join a merchant company, simply because our enemies would not expect it of us."

"Enemies." She shivered. "Is it possible, you think, that Tylanok knows what we were sent to do, and he sent spies and other people after us to block our way, to rouse the people of these lands against us?"

"Tylanok wants to command the gifts of Verdidan for himself. If he told the kings and priests of these lands about us, he would have to share the very gifts he wishes to command. Why should he negotiate and persuade others to agree with him, when it is easier to wait until he is strong enough, then send his soldiers to destroy and subdue?"

Her brother's words were little comfort as Sholeh returned to helping prepare to leave the port and head out to the stormy, open water. She wasn't sure what the crew decided to do with the man who came to kidnap her, but she heard the feet thudding on the deck and down the gangplank, and then return, running, only a few minutes later, followed by a shout to lift the anchor.

To her relief, the bouncing and thudding of the ship lessened as the ship moved away from the docks and headed out into deeper water. Sholeh supposed it was because they were moving with the waves, instead of being hit at an angle and bracing against the docks. Finally, there was nothing for her to do but settle into her sling bed, wrap a blanket around herself against the cold, and wait. And pray.

The call to arms didn't come when she expected it. Neither did anyone call down to her, letting her know the ship had passed out of the wide harbor without challenge, and it was safe for her to come above decks. Sholeh supposed it was safer for her to stay below, out of the rain drumming against the deck over her head, and out of the way of the crew as they guided the ship. Soon, the swaying of her sling bed grew too rough for her. She unhooked the ends and folded it into a pad to sit on. The ship jolted sideways as well as up and down, knocking the baskets holding her clothes and other possessions to the floor. Sholeh imagined the ship rocking so violently that it tipped onto its side, dumping them all out into the water. Though she trusted Captain Wylles to keep control of his ship, she thought it might be wise to put as much into her waterproof pack as she could. She would appreciate dry clothes when the storm was over.

If it ever ended. She was sure only an hour or two had passed since leaving the docks, but her queasy stomach seemed to have been suffering for half a day or more. The bouncing and swaying and fighting not to get sick exhausted her. She was relieved to give in and close her eyes, and swirl down into uneasy sleep.

Shouts coming through the howling winds yanked her out of a twisted, strange dream where Sholeh couldn't keep her eyes open to see what was around her. She sat up, gasping, heart racing. Shivering, she gathered the blanket around herself again and listened. The shouts said something about a ship.

Had they reached the place where Cleita and Loree's ships were supposed to wait for them? Were her cousins' ships in trouble? Sholeh fought down the queasies and got to her feet. She staggered across the rising and dropping deck, until she had the idea to lean into the wall as she made her way to the stairs. She fell twice before she reached the upper deck. The wind yanked at the blanket she had wrapped around herself and she was instantly soaked.

She found Captain Wylles and Indago hanging onto the ropes wrapped around the lower half of the center mast, their heads tipped back, shouting back and forth with two men who perched on the top beam holding the sail, on either side of the mast. They had tied themselves to the mast and leaned out, shielding their faces from the wind and rain with their hands, visibly searching for something.

"Little fool," Indago snarled, when Sholeh staggered and stumbled her way across the deck and joined them. He put her between him and the mast, with both his arms bracing her.

"What has happened? They aren't here where we left them, are they?" she demanded.

"No," Captain Wylles shouted. His voice sounded as if he were several ships' lengths away, instead of just on the other side of the mast. "They're gone. Chased, I think."

Sholeh didn't have to think long to understand what he meant. Especially when the men at lookout in the mast shouted down what sounded like descriptions of several ships and estimated distances. She guessed that enemy ships had appeared out of the approaching storm and her cousins' ships and their captains made the wise choice to flee.

She prayed they had fled, and they hadn't been attacked and captured, maybe even sunk. When Indago ordered her to go back below, she obeyed, shuddering. What would she see the next time she came above the decks? The enemy ships closing on them, or her cousins' ships, somewhere ahead of them, fleeing before the storm?

"Where are we going?" she asked her brother, when he came below decks at one point to retrieve food for those fighting the sails.

"North. We agreed on several ports to take refuge, if we were pursued. Let's hope ..." He wiped his face with both hands, ending by raking his fingers through his hair and sending splats of water to the cold, damp deck. "I don't want to frighten you."

"Be prepared for the worst?" She tried to smile. "Father always tells us that. Be prepared for the worst to happen, and then all outcomes will be sweet."

"Arm yourself. Try to sleep." He drew her into his arms for a hard, tight, far too brief embrace. Then he hurried up the steps, staggering with the lift-twist-drop motion of the ship among the waves.

Sholeh dug through the chest of weapons, trying to distract herself by searching for the perfect fit and weight. She strapped a short sword to her side, threading a leather thong through the hole at the bottom of the sheath to bind it tight to her thigh, rather than just belted at her waist. Then she found two knives and strapped one around her upper arm and the other to her calf. She repacked her waterproof pack, exchanging her spare dress for rough trousers and a shirt and blanket, wrapped tight around her bundle of healing herbs. She slipped two more knives into the pack. Then she stripped down to her underclothes and put on trousers and a sleeveless shirt, re-fastened her short sword and knives into place, and put her dress on over it all. She would definitely be warmer, no matter what happened. As a final precaution, she wove a strap through the arm loops of her pack, fastening it low across her chest, so that if the worst happened and she was knocked unconscious by the rocking and jolting of the ship, the pack would not come off.

Wearing the pack made for uncomfortable sleeping, but she didn't really expect to sleep, did she? Sholeh curled up in a nest of two blankets and the sling bed, lying on her side with her knees pulled up to her chest, and pressed into the corner of her sleeping nook as far as the pack would allow. She closed her eyes and softly sang prayers until exhaustion took her. She slid down into spinning blackness that muted the roar of the storm and the shouts of sailors, where even the rise and jolting fall of the ship couldn't reach her.

~~~~~

Icy water, harder than stones, slapped her face. Sholeh bolted upright, a massive thud reverberating through her body. She lay on her back, gaping up at the stormy sky through a jagged hole in the blackness that had swallowed her. Lightning flashed, then another black wave slammed down on her. She closed her eyes and flung her arms over her head to shield against the force, but it was no use. The water crashed into her, shoving her across the tilted decking. She jolted into another tilted surface.

More lightning. She blinked against salt water that blinded her. Water caught her, lifted her, flung her in a tangled heap, slamming into a hard, flat surface from the waist down. The impact sent her tumbling headfirst downward. She hit hard, then sank into churning waves.

The ship. Where was the ship? What had happened?

A massive blackness pushed her under the water and kept moving, scraping above her. Sholeh fought not to scream as understanding painted the image in her head. A ship foundered over her, pushing her down into the water. Her ship? Or had the enemy caught up with them?

Holding her breath until stars shimmered in front of her eyes, she struggled to push herself away from the wooden shape that rocked and churned and seemed bent on dragging her down with it. Sholeh strained to see something, anything, though the salt water burned her eyes and there was nothing to see but blackness. Even the stars faded from in front of her eyes.

Please … Verdidan …

The darkness wrapped tighter and squeezed at her lungs, like a massive, angry fist trying to force her to breathe her death.

~~~~~

Sholeh woke to the roaring of the surf and the feeling that all the sea tried to reside inside her skull. The taste of blood and brine and sand lay heavy in her mouth. Her stomach tried to turn inside out when she swallowed.

The sense of her body returned to her by degrees. She lay still, accepting the pain and weight as proof that she indeed lived, until she felt the incoming tide tugging at her ankles. Panic shot fire through her muscles and she scrambled on hands and knees away from those soft fangs. Her abused stomach emptied its load of seawater and she cried out as smiths banged on her temples with hammers the size of the moon.

She thought she heard the cries of warriors and the thudding of war drums. Sholeh refused to look over her shoulder at the storm-tossed sea. She reached dry sand and the pebbly shingle of the shore without hearing the scrape of enemy keels on sand. Despite herself, she looked back and found the frothing shoreline empty.

Entirely empty, as far as she could see, in the gray light that was all storm and gave her no idea of the time of day.

No one and nothing moved but the water. And Sholeh.

The agonized throbbing inside her head made thinking hard. It dimmed under the jagged sensation enclosing her heart.

Alone? Please, Verdidan ... no ...

Sholeh lay still and limp until the torment softened. Enough that the breeze enfolding her body emphasized how wet she was, and how little covering her torn clothes gave her. Moving slowly, feeling as if every fiber of muscle had been battered, she checked herself. By a miracle, a gift from Verdidan, her pack was still strapped to her back, though it felt heavy enough it had probably filled with water during her night of semi-conscious drifting. The knife strapped to her calf was still there, and the short sword. Her dress was shreds held in place with her leather belt. The trousers were in slightly better shape, offering her some modesty. The same for the sleeveless shirt under her dress. She shuddered to think of how little she might be wearing now if she had only been wearing a dress, or even just a sleeping shift, when the ship capsized.

Her entire body stiffened as memories of that short, battered, drowning struggle filled her head to the point of aching. She couldn't be sure if she had actually heard the sounds, or if she filled in the pieces in her memory with her imagination. Sholeh remembered that frozen, brief moment, looking up at the stormy sky, lightning accenting the jagged hole where the decking above her had been shattered.

She feared the enemy had rammed their ship, sinking it. Whether an accident caused by the stormy sea, or deliberate, what did it matter now? She was alone, with nothing but rags, a knife and sword for defense, and the contents of her pack. What should she do? Stay here on the shore, looking for other survivors? Make her way inland? Sholeh felt sick at the thought of trying to find Mount Aerno without her brother and the company of warriors sent to protect them. How could she get there on foot? How long would that take?

Chapter Six

First, Sholeh had to determine where she was, how long ago the storm had struck, and how far she was from the last port of call. Maybe she could find someone who knew the currents, who could help her determine where others would wash ashore. If anyone would wash ashore.

Indago would look for her. He would spend the rest of his life searching for her. Could she do no less for him?

Sholeh looked out at the churning water, the waves still crashing down with gray foam when they reached the shore. If there was anyone out there, she couldn't see them, with heavy clouds blocking what little sunlight remained. If it was morning or evening, she couldn't tell. The pounding in her head eased a little more, but her legs grew weaker with every minute she stood there, staring at the water. If anyone came ashore, they would be pulled by the same currents and waves that caught her, so wouldn't they indeed land here, or somewhere close by? Common sense said to stay here.

Yes, she would stay here and wait. She had to find shelter. Turning, she almost pushed herself off her feet. Sholeh caught her breath against a surge of nausea and the illusion of the world tipping from side to side around her. The shore was a ragged place, high dunes tufted with grass and pockmarked with massive chunks of dull gray-black rock that wouldn't yield to the scouring of wind and water and sand. She staggered over to a cluster of slabs of rock, leaning against each other to form a rude kind of shelter. A sigh escaped her when she went slowly to her knees and felt the instant relief from the wind. She didn't realize how cold she was until the wind stopped sucking away what little warmth came from moving. Sholeh fumbled with the strap holding her heavy pack to her back, but her water-shriveled fingers were too achy-cold-stiff to cooperate. She finally settled down with her back to the rock, the pack cushioning her somewhat, and her legs stretched out in front of her. With the stormy sea in front of her, she fought to keep her eyes open and keep watch.

She was far too tired to even weep as her eyes closed against her will and sleep took her.

The sea grumbled and snatched at her in her dreams, but she evaded its dragging clutches. *Sholeh ran through ragged gray mist. She climbed higher with every step, over rocky terrain, into a forest where shadows crouched and* green-gray eyes peered from between the black trees that blocked the sunlight.

"Don't fear, little one," a rough voice whispered. "Come up, come in, and you will find friends."

"All my friends are dead," Sholeh snarled. "I know better than to trust the men of Nedaia."

"That is wisdom." The voice softened. "But we are not men, and our words are true."

An enormous black wolf limped out of the shelter of the shadows. He walked on three legs, holding his foreleg out. Blood smeared the sleek ebony fur, and Sholeh saw the extra bend where the bones had broken and punctured muscles and fur.

The healer in her pushed aside the fear she should have felt. She reached for the wolf, silver flickers of magic dancing in her fingertips. The wolf backed away.

"Let me help you. I have come here to find you. The guardians. Do you remember anything of your duty, your ancestors' vows?"

"What can brute beasts remember, except hunger and hunting and blood?"

The voice in her head sounded so mournful and full of pain, Sholeh choked on sobs.

"Help me find you. Help me find the mountain where you live."

"What do you know of the mountain?"

"I have come to bring you back to the Isle of the Moon."

The black wolf leaped forward so he towered over her, enormous, blocking out the light. His eyes were a man's eyes, wide with fear.

"The crescent moon? Do not lie to me, to us. All our hopes rest on the crescent moon." The wolf tipped his head back and let out a howl that rang off the sky and the trees and made the ground beneath her shudder.

"Yes." She gasped, fighting the need to sob and to flee. "I come from the island shaped like a crescent moon, searching for you, for the guardians. Let me heal you, and then we can look for my brother, our warriors, and we will go home in safety." She held out her hand. The wolf was close enough she could have grasped his leg, but she knew better than to touch a wild animal uninvited.

"My injury is nothing you can mend. Little one, never go outside at the full moon. Come up, come in, and we will care for you." Then he vanished back into the shadows.

Sholeh puzzled over those words until the crashing of the waves crept up behind her. She turned to flee, as the waves slipped up and brushed at her heels, but no longer screamed, trying to swallow her up again. She fell deeper into sleep and the crashing waves softened.

Through her sleep, the pounding hiss of the water softened to voices and then to words. Sholeh woke slowly. Her bottom ached from sitting. She pressed her hands against the sand and determined she still sat against the rock where she had found shelter. She heard three people talking, two men and a woman. She heard the muted rumbling of waves on sand, the normal music of the shore and not the screaming and crashing of a storm. Her eyes were crusted shut with salt and she winced as she opened them. Sholeh held still as she took in her surroundings. Someone had draped a ragged, thin blanket over her up to her waist. The gray cloth might have been creamy brown when it was new and clean. It felt gritty with sand under her fingers and smelled of fish.

The people sounded so close to her. The blanket hinted at kindness, yet how could she trust strangers? Especially Nedaians, after all that had happened to her and her people. Sholeh was faintly surprised not to be bound hand and foot already, and the pack stripped from her back.

She wasn't surprised, when her clearing eyesight revealed that someone had removed her knife and sword. They had made it to shore on her person, despite the tumbling of the waves, so whoever had put the blanket on her had taken her weapons. No, she had not fallen among friendly folk.

The three people sat around a small fire with their backs to her, maybe four steps away from the shelter of the rocks. The men, clad only in loincloths, were hairy and gnarled with muscle, their brown hair tangled, matted and shaggy. It escaped Sholeh how people who lived at the sea's edge didn't bathe regularly.

The woman sat between them, her long, dull black hair hanging freely down her back, just as tangled as the men's. She wore a threadbare, beltless dress of some dun material.

Sholeh guessed they were fisher folk, rather than slave traders. Would that be good for her, or bad? Her head ached too much to let her speculate long in that direction.

Her head felt tender on the right, and her flesh stung from bruises when she pressed fingers to cheek. She explored her face, down her other arm, her chest, finding bruises everywhere.

She had to move quietly, slowly, to avoid attracting any attention until she understood her situation. Until she had found her brother, their ship, their warriors, she dared not trust in anyone to defend her. Dared not trust smiles or promises from strangers. Not here. Not from someone who had taken her weapons. She was her only defense, and could depend on no one, no matter how defenseless she felt. Cold and ragged, bruised and hungry. And alone.

"You're only helpless if you decide to be helpless," her father had scolded, after one of her in-fighting lessons.

A shiver raced up her spine as common sense came awake. Years of training returned from the black depths of her battered mind. She had vowed her life and her soul to Verdidan's service and care, so what right did she have to sit and despair and give up? More important, only a fool sat still and waited for her enemies to come to her.

She had to get up, find a weapon, find a place to put her back to, and settle in to battle for her life. And then, somehow, some way, by Verdidan's grace and mercy, find the way to Mount Aerno. The dream gave her hope, a gift of guidance and encouragement from Verdidan. Wolves did not speak with the voices of men, except in the tales from Isle of the Moon, and in dreams.

The breeze shifted, carrying to her the odors of dirty flesh, salty sweat, and sour wine through the fresh salt smell of the sea. The stench made her empty stomach revolt. A spasm moved through her, straining her bruised and aching ribs. She bit her bottom lip hard to stifle a groan. If that slight movement was agony, how could she get to her feet to flee?

Yet flee, she must. Her life and freedom depended on it.

Sholeh tasted blood by the time she gained her feet and took the first tiny, soft step backward and away, always watching the three sitting by the fire. She shivered in her wet rags, but she knew better than to take the dirty blanket with her for warmth. She couldn't trust anyone in Nedaia to act from mercy. If she took the blanket, they could brand her a thief and make her a slave.

She did not dare make a return claim on them, demanding they return her knife and sword. They would call her a liar, and being a stranger, a foreigner, she would not be believed.

A constant, wordless prayer writhed through her thoughts as she fought for every soundless step away from the shelter, away from the water's edge, toward the jagged cliffs and blunt, raw landscape. Inland lay her hope and her only possible allies, even if the journey by foot took her several moons. A forest would provide shelter. Her healer's gift helped her to calm animals. The animals of Nedaia would be more friendly than the people. She thought of the dolphins who had come readily enough to the call of her mind. Perhaps she would be safer escaping into the water, now that the storm had calmed?

She turned her thoughts to the rolling waves and reached for those friendly minds, so warm within the cold water. A gasp escaped her when she felt an answer almost immediately. Seconds later, she heard the first screeling cry.

"Awake, are you?" a rough, yet warm male voice asked.

Sand and pebbles crunched behind her. Sholeh ducked aside, sensing the hand reaching for her, and turned to face the three strangers.

"Agantes is kind," the other man said. His voice crackled, sounding like someone had tried to strangle him. His shoulders were wide, his build like an ox. His chuckle sounded like gravel in a wooden tub. "I'll take her."

A scar bisected his square face diagonally, from high in his forehead, across his eyelid to make it droop, then in a knotty white line down and across his broken, bulbous nose. Then it twisted down to turn his mouth to a permanent leer. Saliva dripped from the corner of his mouth, and broken brown teeth showed in the gap.

"Until her owners appear," the woman said in a tired voice. She didn't even look at Sholeh as she spoke and stepped up behind the first man, the one with the kinder voice. "Her clothes are stained and torn by the sea, but they were once rich. She has royal blood or is the plaything of a king."

"Doesn't matter. She's mine now," the scarred man said as he reached for Sholeh. He cursed when she evaded his hand. "Stand still!"

"No." She took a step sideways, braced to run.

"Learn this now, girl," he snarled. "You obey me or you'll taste my fist. Agantes gave you to me to warm my blankets. I don't care if you like it or not."

"Agantes has no power over me, to give me to you or to anyone." Sholeh took a step back, feeling the dampness in the sand. How many steps until she could reach the water? She stretched out her thoughts for the dolphins.

The dolphins chattered angrily. The three people turned, startled and staring. Silvery bodies danced out among the waves. Sholeh stretched out her hands in silent thanks to Verdidan. With a snarl, the scarred man caught hold of her upper arm.

Sholeh flung herself backward, breaking his grip. She got one leg under herself and brought up the other knee. He roared and flung her away to evade the blow. She used the momentum to tumble head over heels. She ignored the twinges in flesh and bones as she twisted to land on her feet. Her pack pulled her off balance. Common sense said to throw it away, but all that remained to her in the world was in that pack.

The two men cursed and lunged at her, but Sholeh danced out of their reach and raced into the water, knee-deep in just a few steps. Fins cut the rolling waves. A long, blunt nose and eternal smile appeared above the highest crest only a dozen paces out from shore. More dolphins danced further out, waving fins like welcoming arms. The screels and clicks of the dolphins rose in a chorus above the sounds of gulls and surf and the growls of the man who stumbled across the wet, packed sand to snatch at her.

Sholeh submerged and writhed like an eel to cut through the drag of the surf. The pack slowed her, gave the current purchase on her, and she had to fight. She emerged for air ten paces out and let out a cry to mimic the dolphin. Angry shouts rang from the shore.

A dolphin clicked and chattered as it slid up in the water next to her. Sholeh licked salt from her lips and wrapped her hand around its fin.

"You're mine!" the scarred brute shouted. "Agantes gave you to me. There's nowhere you can go that I won't find you."

"Agantes is no god and has no power over me," Sholeh muttered. Then she turned all her attention to the dolphins circling her, begging them with all the strength of her soul to take her far away from this place.

She called up an image of the forest from her dream as the first dolphin tugged her out into deeper water. In moments, the three people on the shore were barely discernible against the rocks. The dolphins clicked and screeled, confused by the images she used. How could they understand she wanted to find that particular forest? Sholeh held on with both hands as the dolphin dragged her farther out to sea. She tried to convey with images that she merely wanted a place on land where she could hide. The other dolphins darted through the water on either side of them. Sholeh closed her eyes and thought of the dream and the wolf who had spoken to her, offering shelter and protection.

She showed the wolf in her mind to the dolphins and tried to convey to them the need to hide from other people. Clicks and chirps and whistles went through the pod of dolphins. They slowed to confer. She was too tired to spare the effort to try to decipher the images that flicked between the creatures' minds. She held on and thought of the black wolf, and prayed Verdidan would guard her just a little longer.

The dolphins set off again, so swiftly she had to close her eyes against the water splashing her face. They changed course, going up along the coastline. Before her bruised arms could get too tired to hold on, the dolphin conveying her darted in toward the cliffs that rose high above the boulder-strewn shore. Sholeh blinked salty water from her eyes. Just when it seemed they would run aground on the rocks, a vertical black streak in the cliff face opened before them, revealing a gap reaching inland. The dolphin swam a bowshot up the narrow channel that ran into the heart of the cliffs. Then the water grew shallow enough that Sholeh's feet touched the bottom.

A flickering image of many wolves, men in armor, and a thick forest touched Sholeh's mind. How did the dolphins know of the forest beyond the cliff tops? Maybe they gathered the images from other minds? Were there people nearby who spoke with the dolphins, accepted by them, perhaps with gifts like she had received from Verdidan? The dolphin clicked once, then shook himself, dislodging her hold. Sholeh pulled her arms back, freeing the helpful creature. Looking back, she saw the other dolphins leaping and dancing along the tops of the waves.

"Thank you," she whispered, and took a step toward the pebbly bank of the stream.

Sholeh watched the dolphin dart away, back toward the open sea and his friends. For just a moment, she wished she had the power to change herself into a sea holder, to slip into the water and swim away and dwell with the dolphins for the rest of her life. Or perhaps not the rest of her life? Perhaps just until she crossed the sea and reached the Isle of the Moon.

Her pack felt heavier than before on her back and Sholeh sighed, knowing she could not discard her Human form any more than she could discard the pack and the heritage and treasures it contained, or the duty given by her mother and the Council. She settled down on a boulder and struggled to untie the strap that held the pack on her back. No wonder the three people who had thought to take her prisoner hadn't been able to unfasten it. Her fingers were sore and several nails had torn by the time she untied the water-swollen strap and slid the pack off and emptied it.

Her spare clothes were damp, but not soaking wet, and they smelled fresh compared to the salt-crusted rags she wore. Sholeh spread them out on a straggly bush to dry in the sunlight that pierced the ravine where she sat and examined the rest of her pack. Whatever water had penetrated the seal on the pack was very little and had been absorbed by the cloth wrapping her healing kit and the bound bundle of gold sheets. She spread everything out to dry that she could. She still had the knives she had put in her pack, not that they would have done her any good in defending herself against her captors. They had her sword, after all.

A thin trickle of water glistened on the rocks far to her right, falling from a spring high in the cliff face. Sholeh followed it with her gaze, until she found the shallow cup in the rock. It held more than enough water, sweetly fresh and tasting of sun-warmed rock, to quench her thirst. She drank up everything she could gather in her palms, startled by how the taste of water awoke her thirst, rather than quenching it. When her belly felt heavy with water, she stopped, fearing she would make herself sick. Carefully, constantly listening for the sounds of voices, any hint that people were near, she peeled out of her ragged clothes. Using what remained of her skirts, she sopped up water from off the rock face and washed herself as best she could. Her hair was matted and thick with salt, and it would take too long to wait for water to collect enough to let her wash it. Sholeh resorted to rubbing the damp cloth through her hair.

When she finished, the angle of sunlight had changed enough to make her conscious of the passage of time. Sholeh shuddered at the thought of being caught halfway up the cliff face when night fell. Or worse, reaching the top as darkness came, and being vulnerable to attack from the people who might live there. She had to pack up her few remaining belongings and start climbing.

No ships broke the smooth line of the green-blue horizon behind her. Sholeh kept careful watch as she packed. No merchants, no fishermen, no warriors in their black-keeled ships to find her.

She thanked Verdidan when she discovered the narrow inlet continued further inland. As the ravine gradually sloped upward, she found a stream, five times larger than the trickle she had washed in. The silver water sparkled in the stray beams of light that penetrated the high cliffs on either side. It bubbled, sounding like a child's laughter, falling down the natural stairs from high above. Water and a hiding place, gifts from Verdidan.

Sholeh thought about the dream of the wolf and the mountain and how she would find the home of the guardians, as she walked up into the stony heart of the coast all through the afternoon. She gleaned a handful of sour berries and scooped up a few handfuls of water as she climbed through the increasingly narrow chasm, following the stream to the spring at its source.

Sunset spilled thick shadows down on her from the eroded lips of the ravine, and she estimated she was only halfway to the top. When she did emerge into the higher landscape, where would she go? What would she do? Sholeh's steps slowed and her aching body felt heavier with every heartbeat. The possibility of meeting up with unfriendly people in the shadows pushed all other thoughts from her mind.

With the coming of dusk, the increasing cold of the shadows and the aches filling her weary, starved body overruled all her other concerns. Why risk meeting up with people in the dark? She found a relatively smooth spot to rest, in a pocket of sandy soil in the shadows of several bushes and a larger spine of rock. Better to rest here, out of sight, than push herself to walk through the thickening shadows and perhaps fall and break a limb. Or reach the top of the cliffs in shadows, unable to see danger approaching.

Sholeh bent down to creep through a gap in the bushes in the hopes of some warmth captured by the leaves. A low growl greeted her. She went still, then cautiously, tipped her head to look behind herself.

Nothing but shadows crept across the stony ground. She looked up, to the bloody sunset sky. No shadows of some predator about to leap down on her.

That meant the sound came from deeper among the bushes. She closed her eyes and called up all her strength and sent her thoughts to the hiding creature. Sholeh's arms buckled as the effort sucked away what little strength remained. She nearly went face down in the dried leaves and pebbles.

Her mind touched the beast. Its pain. Fire ate at its leg and sent vines of agony into its head and throughout its body. Pity pushed away the first chilly fingers of fear. Sholeh concentrated, sending thoughts of comfort to the wounded animal, and continued creeping through the bushes.

She froze, didn't blink, didn't breathe, at her first glimpse of the black wolf from her dream, with the broken foreleg.

Chapter Seven

The wolf stared at her. Perhaps he was so sick from his pain he couldn't react to her presence? She would use that stillness.

Crooning a healing prayer-song, Sholeh crept forward, slowly, holding the wounded wolf still with her gaze and the power of her mind. Healing his broken leg would likely take more from her than she could spare. Yet if her dream had been true, her quest and her sacred duty demanded that she heal the beast.

The wolf closed his big, green-gray eyes and let out a sigh when she came within arm's reach. Sholeh continued her song and slowly stretched out a hand to touch the beast's head. His ears went flat against his skull. He lowered his head, allowing her to stroke his thick, unexpectedly soft, blue-black fur.

The wolf's pain flooded into her, red and jagged, like broken pottery fragments caught in a flood, lacerating everything they touched as they tumbled along. The sickly yellow heat of fever crept into the creature's flesh from his wound. She saw her own fear, tingeing the golden and silver glow of her healing power a faint, poisonous green.

"Blessed Verdidan, All-Maker who gives me my gifts and duty, work through me. One of your creatures suffers. I answer the call, as I vowed on my day of consecration," Sholeh whispered in her mother's language full of liquid vowels, so very different from the sharp, hard sounds of the Nedaians' language.

The wolf opened his eyes and stared up at her. Human wonder gleamed in his eyes. Sholeh sensed something stirring beneath the pain and the eternal *now* of a wolf's mind. Quickly, before she lost her nerve entirely, she focused all her power on the broken bones and torn flesh.

"Forgive me, friend," she said, and grasped the wolf's leg in both hands, above and below the break.

The wolf howled and started to yank his leg away. Sholeh held on, eyes closed, reaching with mind and soul into the bones of the land for her strength. It flowed up through her feet, drawn from stone and water and the power that made seeds sprout in the spring. Golden light enfolded her and the wolf, wrapping them like a newborn's swaddling cloths.

In a heartbeat that touched eternity, the healing was done. Sholeh kept her eyes open, to watch the wolf finish struggling to his feet. She slowly collapsed and settled her weary, sweaty head on her crossed arms.

The wolf stared down at his healed, straight leg, so much like a man in shock that for a moment, she thought she saw a tall, lean, bronzed warrior in full armor standing over her. He had a thin, blue-black beard and green-gray eyes, and stared at her in wonder. She blinked. The wolf took a step toward her.

As she sank down, spinning into nauseated exhaustion, Sholeh heard the wolf whimper. She felt his cool nose against her neck. Felt his tongue lick the sweat from her forehead. She shivered, drained of all energy and warmth, and then knew nothing.

~~~~~

In her dreams, the wolf became a warrior and stood over her, watching her, concern wrinkling his face. A wolf again, he curled up next to her, sharing his warmth. The dusty, musky scent of his fur filtered through her dream, comforting her. Sholeh rested her head in the soft, thick black fur and felt safe for the first time since her ship headed into the storm.

"It's all right, little one," that familiar voice whispered. "You're safe now, and among friends. Stay. We'll find you a place to hide, and food." He sighed. "If you spoke truly about the crescent moon ... You're a gift from the gods. If the gods ever truly existed."

"Verdidan is," she responded sleepily. "There is only one god. Verdidan Who Gives Life."

"Then stay and teach me about this Verdidan. Sleep now, little one. You are safe."

When Sholeh woke, the wolf was gone, but the extra warmth and the depression in the fallen leaves next to her showed that her companion had left only moments before. Sighing, knowing as she woke the warmth would vanish, making the wolf a dream as well, Sholeh rolled onto her back.

Noonday sun burned down into her eyes, piercing the shelter of the bushes around her. She raised one hand to shield her eyes. Her arm trembled. Not from cold or weariness, but hunger. Sholeh wanted to weep. All her climbing yesterday had brought her perhaps halfway to the top. Maybe a little more. She didn't want to climb anymore, she couldn't go back down, and she refused to stay here and simply give up and die. She was a healer, only daughter of Adastra. She refused to be weak.

But she was so very hungry and bruised and alone.

Sholeh sighed for the wolf's company even more than his warmth. At least she could pull the damp blanket from her pack to wrap around herself to solve that problem, but how could she climb like that? She crept out of her shelter, knowing she had a long way to go until she reached the top of the cliffs. Perhaps there would be farms on the level ground, high above the waves. She wondered if she had the skill, let alone the strength, to sneak into the fields and steal a handful of wheat or oat stalks and beat
~~~~~

out the grain, to eat raw. Maybe some vegetables or early grapes to glean off the vine, while staying in the shadows.

The thought of stealing occupied her thoughts for the first few difficult moments, as she struggled to start climbing again. She had never been in need before. Hunger had been an affliction in others, which she had been glad to alleviate. Bruises and rags and cold had also been something that tormented others, never her. Steal? She had never needed to steal. Sholeh the fugitive, however, would do whatever it took to survive. Steal, fight, flee. Anything to keep herself alive. Except submit to the abuse and ownership of a Nedaian man. She would rather slit her throat or die alone and broken.

Very well, then. She would steal. She would hide. But hide where? Those thoughts occupied her as she came to the first series of rough steps in the rocky pathway, littered with debris and splash from the stream, so the way become slippery.

A man-shaped shadow slid across the sandy ground to her right. Sholeh froze when she saw it. He stood above her on the steps, maybe two man-heights. One leap would bring him down on her. In her weakened condition, with such unsure footing, she had no hope of escape. Sholeh refused to look at him. She concentrated on his shadow and tried to find a sharp stone within arm's reach, to defend herself.

"No need to fear, little one," the man said. His voice was the low, sweet rumble of hooves on a meadow thick with sweet grass. "You're among friends now."

She almost snorted her disbelief. A gasp escaped her when a bundle of cloth dropped down almost on her toes.

"If you want to be alone, we'll leave you alone," he continued. "But we will watch so no one harms you."

A whimper escaped her when the sweet, yeasty smell of fresh, warm bread seeped through the cloth.

"Why?" she asked, her voice catching in her raw, dry throat.

"For the sake of the night hunter whom you healed. Because some of us heard you speak to the wave dancers. And because no child should be harmed simply because she is beautiful."

Sholeh reached for the bundle of cloth and sighed when his shadow retreated into the larger darkness of the rocks and bushes above her. When she struggled up another step and turned to look for him, he was gone.

The cloth was a thin blanket of clean, dun-colored cloth with a scrollwork pattern around the edges, and a simple pin to hold it together. Tucked inside were simple sandals, little more than lengths of fire-toughened leather and straps to fit them to her feet. Sholeh gasped in delight when she saw them. Her climbing had been slow because of the roughness of the ground and the soreness of her feet. Now she could move three times faster, with no fear of cuts. When she lived on the Isle, she would have laughed at the thought of wearing such ugly things, but these were blessed gifts from Verdidan.

More important than all the other gifts was the bread. It was an entire loaf, wrapped in thin cheesecloth, still warm from the oven and large enough to feed three people. At least, three people who weren't as empty and ravenous as Sholeh felt at that moment.

"I am not a beggar or a barbarian," she whispered, and put the bread aside. She had to remember to do things properly, or she would become something shameful.

Sholeh tucked the blanket into the straps of her pack, to make it easier to carry. She would be very glad of its warmth when night came again. She took care to fit the sandals to her feet, neither so tight they hurt her feet, nor so loose they would fall off in the climb. Giving thanks to Verdidan and asking a blessing on the stranger who had brought her such gifts, she tore off a small piece of bread and tucked the remainder back into the cloth that had wrapped it. She knew better than to strain her aching stomach with too much food all at once. After eating slowly, she sang a short prayer of thanks, drank deeply from the stream, and continued climbing.

The top of the crevice had seemed like days of climbing away when her stomach was empty and her feet were bare. Sholeh reached it in two hours. She laughed quietly, pausing in the shadow of the boulders near the top, and allowed herself another couple mouthfuls of bread.

The black wolf met Sholeh when she stepped out onto level ground. His mouth dropped open in a canine smile and he waited for her to approach. He whined when she dropped to her knees and reached to stroke his head, down his back.

"Will you help me, my friend?" she whispered. The wolf whimpered as if he understood, then licked her cheek.

Sholeh stood, and when the wolf got to his feet and trotted through the spindly trees at the top of the cliffs, she followed.

The wolf led her through the hazy afternoon quiet. Past a farm golden and green with shoulder-high wheat in the fields all around it. Around a vineyard, where the tangy promise of ripening grapes freshened the air. Into another long wall of trees that stood against the sea winds that moaned continually along the tops of the cliffs. He stayed by her side, keeping watch as she gleaned berries along the way and tucked them in a pouch made from the bread cloth.

The forest deepened, thickened, darkened. Sholeh felt a little safer with every step further into the shadows. The quiet reassured her. Not the deathly silence of wild creatures watching an intruder, but a stillness filled with peaceful rustling of feathers and scampering of little feet along the forest floor and through leaves in the treetops. The wild things accepted her, making no alarm cries at her presence. Sholeh was no fool. She knew this quiet welcome came because of the wolf walking at her side.

What sort of place was this, where a wolf didn't walk as predator and the smallest creatures didn't freeze or scamper away in terror? Sholeh didn't care. It was enough to be here and know she was safe from people. If only she could persuade her new friend to walk with her all the way inland to Mount Aerno, to find the guardians. They were wolves, yes, but the legends said they possessed intelligence, a gift and duty from Verdidan. If only she could tame this wolf and his pack-mates, so when she found her brother and their ship, they could flee back home across the sea. Sholeh knew better than to disobey the visions that had sent the searchers out into the world. She had to find guardians, not ordinary wolves.

Although, now that she had leisure to think beyond safety and food, who would ever call this wolf ordinary?

The wolf led her to an empty hut in a clearing slowly being reclaimed by the forest. Sholeh almost walked past it, but her guide stepped in front of her to block her path. She looked again at the tangle of vines and stone and rotting wood and saw part of one wall had fallen inward, taking a large section of the roof down with it. The roof looked intact, or perhaps the gaps had been filled in with vines and plants sprouting in the soil that had accumulated over the years.

Sholeh walked around the hut and found the gaping hole of the door, squeezed to half its width by the collapse of a second wall. The way was blocked by a plank table that had fallen over inside, and by more vines. She climbed over the barrier and inside. Thoughts of animals denning inside the abandoned hut made her move cautiously.

The hut was dry inside, lined with blown leaves and accumulated dirt. Sholeh smiled and sent impressions of thanks to the black wolf. She reached out a hand through the doorway to him and he licked her fingertips. A whimper escaped him as he took a step closer and nuzzled her arm. Then with a flick of his tail he turned and left, faster than thought.

~~~~~

For three days, the black wolf accompanied Sholeh whenever she ventured out of her hiding place at dusk to forage for food, materials to make her hut more secure and comfortable, and to explore the countryside while people slept. She stayed in hiding during the day, letting her bruised, aching body rest, weaving baskets to hold the food and the healing herbs she gathered, or fashioning tools from wood or stone for cooking. Not that she dared to try to light a fire, but she hoped to be safe enough for that someday.

She learned to sleep the daylight away and wanted nothing to do
~~~~~

with people. She always returned to her hut from foraging when the moon began its descent toward morning. Each night, the wolf leaped over the barrier of the table, which she left in front of the door, and curled up with her, sharing his warmth in the chill that settled in before dawn. She whispered to him tales of her island home and taught him of Verdidan as if he were a child. The wolf listened, watching her, his eyes seldom blinking, as if fascinated by her stories. That was company enough for her.

The fourth morning, a dark shadow sat by the spring where Sholeh came to fetch water. She used a basket she had woven and lined with leaves which, when crushed, created a sticky paste that sealed the basket weave, to hold water. The shadow stayed still, and she would have ignored it but for the prickling of warning that raced up her back and across her scalp. She had her knife and a long, pointed stick she had sharpened, to help her with digging when she foraged.

A snuffling sound broke the waiting silence. She stared, self-mocking laughter catching in her throat when a silver-gray wolf stepped from the shadows. It carried a hare in its mouth. Her stomach twisted, imagining the taste of fresh meat. With a whine that sounded like a question, the wolf approached her, and a moment later dropped the hare at her feet. Before she could gather her thoughts back from shock and hunger, to touch the wolf's mind with her thanks, the beast licked her hand, turned, and fled into the darkness of the trees.

Laughter escaped her, soft with the caution she learned from the wild beasts. Sholeh picked up the hare, tied it to the end of her belt, then scooped up her water for the day and went back to her hut. She didn't dare try to cook it during the day, when people might be abroad in the forest, and smell the meat or smoke. If she managed to start a fire, of course. She skinned the hare as best she could, careful to save the skin, to use the soft fur later. She wrapped the cleaned carcass in wet leaves, to preserve it until evening, and slept, smiling as she dreamed of hot food.

~~~~~

Her fingers were bruised and sore, scratched and full of splinters by the time Sholeh got a fire going. She laughed in pure triumph, carefully settled the hare on the makeshift spit, and prepared to sit and wait until her dinner was ready.

The black wolf arrived for their nightly walk and skidded to a stop when he saw the fire and the hare. His eyes widened and he darted from one side of the clearing to the other, sniffing and sticking his head into dark spots of shadows. Sholeh laughed at the image of a jealous suitor looking for a rival.

"A big silver wolf met me this morning and gave it to me," she said. The laughter caught in her throat and died when the black wolf growled and ran to her. He sniffed at her hands, her dress, then found the skin she
~~~~~

had stretched on a makeshift drying rack.

Growling, he ran into the darkness. Sholeh shivered, wondering if the beast truly understood her. If so, why would he be angry that another wolf had fed her?

When the black wolf returned, the meat was only half-cooked and Sholeh had given up trying to keep the fire alive. She let it die and took the partially cooked carcass off the fire. Hot and dripping with juice was fine with her. She offered the wolf half. He snorted and stalked away from her.

"We can still take our walk. I want to walk with you," she called after him. The wolf growled but didn't look at her.

She ate, watching him as he circled the clearing. The meat caught in her throat when she saw the black wolf carefully mark a wide circle around the clearing, then another, smaller circle around the hut. He scratched in the dirt and lifted his tail and she smelled the sharp wolf musk filling the air. Then for added measure, he lifted his leg, doubly marking the territory.

Had she been claimed as part of the black wolf's territory? Something about it repelled her, conflicting with her sense of safety. Yet what could she do? Flee past the farms to the village, and beg sanctuary?

The thought of the wolf being hunted and killed by the villagers terrified her. That helped her settle her thoughts. She had to trust that Verdidan had sent the black wolf to watch over her until she could find her brother and their warriors. Hints of jealousy, of hurt feelings, were just her imagination.

Another wolf, dark brown like rich soil, sat at the edge of the clearing two nights later, when Sholeh and the black wolf returned from their nightly walk. A half-grown deer lay in the moonlight, its throat torn out. The black wolf rubbed noses with the brown wolf, caught the deer in his jaws by its hind legs, and dragged it into the clearing.

"I thank you, friend," Sholeh murmured, when the black wolf left the carcass in front of her hut door, then flipped his ears at her in his usual farewell and left. She stood still, clutching her basket of berries, nuts and roots, and watched the two wolves run away, side-by-side.

She spent the night processing the meat the wolf had left for her. Some went into a stew, to eat right away. The rest she ground up with herbs to dry and preserve it in slabs, in the makeshift smokehouse hidden behind her hut. She was especially proud of the smokehouse and prayed the smell of smoke and highly seasoned meat wouldn't give her away.

~~~~~

"You are well, little one?" The male voice came from the shadows the next morning, when Sholeh knelt at the spring to fill a basket with water to get her through her day of hiding.
~~~~~

"Very well." She held still, listening with every fiber of her being. The man's voice stirred something warm and pleasant inside her.

"I think you might be tired of nothing but berries and meat. A gift, waiting at your door. Rest well."

She caught her breath, wanting to ask him to stay and talk a little longer. Wanting to ask his name, where she was in Nedaia, and how to reach Mounta Aerno. She should ask if he had heard about other strangers washed ashore. The words caught in her throat, and after a few heartbeats had passed, she sensed her unseen friend was gone.

Two loaves of bread and a comb waited in the doorway of her hut. Sholeh laughed, more pleased with the comb than the fragrant, warm loaves.

~~~~~

Slowly, she grew to hunger for the few words of greeting from her unseen friend. Every morning after that, when she came to the spring, he waited in the shadows to speak with her. He always left gifts for her to find when she returned to her hut. Necessary, simple things, they were riches to one who had nothing. More bread, warm from someone's oven; clips and braiding cords for her hip-length tangle of hair; new sandals; a shawl; another knife; simple platters of wood and pottery bowls.

Their morning ritual never changed, for eight days. He greeted her, never showing his face. She greeted him as she knelt to gather her water from the spring, never looking deeper into the shadows where he waited. He would warn her if people from the nearby town or farms might be in the forest.

On the second day, she asked him if he had heard about other strangers who came from the sea, and he promised to ask. Every day, he told her no news had come.

Usually, he followed her to her hut, disappearing into the forest shadows once she reached shelter. Sholeh always let him leave, silently praying a blessing on him, content with her silence and solitude. Until the eighth morning.

"Please. Stay, friend?" she asked, as she approached her door.

"Am I your friend?" He chuckled, and the sound was warm honey against her bruised and dry spirit.

Her heart skipped a beat in pure relief and delight that he had stayed, instead of vanishing immediately.

"Yes. May I see you?" She put down her container of water and stayed facing the doorway.
~~~~~

Chapter Eight

"That may not be wise," he said.

"Why?"

The silence lasted so long, she feared he had faded into the misty morning. She turned quickly, hoping to catch a glimpse of his back as he fled into the forest shadows, and came face-to-face with him.

He wore the short kilt and leather overtunic and leggings of a soldier. Bronze strips reinforced his sandals. A long knife hung from his belt instead of a soldier's short sword and he had no armor. Something about him told her he would wear the bronze breastplate and leg shields, and plumed helmet of a commander, rather than the wood-and-leather bowl-shaped helmet and breastplate of a common foot soldier.

His eyes were a familiar green-ringed gray, his blue-black hair thick and darker than a moonless night, clipped short for comfort under a helmet. His beard was close-trimmed to frame his cheeks and chin and give enemies nothing to grip in battle.

He was the man from her exhausted vision immediately after she had healed the black wolf. Her legs folded and a whimper of pure terror crawled through her throat like a snake.

"Little one?" His voice broke and he reached out to grip her arms.

His massive hands filled the same place where the brute fisherman had bruised her flesh, but his touch had a gentleness that belonged to a harpist, a scribe, an artisan who sculpted in gold and jewels.

"You're a soldier," Sholeh whispered.

"Mercenary." The corners of his mouth twitched.

Sholeh wanted to see him smile. It would be a kind smile. A foundation for good laughter. No cruelty on those lips, in those deep eyes.

"Mercenary?" she echoed.

"Disappointed, little one?" A tiny sigh escaped him as he released her. "Well, we all have to find a way to live. Men who roam with no women-folk or children among us … we're more acceptable, less dangerous to the townsfolk, as mercenaries looking for work. Otherwise, we're bandits and brutes, on the prowl for innocent flesh to devour."

"Why are you helping me?"

"Some men can't avoid shedding blood. When they are able to protect someone, they should do it before the Furies call them to an accounting. Don't you think?"

"Furies? Who are they? Why would they call you to an accounting?"

He laughed. "Oh, little one, you truly are from a far-off place, aren't you?"

"I'm not that little. You're a giant." She smiled at him, despite the snap in her voice.

He stood more than a head taller than her, his shoulders a few fingers higher than the top of her head.

"You've left the winter's sleep of your pain if you can think about the world around you." He nodded as if pleased. "Will you share your name?"

"Sholeh," she whispered.

He settled down on the ground a few steps away from her in a fluid movement. "I am Steffyn." His serious expression melted into a smile that made her smile in return. "Your name is foreign, is it not?"

She knelt facing him. "My people come from far over the sea. Our ship was rammed by whoever chased us into the storm that hit half a moon ago."

"Yes, I guessed so, when you asked for news of others coming from the sea. Tell me more of them? Why did you come to Nedaia?"

"Legends, tales of wolves unlike any others. They were once guardians of the land where I live. We are endangered by a powerful enemy with the power of Biss, and Verdidan sent visions to our elders, directing us to find the guardians and bring them home again."

"Who is Biss?"

"Pure evil. All the cruel, terrible things the gods of Nedaia do are nothing compared to the evil and the power of Biss."

Steffyn nodded slowly, studying her face, until Sholeh thought he could touch her thoughts. He got to his feet again, moving stiffly as if something pained him.

"We must find your brother then, and make sure you are safe, and send you on your way." He took a step back and his smile turned so sad, it yanked a sob up into her throat, choking her. "Sleep the day away, Sholeh-child. Remember you are surrounded by friends, warriors all, and sleep sweetly."

"But you will go to war and I will be alone again." She caught her breath, surprised at what slipped between her lips. Was she already so dependent on him?

"There will always be someone to guard you. I swear it on my mother's blood. That is the strongest Quest oath my people can swear, and it is never given lightly."

"Who are your people?" Sholeh whispered. She obeyed when he gestured for her to turn and go into the shadows of her hut.

"The Kreefa."

No rustling of cloth or underbrush marked his retreat, but she knew he had vanished into the coming day. It wasn't so much a movement or sound, but a feeling of a sudden void in the very air around her.

"Kreefa?" Sholeh brought her basket of water into her hut and tugged the concealing vines back over the doorway. She curled up in the springy nest of pine boughs covered in her blanket and pillowed her head on her bent arm. "That tells me nothing," she whispered into the darkness.

~~~~~

The black wolf waited at her door when she crept out at sunset. He kept her company the entire time she gathered her herbs and explored another portion of the surrounding countryside. Sholeh wondered why he didn't wander off on his own to hunt or roam with his pack, but she was grateful for the company. After talking with Steffyn, loneliness hovered closer around her heart than before. The wolf nuzzled her hand often, as if sensing the drooping of her spirits. When she returned to her hut, he stayed with her instead of vanishing into the night to return to his own kind. Sholeh welcomed his presence. She sat outside, watching the moon travel the bowl of the sky, and thought long and hard. The wolf rested his head on her thigh and she fancied he enjoyed her touch just as much as she enjoyed stroking his fur.

How long should she wait before she went to the shore to search for news of survivors? How long until she began the long journey to Mount Aerno on her own? Sholeh thought of leaving her safe little haven, the protection of the black wolf, and Steffyn, and she shivered. Steffyn called himself a mercenary, and she knew such men went where there was pay. How could she pay him and his warriors to guide and guard her on the journey to Mount Aerno? How could she convince him to do it for free, other than play on the sympathy he already felt for her?

It would take a miracle of Verdidan even greater than all the blessings she had already been granted. Did she dare to hope and dream and pray?

The wolf left her as the near-full moon settled into the horizon. She wondered if he had heard her thoughts of leaving this sheltered spot and became angry.

Sholeh couldn't sleep. She got up and moved like a shadow through the forest, following the unseen path that led her to the edge of the forest, at the top of a shallow hill. From safety, she looked out at the village in the distance and the rolling blanket of vineyards and farms that lay between it and her safe haven. She watched the world of men, shrouded still in darkness and sleep, and prayed in whispers, begging Verdidan to give her guidance for what to do next.

When day came, she returned to her hut and found Steffyn waiting. He knelt by the doorway, gutting a wild piglet. Sholeh almost fled, but he greeted her with a smile and didn't scold her for being away from her safe little hut. After a few seconds of hesitation, trying to guess what he
~~~~~

thought, she approached and knelt facing him.

Steffyn handed her two wedges of metal. One was iron, and the other a silvery-black she didn't recognize. When she just looked at the pieces in her hand, he frowned for a moment, then laughed.

"How do you not know how to make fire?" He finished dressing the piglet and took the wedges from her hands. His were still bloody.

"Fire? With this? But you make fire with a lens of glass, filled with water, to focus the rays of the sun until the tinder burns." Her face warmed as she remembered how she had struggled to make fire with wood sticks and friction. What made her think there was only one good way to make fire?

"Glass? Who but royals are rich enough to own it? This is the way we common-born do it. Less breakable, too, if you must travel." Steffyn winked at her, just when she thought he might be mocking her. He tipped his head to the side, inviting her to sit next to him.

It took nearly ten minutes before she quite got the knack of striking the two wedges of metal together until sparks sprang from the collision. Until enough sparks rained out to catch in the feathery pile of tinder. They laughed together as they took turns gently blowing on the infant flame until it caught. Sholeh told him what a struggle it had been to make fire with just tinder and dust and a sharpened stick, and they laughed together over that, too.

"Do you know how to season this for cooking?" he asked, lifting the cleaned piglet carcass by its heels.

A quick trip into her hut brought out packets of leaves she had collected during her night rambles. She had pierced their stems to weave them together into garlands and hung them from the slanted ceiling to dry. Steffyn produced a skin bottle filled with water to wash the piglet, then they rubbed it with crumbled seasoning herbs and stuffed the body cavity with chopped tubers.

"It will take some time until we have good coals for cooking. I thought instead of spending the hours in sleep, we could ... talk."

"About what?" Sholeh found it hard to look at him for a moment.

There had been a catch, a dropping in his voice that made her think he wanted something besides talk. She was grateful, remembering the brute on the shore. Yet she had quite enjoyed the warmth whenever their hands and arms had brushed against each other while they worked together. She liked Steffyn's presence. Her healing gifts helped her see great depths and harmonies in his spirit. His heart and mind were well-ordered, as clean and strong as his body.

"You are from a far distant, foreign people. You know so little, you will make mistakes and people will notice you. Far more than your beauty already demands," he added, his voice going husky. Steffyn looked away for a moment. She saw his throat contract as he swallowed. "I will try to help you find your people. Until then, I will teach you about Nedaia, our gods and customs, so you will be safe."

"You should be a minister in a king's household," Sholeh whispered. "That is great wisdom."

"No, little one. That's common sense, which has nothing to do with the wisdom of kings and armies." He winked at her. "Hand me my pack, will you?" He gestured at the pile of gear he had left on the far side of her doorway; cloak, spear, and heavy leather pack. Steffyn reached into it and grinned. "A celebration, I think. Perhaps it's not wise to drink so early in the day, but since we are both creatures of the night, this is our evening meal, eh?" He sighed when she laughed at his words, and brought out a wineskin. "Such lovely music, my Sholeh-child. Your father, the king of some far-off land, had no need of musicians."

"My mother rules us."

"Ah, and how many folk are wise enough to be ruled by their women? The Kreefa survive our bloody nature only by the strength and wisdom of our women." The light left his eyes. He yanked the plug from the neck of the skin and tipped his head back to squirt a stream of dark red wine into his mouth.

"Is the king of Nedaia named Agantes?"

Steffyn choked and nearly dropped the wineskin. Sputtering, he bent his head to wipe his wet chin on his shoulder. His eyes watered and his fingers shook as he jammed the plug back into the wineskin. "Why do you ask that?"

"The man who … a man said Agantes had given me to him. I thought perhaps he spoke of the sea god, but Nedaia is a strange land, and perhaps there are kings named after gods."

"The only Agantes hereabouts is the god of the sea. Just as Xoris is the god of the sky, with Anieri the queen of the gods and Pallon drives the chariot of the sun across the sky."

"I know of Pallon. Some of his priests tried to take me and my cousins to serve in his temple. And I know of Agantes, Xoris, and Anieri, but there are so many other gods in Nedaia that I do not know."

Steffyn's puzzled little frown faded into a compassionate smile that made her want to cry. He gently touched her chin with two fingers and tipped her head up so their gazes met.

"We have much to learn today, Sholeh-child."

As the flames burned down to coals and they buried the piglet in leaves and coals and waited for it to cook, he told her about Nedaia, and the people who thought it was the center of the world. He named the gods and their offspring and rivalries. He explained the different cities and petty kingdoms of Nedaia, the many kings who held loose allegiance to the high king.

When the piglet was cooked and steaming delicious, Steffyn told her of distant lands Nedaian merchants visited, Gallis and Aegyps and the desert lands of the Sandmen. After a time, Sholeh forgot about trying to learn and simply enjoyed the warm, sweet rumbling of his voice, the musical drumbeat of his laughter, the excited glimmers in his eyes.

"You would go to other lands if you could, I think," she said, sleepy from an overfull stomach. She was closer to being drunk on the rich food and Steffyn's company, than the wine.

"If I could." He shrugged and squeezed the last of the water from the skin into a cloth. He handed it to her. "You'll attract itchy visitors if you don't wash before you go to sleep."

Sholeh made a face at him, but she complied. The fat smeared on her face and hands was a comforting feeling that went with her full stomach. While she had plenty of meat from the deer, dried meat didn't satisfy like hot and freshly cooked food did. Foraging permitted her to avoid the notice of people but didn't fill her stomach properly.

"One more gift for the celebration, and then I must leave you to sleep," Steffyn said.

He smiled at her as he reached for his pack, but the light didn't touch his eyes. She wondered what bothered him, until he pulled a wad of cloth from his pack.

It unfolded into a dress of soft reddish-brown, little more than a tube with bronze pins to hold it together at the shoulders. Another length of cloth of a dull white edged in dark brown squares was a mantle.

"You are skilled at hiding, and the few friends I trust to guard you will do all they can, but you cannot avoid notice forever. Clean clothes, a change of clothes, will do much to persuade the people who see you in the forest that you are not a runaway slave or a madwoman." Steffyn held the two pieces of clothing out to her.

Sholeh's hands trembled as she clutched them close. "How can I thank you? For all you have done for me?" she whispered.

"Be careful, Sholeh-child." He reached to touch her face, gently curving his fingertips along her cheek. "Don't venture out of your safe little den during the full moon. I have done all I can to protect you."

"The black wolf—"

"The black wolf will not come near you at the full moon. It's too dangerous, for both of you. Don't go out no matter how your blood burns and you want to dance and sing and run in the hot moonlight. Please."

She wanted to ask why, but she looked into his green-gray eyes and saw shadows there. Fear for her. Pain he suffered in memories. Shame that silenced his tongue. How she knew such things, she wasn't sure, but she trusted what she sensed in the depths of her soul. Her mother could read the spirits of people. Sholeh thought perhaps she had matured enough to share the gift.

"I will stay."

He kissed her forehead, a light brushing of his warm lips like a blessing, then snatched up his empty pack and weapons and vanished into the depths of the forest shadows.

~~~~~

The black wolf sat in the doorway, watching her when she woke that evening. He cocked his head to the side and his long tongue lolled out and he looked so sad and neglected, she couldn't help but smile. Sholeh dropped to her knees next to him and wrapped her arms around his neck. The wolf trembled and whined softly, but otherwise did nothing until she released him.

Then he pinned her to the ground and washed her face with his long tongue until she shrieked laughter.

She was glad there was still meat left from the piglet. The black wolf was as much her friend as Steffyn, and she owed him much for guarding and guiding her. Sholeh pulled out one of the wooden platters Steffyn had given her and gave more than two-thirds of the leftover, cold, greasy piglet meat to the wolf. She watched him devour the meat and thought hard.

Tomorrow was the full moon. If Steffyn was right, the black wolf would leave her as soon as the moon rose. Would she have no company at all? What did he fear befalling her, in the brightness of the full moon? Discovery?

"I think people eventually will find me," she told the wolf.

The wolf's eyes held intelligence and he cocked his head to listen when she spoke, as if he really did understand her.

"What would be wiser? To accustom the local people to my presence? Or to hide every time I hear a voice or a footstep? I think I must find some way to meet the people hereabouts, so they see me as a friend. They might tell a friend news of other strangers and newcomers to the coast, when they wouldn't tell a stranger. But the how of it ..."

She remembered all her bundles of herbs, carefully preserved and dried. Far more than she would ever need or could use, if she continued her pace of harvesting and preserving. She worked simply to keep busy, to occupy her mind and avoid the despair that came with sitting and brooding. She could sell the fruit of her labors and earn herself a place in the community.

~~~~~

Sholeh curled up and tried to go to sleep before the moon had reached the high point in the night sky. She needed her sleep, because she would be awake most of the next day, walking to the village and back. The black wolf seemed happy to come back early from their wanderings. He curled up next to her, making a little crooning sound in his chest. When she draped her arm over him, he licked her hand.

Morning came with no Steffyn to greet her and no black wolf lying next to her. Sholeh didn't like that. A shiver of fear rippled up her spine as she imagined both of her guardians wounded somewhere. Steffyn would have other mercenaries with him, but that was no comfort.

Sholeh saw a few paw prints in the dirt outside her hut, but no other proof of the black wolf's presence. She blinked away ridiculous tears as she braided her hair, then selected and gathered up her preserved herbs. Her hands shook a few times as she made up bundles with the scraps of cloth Steffyn had left and wrapped them in the end of her mantle. She tucked it into her belt and wrapped the rest of her mantle around herself to cover her head. Then, taking a deep breath, she turned her feet to the path out of the forest.

There were men working in the fields. The sight of them, the sound of their voices made her muscles cramp with the need to flee. Running would only attract unfriendly attention, so she forced herself to walk. She walked past the fields, staying in the shadows at the edge of the forest. If she acted as if she belonged, as if she had nothing to fear, nothing to hide, no one would notice her. She hoped.

This farm closest to her hut was too large, had too many people. She passed it by.

At the vineyards, she did the same.

The next farm, however, seemed smaller. The house sat between the cart path and the fields. She thought she heard a child laughing and a woman singing beyond the high, white plastered walls. The warm, rich, hunger-rousing aroma of fresh, baking bread slithered through the air like the tentacle of a hydra or a siren's song to pull her closer to the house.

Sholeh stopped, halfway between the trail and the doorway. Her legs shook and she nearly lost her grip on her bundle of herbs and roots. What had made her think she could do this?

Chapter Nine

A chorus of barks broke the drowsy warm hum that filled the air. Sholeh turned to see a knot of snarling, growling, filthy dogs streak around the corner of the house, maybe thirty paces away. She took a step back, ready to flee.

Her father scolded in her memory. How many times had he told her never to show her back to her enemy? The only way to win a battle was to advance, never to retreat, and certainly never to turn and run.

"How?" she snarled back at the memory. Anger stiffened her joints and she stomped two steps forward. "No closer!"

The dogs didn't listen. Now they were only ten paces away.

Hadn't she been living with a wolf for a friend all this time? She refused to be intimidated by stupid, noisy, filthy dogs.

"What Verdidan put between our ears is stronger than all our muscles combined," her mother said in her memory.

Sholeh flung her thoughts at the dogs. She wrapped up her frustration, her fears, the tears she cried in her sleep and turned them into a cudgel. She added the black wolf's fangs and claws and his growl.

The lead dog yelped and turned a somersault in the effort to flee. The three behind it twisted in midair, split in different directions and kept running. The last two skidded to a stop, their claws and paws digging up bits of moss, dust and pebbles. They whimpered, stretched out on their bellies in front of Sholeh and wriggled as they looked up at her with pleading eyes.

"Away with you, vermin!" a woman shouted from the house. She charged out through the main door, swinging a bread paddle in one hand and holding a naked infant to her uncovered breast with the other arm. "One bite, and you'll be sandals come winter!"

She skidded to a stop. Her mouth moved, but no words came out. Her wide eyes took in the sight of the fawning dogs. She took a few steps closer and looked Sholeh over.

"Are you all right?" she finally asked.

"Yes. Thank you. I'm sorry … I have disturbed you. I will go now." She touched her lips then her forehead with one hand, fingers fanned. "The blessings of Verdidan be on this house."

"Whoever this Verdidan is, he's a mightier god than some I've heard about," the woman said with a chuckle. She held out a hand to halt Sholeh.

It was full of bread paddle. She dropped it and extended the hand again, palm up. "There are precious few women in this part of the country. Come sit? Let me give you wine to ease the dust of the road."

The words were ritual, politeness required by the small household gods of hospitality and security. Steffyn had told her of them yesterday. Sholeh almost refused because it was not required of her to accept. But she needed to speak with a woman after so long. She smiled thanks for the farmwife's hospitality, and let her lead the way into the two-story, plastered stone and log building.

They exchanged names and her hostess settled her in the courtyard on a bench. The household spent most of its time in the courtyard, judging by the benches and two low tables covered with tools, bowls with scraps from the last meal and other articles of everyday life.

"How did you keep those beasts from ripping you to shreds?" the woman, Annis asked, after settling the baby in her cradle. She caught up a knee-high, slender jug with two fingers through the handle, dipped water into a bowl, and splashed in an equal amount of wine.

"My mother … had many dogs around our home, and she taught me how to act and speak so they wouldn't harm me." Sholeh set the bundle of her mantle on the bench next to her and started to unwrap it. She could offer the woman some herbs in thanks for her hospitality. If Annis wanted more, they could trade. This was far easier than she had anticipated.

"If you could teach me such tricks for men, my master would be gentler." Annis smiled as she said it, making the words a joke. Sholeh barely noticed, sickened by this further evidence of the cruelty of life in Nedaia.

A clattering sound from inside the house answered before Sholeh could speak. Annis sighed and shook her head as she scooped up wine into pottery cups for them. She poured out a few drops on a slab of stone as wide as a hand, set before a chunk of stone roughly carved in the shape of a person. Sholeh couldn't tell if it was to represent a man or woman. It would be rude to stare or ask questions.

"Are you Deuteron's new wife?" Annis asked as she handed Sholeh her cup. "I'd heard he went all the way to Arkady to find a girl, but I hadn't heard he had returned."

"No. I live in the forest. I've come to sell herbs," she improvised quickly, when Annis' eyes widened and she seemed to go pale at the mention of the forest.

Annis leaped to her feet and fled indoors. In the silence, Sholeh heard little coughing sounds, coming from the house. Then Annis screamed. Sholeh ran to find her.

A naked little boy with a head of blond curls writhed on the floor. His face was an odd, waxy shade of blue-white and his eyes rolled back in his head. Brightly colored clay and wood beads littered the floor. Annis snatched up the child and clutched him to her breast. She stuck a finger down the boy's throat, but couldn't make him gag.

"Nicos! Anieri and Narva, help me!" Her face went even whiter than her son's.

Sholeh snatched the boy from his mother's arms and turned him upside down. She smacked his bottom sharply and then wrapped her arm around his middle, just under his soft ribs, tightening with a hard jerk. The boy coughed with a loud, popping sound.

Then he went still. For what felt like a dozen heartbeats, total, ringing silence filled the room.

A blue wooden bead as large as Sholeh's thumb fell from the boy's mouth and clattered to the floor. The boy gasped a loud, ragged breath, then screamed loudly enough to shake the tiles from the roof. Sholeh trembled and she gladly gave the wriggling, protesting little red-faced boy back to his mother.

Annis slid to the floor weeping, cradling the boy close, calling on the names of half the goddesses Steffyn had taught her. Sholeh returned to the courtyard. She needed to sit down, and she especially needed that cup of wine and some sunshine bright and warm on her face.

"Blessed Verdidan, thank you that I remembered my lessons," she whispered. Sholeh tipped the cup and spilled a few drops into the sunlight pooled hot at her feet, to honor the Creator.

Kantor, the boy's father returned from the fields, summoned by another slave who had heard Annis screaming. Sholeh watched him as he comforted the weeping woman and assured himself the boy was all right. Perhaps he couldn't see the difference between owning the mother of his children and making her his wife, but he did seem to have a good heart otherwise.

"A healer?" he said, when Annis told him about Sholeh and he looked over the contents of her bundle of herbs. "Pallon sent you, and I will gladly show my thanks. Is this what they teach in his temples now? How to give breath back to a dying child?"

"I don't know," Sholeh admitted. "I merely did what seemed right."

"We are grateful." He bowed to her. "The best this house has is yours for the asking."

That wasn't what Sholeh wanted, but she knew better than to tell this wide-shouldered, square-faced, sunburned farmer she didn't want his gifts. She was in a foreign land, dependent on the mercy of the inhabitants.

Kantor returned to the fields, leaving Annis to dispense the gifts. There were plenty of baskets, woven from river reeds and willow wands, and an abundance of pottery cups. Sholeh let Annis give her a basket and two cups, knowing it wouldn't deprive the household. She put her bundles of herbs in the basket and convinced the grateful, tearful woman to accept the ingredients for a soothing tea for Nicos's throat. Annis examined all the herbs and roots, the leaves and seeds and bits of bark Sholeh had cleaned and prepared, delighted to see many she needed. She traded herbs for a loaf of bread and a pot of honey, and both women were pleased with the exchange.

Whether it was the excitement or her gratitude, Annis was talkative, glad to discuss the storm that had caused the farmers such consternation a short time ago. No, she hadn't heard of any shipwrecks or survivors washing ashore. The village sat at the northernmost fringe of King Adym's territory. He was friendly with King Martus, so their soldiers shared in patrolling the coast. The soldiers frequented the village's only tavern, and if they had encountered strangers, everyone who went into the tavern would have heard by now.

"Come tomorrow, earlier in the morning," Annis said, when Sholeh left the house. "I will take you to meet other women. They'll gladly trade for your herbs and roots and such. The forest holds riches, but we don't go there alone."

"Why not?" Sholeh barely held back a laugh. She felt far safer in the forest than she did standing out here in the sunshine, talking with her new friend.

"Wolves. Hundreds of them. If not for the soldiers King Adym brought in to guard his daughter until the wedding, we would be terrified for our lives. If all is well and the king remains in good humor, he will leave some of them here permanently."

"Ah. The soldiers." She smiled, thinking of Steffyn and his friends. "Yes, they keep me safe, as well."

~~~~~

The black wolf met Sholeh when she reached the edge of the forest. He sniffed at her hands and skirts and whimpered, as if he had worried about her while she was gone. Sholeh dropped to her knees to embrace the beast and thankfulness rose up so strongly in her heart, she nearly choked. What did it matter that tonight was the full moon and she would be alone? She did have good friends, protectors, and soon she would have more friends among the women of this coastal town of Gytheion.

When they returned to her hut, Sholeh gladly shared bread and honey with the wolf. She laughed, enjoying the tickling of his whiskers as he delicately ate the bits of sticky bread from her hand. She chattered to him about the house and farm she had seen, so different from her childhood home.

"I have made friends, I think," she said. "That is very important. A man who has no friends has no shelter against the storms of adversity."

She didn't resent having to spend the entire night hidden inside her
~~~~~

hut, because she was exhausted by the day's activities. Several times when she woke, Sholeh thought she heard wolves growl and snarl in the silvery moonlight that pierced the forest with hot brilliance. She had no fear. Could she blame that on her drowsiness or the fact that she trusted Steffyn and the black wolf so thoroughly?

~~~~~

The next day, Annis took Sholeh to the farm she had avoided the day before. There were three generations of women in this household; the farmer's wife, her three daughters-in-law, and their five daughters.

The old mother, Callia welcomed them and took them to the courtyard for wine and bread and to examine Sholeh's herbs. She picked through the bundles of leaves and examined a few lengths of roots but seemed distracted. When a daughter-in-law stumbled into the courtyard and gestured for her, Callia mumbled an apology to her two guests and hurried out.

"Something is very wrong," Annis said, when the woman had been gone more than a few moments. She gestured for Sholeh to stay and went into the house to investigate. She came back only a few minutes later, smelling of salt sweat and the sour stink of vomit and blood, and beckoned for Sholeh to come with her.

They went upstairs to the women's quarters. Callia and the three younger women gathered around a sixth grandchild who lay in sweaty blankets, shivering and emaciated. A basin held spatters of bile; another had rags sitting in bloody water.

"Astan," Annis whispered. "The only grandson. I thought he was better, or I would have come to help. He can only drink a little water. Everything else rushes to leave his body from mouth and bowels." She shook her head and tears touched her eyes. "Pallon sent you to us yesterday. Can you help here?"

Blessed Healer, Life-Singer, have you brought me here for this? Help me. Use me to save this child, Sholeh prayed silently.

Astan would have been a beautiful child if he weren't so pale and thin, blessed with ruddy curls and blue eyes and sturdy bones. Sholeh approached the bed and touched the boy's face. The fever encouraged her. Cold sweating in this condition would be deadly.

Annis hurried to tell the other women what Sholeh had done yesterday for Nicos and urged them to let the newcomer help. Desperation persuaded them, when Sholeh suspected they would have ignored her otherwise, just because she was young and a stranger.

When she and Annis left the farmhouse, it was long past noon. Astan lay in a fresh bed in the courtyard, soaking in sunshine and fresh air. Sholeh had done what she could against the sickness that ate at the boy from the inside and turned his own body's healing processes against him.
~~~~~

He faced a long road to recovery because the sickness had done so much that Sholeh could not reverse. She had left healing mixtures in several cups, to be ground to a fine powder in a mortar and mixed with hot water and wine, for the boy to drink at different times of the day. One mixture to reduce the fever and sweating, another to settle his stomach, another to stop the flux of his bowels. She promised to return every morning to see how the boy fared.

Sholeh retreated to the forest as soon as she could politely leave Annis's company. When she thought someone followed her, she ran. Today, she needed the sanctuary of the forest shadows more than ever.

The healing of the boy had drained her, so she gladly crawled into her den and curled up to sleep. It was past sunset when she woke, dry and hungry. And lonely. She wanted desperately to talk with Steffyn or the black wolf and tell them what had happened that day, how she had treated the little boy's sickness, and the gifts his grateful grandmother and mother and aunts had showered on her.

Callia had given her honey cakes and a small skin of wine, a larger waterskin, cheese wrapped in oiled cloth, and a handful of dried apples. Sholeh was glad to have the honey cakes and apples. She ate them slowly, savoring the sweetness, the memories they roused of happier times in her own home. Life in the forest had many benefits, but she grew tired of her simple, often raw fare.

The cheese made her thirsty, and she knew a cup of Callia's sweet wine would only make her more so. The spring was only ten steps from her hut. Would she really be disobeying Steffyn if she went that far? What could happen in such a short time?

Sholeh closed her eyes and listened with all her being, in the way she had learned from walking with the black wolf. She sensed nothing. No movement. Even the forest seemed unusually silent. Why? What made the full moon so much different from any other night? The full moon had been part of why the guardians had left the Isle of the Moon. The ancient records said it had burned in their blood but hadn't explained what that meant. As punishment, or as something the guardians could not resist? When she had asked several of her teachers, they all agreed that either the truth was so shameful the scribes refused to record it, or so common a thing, so well-known, they felt no need to waste ink and space discussing it. Just like everyone knew the sun came up in the east, there was no need to say so in writing.

And after so long, the knowledge that wasn't recorded fell out of all remembrance. To the detriment of all.

Sholeh peered out through the gap in her doorway. No shifting shadows, not even the breeze moved. Somehow, that was not comforting. She remembered Steffyn's words and thought she heard the moonlight sizzling where it touched the leaves. Despite the warmth, she shivered a little when she reached for the water skin and listened again. Still, all quiet.

"I need water," she murmured, as if the black wolf was near and could hear her excuse. She imagined stroking his head, watching his eyes close with pleasure and his ears lying flat against his head, and the little whine he always made when she stopped. "It is near enough. Even if danger approached, I am a swift runner and I know this forest. The villagers are noisy and they stink in their fear. If I hear someone coming, I can hide. I will be safe."

She smiled, reassured. The spring wasn't that far from her hut. How could anything happen in a few short, running steps?

Sholeh moved swiftly and silently as the black wolf had taught her. She stayed in the shadows as much as possible with the moon shining down with a brilliance that seemed hot enough to scorch her skin. Why was the full moon so different here in Nedaia? Could the influence of Biss, hiding behind the masks of the false gods, turn simple moonlight into a fever in the blood? Or was it simply the presence of Verdidan, the dedication to the Creator's service and to healing, that protected the people of Isle of the Moon at the full moon?

Common sense said when the full moon was over, she needed to investigate its impact on the people and animals of this land. Somewhere in her learning, she would discover the secret of the guardians, their flight from Isle of the Moon, and some clue to restoring them to their duty and their ancient home.

A growl came from the shadows when she knelt at the spring. Sholeh refused to stop and listen. She refused to let anything or anyone know she was afraid. Animals attacked the weak and ill and afraid, not the strong and healthy and confident.

She filled the water skin, grateful for the gift from Callia. If she had been using her usual basket and had to run, she would lose all the water. Sholeh tied the neck of the water skin, slung the strap over her shoulder, and paused to look straight up at the moon. Another growl came through the darkness striped with moonlight, so bright it felt as solid as onyx set in silver jewelry.

The hairs on the back of her neck stiffened, making her shiver and want to itch. She stood and took a step. A third growl answered her movement, and a faint rustling among the leaves to her left. The animal had moved much closer just in a few heartbeats.

Sholeh held her breath. That sounded like a wolf. An angry one. She let the water skin slide down on its strap to twist twice around her fist, with an idea of using it as a weapon. The silver wolf and the brown might have brought her gifts, but that was in the daylight. Even the black wolf could be different now, under the heat of the full moon. Who knew what magic roamed the darkness of Nedaia, and turned friends into enemies? She wished for Steffyn. Was he affected by moonlight as well, and that was why he stayed away?

Yet didn't she have a better weapon than knives or spears? She closed her eyes to concentrate and reached out with her mind.

Yes, a wolf crouched there beyond the wall of moonlight. Sholeh bit her lip against a gasp as she touched his mind. It spun and churned like a waterspout on a stormy sea, full of scouring sand and debris that ripped and gouged whatever it struck. All his senses burned. Every hair on his body stood on end.

"Go away," she whispered, as the wolf's turmoil snapped out to invade her senses. Her head spun and fire ate down through her middle, to pool between her hipbones. Despite the strangeness and the accompanying fear, she curled her sense of self around the spitting, crackling coal of the wolf's presence in her mind. She dredged up all her discipline, imposing peace through herself, to flood the beast with calm.

The wolf stepped from the shadows. Sholeh pushed harder, trying to wrap herself fully around the wolf's mind. Her mother could put vicious animals to sleep with the barest effort, in the vast power of her mind. Could she do that now, in this time of need?

"No," she whispered, as panic painted a picture of herself fleeing to the safety Steffyn had promised inside the darkness of her hut, and the wolf tearing through the vines and crumbling walls as if they were mist. Sholeh squeezed harder with her mind, scolding herself into confidence and calm, then forcing it down into the wolf's essence. *Sleep*, she whispered in her thoughts.

A soft whine escaped the beast. His front legs buckled. Sholeh held her breath as the animal slid to the ground and his eyes drooped closed.

The wolf's form melted and elongated, until a naked man lay on the carpet of forest detritus where the wolf had been. He groaned. She muffled a shriek and jumped back a step. The water skin strap slid from her numb fingers.

Chapter Ten

The man clawed at the ground, trying to get his arms under himself. His eyes fluttered as he fought to stay conscious. Sholeh felt with painful sharpness the distance left to reach her hut. The man lay between her and safety. Other wolves respected the line laid down by the black wolf, but this man would not.

She had dropped the water skin. She had no weapon, not even her knife. Panic slapped her with ice. Sholeh turned to snatch up the strap of the water skin and hefted it, judging its weight for a weapon. When she turned back, the man had struggled to his feet.

He was very hairy. Very dirty, sweaty, covered with scratches. And enormously aroused. He smiled and the low, rumbling, hungry laugh that erupted from him filled the clearing. He held out a hand to her, beckoning. Sholeh took a step backward. His smile melted into a confused frown, then he snarled like the wolf he had been.

"You—here," he growled. He leaped forward when Sholeh took another step backward.

His snarl turned into a vicious grin and he snatched at her. Sholeh ducked. He caught handfuls of her hair and yanked, nearly pulling her off her feet. She shrieked at the sharp pain and went to her knees. He released one hand, to snatch at her clothes. Sholeh swung with the water skin, catching him in the gut. He gasped, lost his hold with the other hand, and she leaped to her feet.

The man held onto the water skin, yanking her to a stop. She stumbled, gasping at the sudden pain in her shoulder. She let go of the skin and snatched at the ground with blind hands. She caught up stones and dirt and flung them. The man shouted. She smelled blood. A dark streak ran down his face from above his eye. She tried to run again, and this time when he leaped, he caught her.

"Mine," he growled, and landed hard on her. His mouth slammed down hard on her mouth, cutting her lip. Sholeh twisted her head aside, disgusted and terrified by his tongue invading her mouth. He slapped her hard, stunning her. Then he scrabbled down her leg and yanked up the hem of her dress.

"No!" Sholeh kicked hard, hitting his hand with her foot and his nose with her other knee. The man fell backward. She rolled over, scrambling away on hands and knees. He caught her around the waist and flung her away, so she hit a tree head-first. She saw stars and couldn't breathe. She could only lie in a crumpled heap where she landed and watch the bleeding, enraged, naked man stalk toward her.

A black shadow streaked through the moonlight and hit him. They tumbled across the stony ground. When they crashed to a stop, black wolf fought brown wolf.

Gasping, fighting the shudders that threatened to fasten her to the ground, Sholeh struggled to her feet. She would be safe if she could only reach her hut.

She ran, spurred as much by anger at her stupidity as fear. Lightning prickles raced over her skin, hearing the crashing of struggling bodies rolling through the underbrush. She nearly cried out in tearful relief as she crossed the line the black wolf had scratched in the dirt. Then she leaped over the barrier of the table across her narrow doorway. The dark safety of her hut swallowed her. She stumbled and hit the opposite wall with her face. Her heart thundered in her ears. Through it, she heard her terrified gasps.

Nothing else.

Panic tried to crumple her to the ground, but she refused to allow that. She had almost gotten herself killed or raped, by allowing panic to rule her. Sholeh pushed the paralyzing emotions aside with the same mental wall she had used on the wolf.

Had the battle ended? Had brown wolf killed black? Sholeh refused to be afraid. Now that she had a moment to think, she wondered ... If man and wolf were one, and her mind's power calmed the wolf, could it calm the man? She had been so shocked she hadn't thought to try. She refused to make that error again.

Still, she heard nothing, though she waited, her knife now clutched in her fist, until the roaring of her lungs stilled. How silently could a naked man move through the forest at night, guided by moonlight? Sholeh didn't know. She refused to believe the black wolf had been defeated.

A pained moan alerted her. She almost peered out of her narrow doorway before she caught herself. The healer in her wanted to help, then quieted under common sense.

A howl rose up in the hot moonlight. Sholeh flinched. Another howl answered, muffled by distance and the trees. She crouched low in her hut and listened. More wolf voices joined the chorus.

Fool! she scolded herself, but she looked out anyway.

The man who had attacked her lay only a few steps from the protective line in the dirt. His back was to her. By the very laxness of his limbs, she knew he was dead. Those dark smears in the dirt, glistening in the moonlight, weren't from sweat or water.

The black wolf stood over him, muzzle raised to the moon. His voice wavered, sounding like a man singing a funeral dirge.

Two wolves stepped out of the shadows of the forest and came to attention. More wolf voices joined the chorus, swelling and clashing and filling the night until the moonlight visibly trembled.

Troubled, shivering with a cold that came from deep inside, Sholeh retreated back into the darkness of her hut. She couldn't watch, though she was forced to listen as more wolves came into the clearing and joined the mourning. It went on for what felt like hours.

Silence jolted her out of a half-doze. The injudicious movement awoke her cuts and bruises and aches. She used her dearly bought water to wash and worked blindly, going by texture and smell, to grind several leaves and berries and make a paste for her wounds.

Only then did she look out of her hut again.

The dead man was gone, as were most of the wolves. Two wolves stood with their backs to her door, a silver-gray and a brown. As Sholeh watched, another brown wolf entered the clearing, moving swiftly with his nose to the ground. Following the path of her running footsteps.

She thought of how the man had come after her. She imagined she felt the wolf's eagerness. The full moon awoke lust. Men who were wolves, or wolves who could become men, it didn't matter. These creatures wanted a female.

She was the only woman within an hour's walk in any direction.

The two wolves snarled at the newcomer. He skidded to a stop and whined, stretching out his legs and lowering his head in a begging posture. The brown wolf stalked toward the intruder, snarling, ears laid back, tail stiff and straight.

Sholeh held her breath, forcing herself to calm, and prepared to defend herself with her knife and the power of her mind.

The third wolf rolled onto his back, baring his throat in submission. The silver-gray wolf walked stiff-legged toward him, nudged him with his nose, then stalked back to his post. The third wolf rolled back to his feet and scurried out of the clearing, his tail between his legs.

Sholeh watched the same scene play out four more times until the first rosy glimmers of daylight spilled into the clearing. Of all the things she had seen this night, this last was the hardest to understand.

The black wolf stalked into the clearing. The other two went down in submission. He nosed each one, then they sprang up and ran away from the clearing. The black wolf crossed the line he had scratched in the dirt so many days ago and approached the hut. Sholeh held still, marveling at this proof that the black wolf commanded all the others. He had killed her attacker and set up guards in front of her door for the rest of the night. How could this be? Why?

The black wolf whined once, gazing at her hut. Sholeh had no idea if he could see through the shadows, to where she sat. She counted to ten breaths, then the black wolf turned and fled the clearing.

Steffyn had promised she would be safe.

Was Steffyn the black wolf?

~~~~~

Steffyn didn't came to her door until a full day later. He came in the light of day and called her name.

"I disobeyed you," Sholeh said.

She gave him the news before she stepped outside and lost her nerve. An entire day of silence, of waiting, of trying to sleep and forget what she had seen that night, had given her much time to think. Even going to Callia's house to check on her grandson hadn't given her respite from her thoughts.

"Yes, I know." His voice was so soft with distress it made her ache.

"The man who was a wolf, who died—are you also a man and a wolf?" She couldn't look at his face as she asked. A tiny grunt of affirmation was Steffyn's only answer. "Are all your mercenaries of two bodies?" Another grunt. "He wanted—he would have raped me. It came from the full moon, I think, because no wolves have ever attacked me any other night. Is that why you told me to stay in hiding at the full moon?"

"That and other reasons." Steffyn sank to his haunches and studied the ground at her feet instead of looking at her as he spoke. "The Fever runs strong in my men, especially. All Kreefa suffer the Fever at the full moon. Usually, our mothers and our mates can calm us. Mating and battle, especially the smell of pain and death, help to drown the Fever. We prefer mating. Many children are conceived at the full moon." A soft sound escaped him, as if he tried to chuckle and choked on it.

Sholeh couldn't carry on a conversation with the top of his head. She knelt beside him. "The people hereabouts fear the wolves, but they admire the mercenaries, who protect them from the wolves."

"It is easier, keeping separate from all our women. Human women … smell differently. Mating among Kreefa is for life, but mating with a Human woman, especially a harlot, does nothing but cool the Fever." He raised his head enough to meet her gaze. Pain filled his eyes, and shame, and something else that made her tremble pleasantly inside. "There are many harlots in this town, especially. They were enough, until last night. You are safe now, Sholeh-child, but only until the next full moon. The scent of a virgin is sweet torment to us. How many will die to protect you at the next moon?"

"I'm sorry," she whispered. "It's all my fault. I disobeyed."

"I thought the barriers I made would protect you. I thought my scent would hide yours and be strong enough to mark you as untouchable." Steffyn managed a smile, but it flickered and never reached his eyes.
~~~~~

"Until I disobeyed and stepped outside. Perhaps they will hold at the next full moon."

"We have a moon to decide what else to do. Perhaps you should leave and—"

"No!" The panic that cut through her stole her breath. Sholeh grasped his hand. Steffyn's eyes widened, and he smiled, just enough to give her courage. "I don't want to lose you."

"Sholeh, my ..." Unspoken endearments sizzled through the air. "Did he harm you? Beyond these bruises?"

"I have seen naked men before. As a healer." Her throat closed against further words.

"Did he harm you?" Steffyn's hand twisted to return her hold. His grip tightened, almost to the point of pain.

"Other than fear? And anger at my foolishness? I swear, I will not step foot outside during the full moon, not even if I am dying of thirst. Would it have done any good, made any difference, if I had stayed inside?"

"As a wolf, I marked the ground all around your hut. Even in the full moon, my scent should be enough to keep away even the most moon-maddened among us."

"Then I truly am safe." She tried to smile, but the answer to one question simply prompted more. "I wish you had told me the truth. Last night might not have happened."

"Why burden you with knowledge you will not need when you find your own people?"

"Oh." She looked down at his hand holding hers. Was she mistaken about what he seemed to feel for her? Finally, Steffyn sighed and released her and stood.

"I am most grateful, Sholeh-child, that you were not harmed. I will kill any man who harms or frightens you. Even my closest friend."

Before she could ask the questions that churned in her head, so many she couldn't think what to ask first, he turned and stalked into the morning shadows.

"Are you the guardians?" she whispered.

~~~~~

A wolf followed her every time she left the forest. After a few days, Sholeh came to recognize her guardians. The silver and brown wolves who had stood guard in front of her hut took turns as her escorts. She spoke to them, asked them questions, offered them treats that her friends in the village gave her. Sholeh didn't know whether to be worried or not, that Steffyn never accompanied her in wolf form.

Between the miraculous recovery of Astan and the wolves that walked with her to the edge of the farms and the village, the locals held
~~~~~

her in great esteem. They claimed she was a favorite of the twin-gods, Tamis and Pallon, because of the wolf and her wealth of healing knowledge. Sholeh walked safely everywhere. That same respect opened mouths that might not have answered her questions, asking for news of strangers who searched the coastline in long ships, or who had been washed ashore. Not that the willingness to speak did her any good, because she heard no news, not even of driftwood or dead bodies.

Still, she was grateful for the fear and respect because she had no faith in Tamis or Pallon and whatever protection their supposed favor granted her. Steffyn had told her the Kreefa believed in no gods. If there were other people of magical powers, they used those powers to frighten and gather worshippers. They were not all-powerful, all-knowing, immortal, or impervious.

Those she dosed with healing potions and sold her dried herbs were more than willing to answer other questions. She learned about Steffyn and his mercenary band from the old men and women who sat and dozed in the sunshine in the stone-paved square around the village well. The mercenary band was called the Black Wolves. They had a strong reputation for strength, skill, and honor, and were respected as much as they were feared.

~~~~~

Annis reported that tales of the twin gods' healer had spread along the coast, and men from both kings' councils had been asking questions about her. It would only be a matter of time, the farmwife announced, before one king or the other invited Sholeh to serve him and live in the palace. Then she would be safe and established.

Safe from what? Sholeh toyed with the idea of having the protection of a king. Then she thought of leaving the forest. She much preferred feeling the gazes of wolves focused on her, even knowing there were men inside the wolfskins. Wolves had more honor than soldiers. Even if the full moon made their blood boil, they had more self-control and common sense.

Walking back to her den the afternoon after Annis made her declaration, Sholeh decided she would much rather stay right where she was, in the forest, living simply, and safe from the importuning and interruptions of people. Because of the wolves, people stayed out of the forest. Because they saw wolves following her, guarding her, people treated her well. How long would that respect and fear protect her, once she moved to a village or she moved up the coast in search of news about her brother and their ship and warriors?

She wanted to stay here, even knowing that was rebellion against the orders of the Council and the vision that Verdidan had given the sea holders. Just as bad a rebellion as her cousins choosing to keep their three
~~~~~

ships together, rather than voyaging to their assigned, separate territories. And where were they now?

Was Mount Aerno her destination, her goal? Sholeh looked for the brown wolf that walked as her escort today, but in the forest shadows he was invisible. Perhaps she was foolish, waiting until Steffyn appeared to ask her question. She felt as if he were the only one she could fully trust.

What would he say, if she asked if the Kreefa were the guardians she sought? What would he say if she asked him to lead his Black Wolves across the sea, to the Isle of the Moon?

"Are you there?" she called, trying to pitch her voice so it wouldn't carry far, but at least be heard by the wolf, somewhere in the shadows. "Please, ask Steffyn to come see me tonight? I need to speak with him. Please?"

The full moon was close, maybe tomorrow night. She didn't want to wait any longer to settle the question, to share her most precious secret, her quest and duty, with him.

Sholeh knew Steffyn would not come near her during the full moon, but she hoped he would come to visit as soon as the sun had risen. Annis had given her the makings of a feast when they parted that afternoon. She smiled, looking into the basket of dried apples, bread, another pot of honey, and cheese. She carried another small skin of wine over her shoulder. Perhaps when they had both eaten and they were both relaxed, she could ask her questions and he could give her the answers she needed.

~~~~~

Near midnight, Sholeh woke abruptly and lay still, listening. Not a sound reached her in the shelter of her hut.

The utter stillness of the forest had awakened her. No creaks and chirps and clatter of insects. The bats didn't squeak and slap the air with their leathery wings. No slithering sounds of the furry and clawed night roamers as they climbed trees or scratched at the ground to dig up insects and worms for food. Even the leaves hung still and limp on their branches, no rustling and whispering, as if the forest held its breath.

An intruder, a stranger approached her hut.

Holding her breath, Sholeh got up on her hands and knees and crept toward the sagging door of her hut. How could she see out without making herself visible?

Something moved against the stark silver-white spilling into the hut. A stone sliced through the light, into the hut, and crashed into her drying racks. All her herbs and roots and braids of berries clattered to the ground.

Sholeh clutched at her knife. Attack, or wait for her enemy to come after her?

Another rock flew through the doorway, at a different angle. She ducked and rolled out of the way, and nearly forgot to pick up her knife
~~~~~

as she moved.

The scar-faced fisherman from the shore thrust head and shoulders into her hut. Sholeh lunged, knife leading the way. She sliced the side of his face before he could move. He grabbed her arm with bruising force and dragged her outside.

"Daughter of the gods?" he snarled. He backhanded her, so she tasted blood and saw stars.

The force of the blow knocked her off her feet. He didn't let go, twisting her arm as she fell. She cried out. He wiped the blood from the long, curving slice down his cheek and smeared it across her face. His blood tasted foul.

"Healer guided by Pallon. Guarded by Tamis." He spat disgust. "Forbidden to men?" He slung her up against a tree, smacking the back of her head. "Not forbidden to me!"

All this time, she held onto the knife. She whispered a prayer to Verdidan, a plea for help, and tightened her grip. She waited like her guardian wolf friends waited for a hare to hop within striking range. She kept the knife hidden as he released her and shoved her to tumble down to the ground.

"You are mine," the scarred man growled.

He kicked her in the ribs. Sholeh shrieked, the sound crackling to silence. She couldn't breathe, couldn't move for a few precious seconds, and that gave him time to kneel and force her legs apart. He pulled off his ragged loincloth.

A growl from the black shadows answered her wordless prayer. A black, sleek form leaped from the darkness between the trees and slammed the brute to the ground. The man roared and the sound shattered with a crunch and a gurgling shriek.

Man and wolf tumbled across the clearing, locked in writhing, snarling battle. Sholeh scrambled upright on her shaking legs and staggered after them, clutching the knife.

Chapter Eleven

The black wolf leaped aside and crouched, watching the man thrash and bubble blood from his torn throat. With each staggering heartbeat, his struggles slowed.

Sholeh sank down at the base of a tree. She watched the wolf, and the wolf watched her. The blood fury left his too-familiar gray and green-ringed eyes.

"Steffyn?" she whispered. The wolf shuddered and she sensed his shame as if it were a particularly bitter perfume or a sour note on a harp.

Silence spread out through the clearing, slowly, like the blood soaking the torn ground. She looked at the fisherman. Death made him small.

A whimper escaped her raw throat, turning into a wail that didn't stop until the wolf leaped to her side and pressed hard against her. She shuddered and closed her eyes. His hot, wet tongue licked the blood from her face and stillness flowed through her. Sholeh reached blindly and wrapped her arms around him. Warm, sticky wetness trickled across her arm and she opened her eyes, drawing back enough to see a gouge in the wolf's neck where the brute had clawed him. Tears touched her eyes as she pressed her lips against the spot, and she tasted his blood.

"Forgive me," she whispered.

Cold fire prickled against her flesh as fur melted into skin and cloth and Steffyn gently slid free of her arms. How he could stand there, fully clothed, when he had been a wolf just heartbeats before, she could not comprehend.

"No, my love," he whispered in a harsh voice. "Forgive me. I stayed away to protect you from me, and nearly let him take you."

"Love?" Her heart jerked to a stop. "Do you love me, Steffyn?"

The last time a man who wasn't family had said that to her, she had laughed. She had been ten, and the boy was a playmate. He grew angry and stomped away, but two days later they were racing and laughing together as if nothing had happened.

This was not nothing. She was just shy of her fifteenth birthing day. That laughter and meaningless vow of passion felt like two lifetimes ago.

"Sholeh ..." A world of agony made his voice shatter like broken blades. "I'll take him." He slid his long cloak off his shoulders and flung it around her. "You're cold. Go back inside where you're safe." She heard his unspoken plea to obey, saw the fear in his eyes and heard the struggle for control rasping in his voice.

She took his cloak and went to her hut, and sat in the darkness, listening to the sounds as Steffyn dragged the dead body away. When she closed her eyes, Sholeh fancied she saw the path he followed. She sensed his thoughts, planning where to take the body. She felt his fury, his hatred for the man, and shared his indecision over what to do with the fisherman. Her attacker didn't deserve funeral rites, burning the body to ashes, but neither did she want to foul the forest by leaving it lying in the open where the beasts and birds could feed.

Sholeh argued with herself. What was wise? What was foolish? What was brave? What was right?

She gathered up the wineskin and Steffyn's cloak and went to look for him. She followed the trail left by dragging the dead body, until she came to a place full of rocks and fallen trees. Steffyn was nearly finished covering the body with stones when she found him.

"He will poison the air here if I leave him to rot, and only heroes should be buried by fire," he explained without turning to her. "Go home, Sholeh. It's still the full moon."

"I know."

"This won't end it. Blood spilled in lust and fury only makes it worse." His voice cracked and broke. "We fight, to use up the fire that fills our blood, but sometimes that only makes things worse. Like now."

"I'm not afraid of you."

"You should be." The wolf cried at the back of his voice, growling and howling pain. How he kept it inside, how he controlled it, Sholeh didn't know. Her heart ached for him. "I am less than an animal when the Fever comes."

"You'll never hurt me." She crossed the rocky clearing. "You said I was your love."

"A love that could kill you."

"I calmed the man-wolf who attacked me at the last full moon. When he was a wolf. If you are the guardians, then that explains so much of the legends. I think I could touch your mind, in man-shape, and help you control the fire." She spread her hands, gesturing at him. "If you truly need help. Aren't you cooling the fire yourself now?"

"With great effort and pain." He glanced over his shoulder at the pile of stones. "Granted, fighting eased some of the heat, but the blood …" He shuddered. "Please, Sholeh-child, go back to your hut, where you are safe. I will come speak with you in the morning when the moon has hidden its face."

None of the other men-wolves had attacked her as she followed his trail here. Perhaps the viciousness of the battle, the scent of blood and recent death in the air had driven them away? Or perhaps, as he had inferred, the other Kreefa had found harlots to cool their blood tonight. Sholeh wanted to argue with him and make him promise he would come speak with her, not flee and entirely vanish from her life. Instead, she turned and went back the way she had come.

Any other time, she would have found some amusement in the thought of a strong, brave mercenary fleeing from her. The shame burning in Steffyn's eyes made that all too believable, not amusing at all. She stumbled, momentarily breathless, as she relived that moment when Steffyn had called her his love. Perhaps it was just in the heat of the moment, his fear for her, the pressure of his body's need ... but what if it wasn't? She had heard the tales of young men who used sweet words to seduce girls like her, and she had been warned of all the wiles and tricks and the carelessness in the hearts of those who didn't serve or obey Verdidan. Her father had warned her just as thoroughly as he had warned her brothers, about how men let the hungers of their bodies overrule their souls and their common sense.

Yet what if it wasn't lust that spoke when Steffyn called her his love?

Sholeh thought several times she did sense someone or something following her as she threaded her way through the stark contrasts of shadows and moonlight in the forest. No one bothered her, but she still felt safer the moment she crossed the line in the dirt that Steffyn had scratched and then marked in his wolf form. Sleep didn't come easily, even after she had washed and cleaned up the mess the fisherman had made. She lay down where she could see a piece of the sky, and watched for the edge of the moon as it crossed over her and headed for morning.

When dawn came, Sholeh had her words planned. She filled a clay pot with water and put it in the coals to heat, to make one of the sweet, soothing herbal brews her mother had taught her to make. Then she prepared a meal for her and Steffyn. After all, if they were going to spend a long time talking, they might as well be comfortable and well fed.

"Are you from Mount Aerno?" she said, when he stepped out of the shadows of the trees into the silvery dawn light of the clearing.

Steffyn blinked and shook his head, clearly knocked off balance. Whatever he had expected her to say to him, that was far from it. Sholeh felt better immediately when his lips twitched with some humor.

"I think you are what my people came here to Nedaia to seek. Are you from Mount Aerno?"

"Yes, the Kreefa make our homes on the slopes of the mountain of the gods. Why? What have you heard of us?"

"We have a legend, on the Isle of the Moon—"

"The crescent moon, yes?"

"Yes. Why is that important to you?" She gestured at the cloth she had spread on the platform of smooth stones she had created next to the fire pit. Another knot imprisoning her chest loosened when Steffyn crossed the clearing and sat down at the edge of the cloth, facing her.

"We have a legend, also. There is an island, shaped like the moon at crescent. That is the safest face of the moon, when it gives us strength and yet does not burn our souls. Our ancestors committed some monstrous crime and we were cast out, cast away, but someday when the day-child and night-child have come among us, we will return to the island of the crescent moon, and we will find healing and purification and forgiveness. We will take up our duties and regain our honor."

"Is there more to the legend?"

He nodded and ducked his head, tugging the edge of the cloth straight. "Our women are the keepers of our memories. My mother has all the words of the prophecies and legends. She could tell you. What does your legend say?"

"Our legend says that once wolves were guardians of the Isle of the Moon. Something terrible happened to take them away or drive them away, or they left willingly. The full moon harmed them. After what I have seen, I think I understand what the records never said. The Isle is endangered now, and all the young women of my family have been sent throughout the world to find the guardians and bring them home. Prophecy spoke to us. I dreamed of a mountain and drew what I saw. My brother spoke with an old sailor who had seen the mountain. He said it was Mount Aerno, and he said there were wolves on the mountain, that they served the gods, and they were more than wolves."

"Did he tell you all the cruel legends, the lies and fables that cover the slopes of Aerno?" Steffyn met her gaze, his painfully somber. Sholeh shook her head. "There are no gods, though I will admit strange things happen among the rocks and mist. If there are men who can turn into wolves, and people who can heal with their hands, as you did for me, who am I to doubt that there might truly be folks with strange gifts, who pretend to be the gods of legend?"

"There is no god but Verdidan," Sholeh murmured. She might have laughed, remembering how certain she had sounded the last time she said those words, and how arrogant she now sounded in retrospect.

"I would like to know more about this Verdidan. What you told me, when you thought I was nothing but a wolf ..." He shrugged, and a bit of amusement touched his eyes. "I have sent my men up and down the coast, asking for news of stranded travelers, shipwrecks after the great storm that brought you here. There is nothing so far."

"We were chased. Priests of Pallon wanted to take my cousins and me and force us to serve in his temple."

"Why?"

She told him about their voyage across the sea, and that day in the market when she and her cousins had rescued and healed the boy. Steffyn knew the port cities and even knew some of the priests and officials she described to him. The Black Wolves had been everywhere in Nedaia, hiring themselves out to serve one petty king after another, in defense of merchant bands or standing against invaders from the islands along the coast or northern and southern kingdoms. For the most part, Nedaian kingdoms stood together, but when enemy lands were too busy to threaten them, then they fell to squabbling among themselves.

Steffyn then answered her questions about his people. Sholeh already had much to think about, knowing the Kreefa had legends that seemed to prove the legends of her own people were true. She asked what their name meant.

"In the old tongue, it means 'hidden' or 'secret.' The Kreefa hide among the wolves. Two bodies, one soul, protected and secret."

"Two bodies, rather than one that changes back and forth, like tadpoles and frogs? Is that how you can be wolf one moment and then stand before me as a man, and clothed? I would think that changing your shape would destroy your clothes."

"Two bodies, yes." His mouth flickered into a smile, but it didn't reach his eyes. "One waits while the other wakes. Injury to one body harms the other. The strong among us, in flesh and mind, can carry more than our clothes when we shift between bodies." His eyes took on a distant look. Pain and regret flickered at the bottom of the gray, green-ringed depths. "We see ourselves as men, but we have learned to follow the ways of the wolf because they make us strong." He paused, pressing his lips flat together, as if holding back words.

What did he hold back from her now? Sholeh sensed he had been about to say something important, touching his heart and soul.

After a few more moments of silence, Steffyn went on. The Kreefa were a matriarchal people, living in households headed by a mother or grandmother. When boys reached manhood, they left their grandmother's main house and lived in huts on the fringes of the household's territory. Mated couples did not live together, each one holding stronger allegiance to their mothers' households than to their mates. It was simply safer that way, wiser, because men were killed easily enough, but women always remained at the heart of the household. Uncles had more control over the raising of children than their own fathers did, and men owed their loyalty to their mothers' and grandmothers' lines rather than to their children and mates.

Those men who could control themselves during the full moon met their mates to consume the fire in passion. Others tried potions or wine to drown the Fever or resorted to using harlots. Unmated girls were guarded fiercely, because the spilling of a virgin's blood in mating Fever bound the two together. Men who forced themselves on virgins or another man's mate were killed outright. Women preferred mates who were successful at resisting the fires in their blood or came from fathers who had proven their self-control. The hope was that someday, they could breed vulnerability to the moon's fire out of their race.

"Some think we should establish ourselves as gods," Steffyn admitted to her, when their meal was over, and they sat sipping the herbal brew. "There are no gods on Mount Aerno. The Kreefa have lived there and explored all the slopes for generations, and we have found no signs of them. If the ordinary Humans seek gods, some of us say, why not give them something real to fear and worship? Our Elders do not approve such thinking, however. Our legends tell us that reaching for power and authority that did not belong to us is what caused us to lose the crescent moon and the healing that came from the sweet water and the singers who lived there." He shrugged and offered her a sad smile. "Some of my generation choose not to believe the legends, or to obey the laws woven to protect us. Racc was my closest friend in childhood, closer than my own brothers and cousins. He chafes under the laws of the Kreefa that keep us safe, unseen, unfeared by the villages all around us. His dream of becoming a god will destroy us."

~~~~~

In the days that followed, the older members of Steffyn's mercenary band came to speak with Sholeh and tell her what they could remember of the prophecies and legends. She taught them about Isle of the Moon, the prophecy that had sent her and her cousins hunting the Kreefa, and most important of all, Verdidan. If they were descendants of the lost guardians, then this was the knowledge, the duty their ancestors had forgotten, perhaps deliberately, perhaps in shame. Some of them took gladly to the teaching of one god, a benevolent but stern and righteous father rather than the licentious, self-indulgent, quarrelsome gods worshipped in Nedaia.

The oldest man in the Black Wolves was Nedden, the silver-gray wolf who had brought her the rabbit and earned such anger from Steffyn. Sholeh was relieved to learn that Steffyn had been worried, rather than angry or jealous. Nedden was ill and shouldn't have left their camp. He had been kicked in the head by a horse, while pulling a child out of the path of a runaway wagon. It was not wise to shift from one body to another after a critical injury. Some Kreefa had been lost that way, either dying or so damaged in mind and soul they never retook their Human form. That was why when Steffyn and Sholeh had first met, he stayed in his wolf form with his broken foreleg. He had been waiting until healing began before shifting back to man-shape.
~~~~~

Nedden spent more time with Sholeh than the other Black Wolves and told her many small details about Kreefa life and legends. She was intrigued to learn that her hair had convinced the mercenary band to both defend her and leave her alone.

"One of our oldest tales speaks of a maiden with moonlight hair, who speaks for the gods and holds the power of life and death in her hands. She is the one who knows the path across the vicious waters, to the crescent that will cool the flames in our blood once and for all. After her will come the day-child and night-child, and the time of the journey will be on us. Some believe the moonlight maiden will give us the healing that will allow us to shed our wolf-skins for all time."

"I am not ..." Sholeh sighed. Yes, she could see how they would confuse her with a figure from prophecy, but the truth was that she had no idea how to get across the sea. She had no idea where she was in the world, in relation to where Isle of the Moon lay, other than through the horns of the north and south peninsulas, after heading west. But west from where? "I am only a servant of Verdidan."

"Yet you are a healer. You must know how to kill, to know how to heal, yes?" He chuckled quietly and patted her hand. "Don't let it burden you, child. Be glad of the fear of you and the power you might wield, otherwise you would be besieged with suitors. Steffyn would not be glad of the need to thrash half the company every day, to keep them away from you." His chuckle grew louder as her face heated.

At the next full moon, five of the men who came regularly to learn about Verdidan and joined Sholeh in morning prayers reported that fighting the Fever was easier. They hummed the prayer songs she had played for them on her quartz flute, asking for Verdidan's strength and protection, and the flames were easier to resist. Some who came to learn didn't use the songs, preferring to visit the local harlots. Some were amused and others frustrated, when they found the girls weren't nearly as satisfying or distracting. Steffyn said nothing about his tactics for enduring the torment of the moon's fire. He was only slightly amused by the frustration of his men, and relieved for those who found some easing of the struggle. Sholeh wondered if he used harlots to cool the burning in his blood. She didn't like that possibility, and then scolded herself as a fool for letting herself care.

Yet why did she care? None of the Black Wolves had made the vows of purity and self-control and service to Verdidan. One of the key precepts taught on the Isle of the Moon was to never be so arrogant and cruel as to stand in judgment of those who served another master, even though, in the end, the only true choices were between Verdidan and Biss. Proclaiming the law and teachings of Verdidan was very different from criticizing and condemning others for not following them. Early in life, when she realized just how powerful and influential their family was, her parents had taught her that those who stood closest to Verdidan had a duty to constantly weigh their own actions and thoughts and compare themselves only to the Creator. Never was she to compare herself to others, especially not to focus on their failings, because she herself could never claim to be perfect, a mirror image of Verdidan.

Who was she to judge the men who did whatever they could to resist the pull of blood and the animal instincts and needs that came from their second body?

"Because Verdidan expects purity of our hearts and minds and bodies," Nedden said when she confided her questions to him. This day, he accompanied her on the long walk back from the village when she had sold most of her stores of healing potions and dried mixtures. "You see his laws as something that applies to the entire world, because Verdidan made everything. So you expect others to follow the same laws that you were brought up in. You know we were not raised to think as you do, so you try not to expect us, especially Steffyn, to live as you do. And yet you still do."

"Am I really so foolish and self-righteous as you make me sound?" She managed to smile at the man who was becoming like an uncle or a much older brother to her.

She had decided that Nedden spent so much time with her as a favor to Steffyn, to keep the other young men from getting too close and trying to claim her affections.

"Innocence and certainty of what is right and true and proper are not self-righteousness." He paused and winked. "Not exactly."

Chapter Twelve

Sholeh needed to learn about the way people thought and lived in Nedaia. That lesson was thrust home with shocking clarity only a few days after that conversation. Annis informed her with a shocking casualness that the surrounding countryside was of the belief that she had not just become the healer for the entire mercenary band, but the leaders of the Black Wolves shared Sholeh between them. Before she could come up with the words to assure her friend that no, she did no such thing, Annis went on to say that she thought her very wise and prudent in such an arrangement.

Widows were easy prey in Nedaia. When a man died, and his sons weren't old enough to claim their inheritance, or he had no sons at all, his relatives swooped in and divided up the property among themselves, however little or much there was. An uncle or grandfather usually stepped in to defend the young son's inheritance, but if there wasn't genuine affection and respect between the widow and her husband's family, her defenders were few. The widow and her daughters were often left homeless and defenseless, unless the girls were of marriageable age and could be used to create marriage alliances profitable for the clan or family line. Annis considered Sholeh's arrangement very wise, because there would always be a man to defend her and keep her from being confiscated by some king or prince.

Sholeh left Annis's home as soon as she could and felt like she would burst out in screams on the walk back to her hut. Yet she didn't dare make so much noise and attract attention. Steffyn was the first to come near her and she blurted all her confusion and indignation to him. He didn't react, either with embarrassment or amusement or anger that such things were being said about her. Sholeh realized he had heard the rumors already.

"What am I to do? How can I face those people?" she raged, pacing between the fire pit outside her hut and the hut door. As if she could dart into the comforting shadows and hide from the uncomfortable rumors.

"You are already facing them. Some of those you deal with every time you go into the village are the ones who started the tales," Steffyn said. "I realize you have different standards—"

"Yes, yes, I know. Hardly anyone thinks what I'm supposedly doing is wrong at all. Annis thinks it's a wise move. But I am not that kind of woman. Even though we know the truth ... it is still wrong, that others believe such things about me. What if my brother heard? What if someday the tales crossed the sea to my parents?" She turned to face him, desperate for him to say something, do something that would calm her roiling feelings and ease the shame she felt. Knowing it was ridiculous to be upset about such lies and rumors did not make those feelings go away.

Steffyn's expression suddenly caught her attention. He was somber, yet she suspected he had thought of something. She saw it in the soberness of his eyes, the slight downward turn of his mouth.

"What is it?" She reached out a hand to him and Steffyn took it, interweaving his fingers with hers. Sholeh liked when Steffyn did that, although right that moment, she would have preferred if he held her tight to his chest and promised everything would be right again, soon.

"Perhaps we should leave. The duty that brought us here has ended. To guard the king's daughter from kidnappers until the wedding festivities and the two kingdoms' alliance could be solidified. Soon, people will ask why we linger where there is no work for us. Mercenaries go where conflict already exists, or where it is about to erupt. A wise king is alarmed when mercenaries go through his territory, or even pass by his borders, because it could signal another king is about to go to war."

"You stay for me, don't you? To protect me?"

"If only a fragment of the things you have told us are true, if the Kreefa are descendants of your island's guardians, then we have a duty in our blood to guard you. Child of the holy bloodline. The child who brings us hope of true healing. We have a debt handed down to us by our ancestors, who spilled holy blood and condemned us to be less than what we had been born to be. Can you understand the weight of that burden, Sholeh-child?"

She wanted to shout that she was not a child, even as something inside her came close to purring every time he used the endearment.

"Silly man," she said, trying to smile. "Of course I understand that weight."

"Forgive me." He raised their interlinked hands almost to his lips. "I don't need to explain, but ... putting into words all the duties and restrictions and the thoughts that fill my head helps me understand, and perhaps find a solution. We stay here for you, first. But we also stay to find the others from your ships. Even if all we find are their graves, so you can shed at least one burden and send up prayers for them."

"Am I endangering you?" Ice filled her chest, so she couldn't breathe for a moment. Had Steffyn brought harm to the Black Wolves by staying here too long on the coast, drawing attention to the mercenary band, and then adding to that by asking for news of shipwreck survivors?

"No. How could you, when it is not your duty to think of dangers?"

"Steffyn ..." She turned, gesturing east and inland with her free hand.

"If after all this time you have heard nothing, then yes, we should go. My duty and common sense say to speak to the Elders of the Kreefa." She sighed. "Common sense also says that even if I could speak and persuade them tomorrow, and all the households were packed and ready to board ship tomorrow, it is already too late in the season for sailing across the open sea."

"We must first persuade the captains of enough ships that we will not fall off the edge once we sail out of sight of land," Steffyn added, with a muffled snort of laughter.

"We have the remainder of fall, and through the winter to persuade and prepare. If you are willing to take me to Aerno to meet with your Elders."

"Ask anything of me." Again, he made the gesture as if he would brush his lips over her fingers, interwoven with his.

Sholeh muffled a sigh, wishing he would do so.

Then something flickered at the edges of her mind. For a brief, dizzying moment, she thought she looked at herself. Through Steffyn's eyes. Before she could draw a sharp breath and try to understand, the sensation was gone.

An impression lingered, however. A sense of sadness. Reluctance. Hesitation. Something he did not want to share with her.

"You did hear something," she said, testing each word before she let it slip off her tongue. "There is a chance. You think someone has found them, or some of them. But you hope the news speaks of someone else?"

Steffyn met her gaze. He said nothing for a few moments, before sighing and looking away.

"Slavers. Armed ships that patrol the coast after storms, seeking those who have been stranded. Easy prey to capture and turn to profit." His hand tightened on hers. "Rumors have come, of women with hair of moonlight. Those rumors have reached us because tales about the healer woman with moonlight hair are traveling up and down the coast. People are curious. More will be hunting for you than just that fisherman."

"All the more reason to leave this place," she said.

"Why are you smiling?"

"Am I?" A brief, sharp little chuckle escaped her. "I suppose it is funny to think that anyone would be foolish enough to come up against the Black Wolves."

"Let's hope that is what makes powerful men, who fancy themselves rivals for the power of the gods, hesitate to come claim you. My fear is that those who have captured your cousins may use them as proof that you, who look like no other woman of these parts, belong to them. For the chance to confiscate you, and the power you might possess, kings could dare to challenge the reputation of the Black Wolves and demand we hand you over to them. I could see wars spreading throughout Nedaia, and then beyond its borders, in the quest to control this power you say comes from Verdidan."

"When do you plan to leave?"

He smiled, sadly, with a sharpness she feared came from pain. "I must wait until my men return from seeking information about those slavers. When we know where they have gone, and if the tales of their goods for sale are true, then we will know where to go."

"Or where not to go. They could be waiting for you, using my cousins or false tales of my cousins as bait."

"You think like a warrior."

"My father oversaw all defenses for Isle of the Moon." Her breath caught, aching for a moment in her chest. "I hope to introduce you to him someday. Soon. I think you will both like each other very much."

"Let us hope your father approves of how I defended his daughter," Steffyn whispered. "I am sorry, but we must consider all possibilities. If the few rumors we have heard are false, then chances are strongest that Agantes has taken them all down to his realm, or they have fled Nedaia entirely. And I don't think they would willingly leave you," he hurried to add, clutching her hand tight when she took a step back, stung by the thought that she had been trying to avoid.

Odd, how she felt some relief, hearing him say what she had feared considering.

"Where do you think we should go, then?" she asked, after gazing into his eyes to the point that she thought she might touch his soul.

She chose to focus on the next step rather than give in to the black wave of mourning that hovered at the edges of her thoughts, most often at dusk and dawn. She knew her brother, her warriors, Captain Wylles and his crew and ship, had all either fallen to slavers or perished. Those were the only alternatives. Indago would search for her until he was old and feeble. He would not return home without her or certainty of her fate. He was either imprisoned somewhere so deeply that he could not break free, or he was dead.

When either of those dreadful alternatives were confirmed as reality, she would fall apart in mourning. Better to focus on other things. Perhaps she should be grateful for the petty irritation of her soiled reputation?

"You have a quest to fulfill." Steffyn tried to smile, and shifted his hands to her shoulders, to shake her gently. As if he knew the mire that tried to suck her down into depression and fear. "No matter what happens, no matter what answers we receive, the destination is the same. We will take you to Mount Aerno, to speak to the households of the Kreefa. If our mothers and grandmothers agree, then we will cross the sea to the crescent moon."

"But?" she whispered, sensing the hesitation in his plan, feeling an odd dread twisting through the elation that shot through her.

"As you said, even if we left tonight and reached Aerno tomorrow, there is not enough time to prepare and make the crossing before winter makes travel by ship impossible."

"If we can find enough ships and their captains willing to risk sailing beyond sight of land and falling off the edge of the world, you mean?"

"There is that, too." Steffyn managed a nearly normal smile. "If Verdidan is guiding us, blessing us, we will be ready to make the crossing in the spring, once the sea has settled."

"If we spend the winter traveling up and down the coast, convincing enough captains with ships large enough to hold all the Kreefa for the voyage."

"There is that too. But one step at a time, my Sholeh-child." His smile faded. "Convincing the Elders of our people could take many moons. We are scattered all over the slopes of Aerno because we cannot live together peaceably. Over the generations, some households have split away and gone to other lands. To repay the debt of blood and treachery, we must find all the Kreefa who have settled elsewhere, to give them the news you bring. If they will come and rejoin us and travel with us ... Who can say? The Fever in our blood makes it easy to resist reason and common sense. While we all may *say* we wish for the fulfillment of the prophecy, the healing to be brought by the crescent moon ..." He shrugged and released his grip on her shoulders.

"Some prefer to let the Fever fill their blood. They enjoy their wolf nature," she said quietly, crossing her arms to press her hands over his and keep them on her shoulders. "Then we must take as long as is necessary to bring fulfillment of the prophecy for both our peoples."

~~~~~

Kratos returned from following the trail of a rumor that led him to the port town of Ayesmosely. It lay just over the northern border of Nedaia, in a small gap of land before the mountains rose quickly to sharp heights, a barrier from the frigid northern third of the continent. Ayesmosely was a trading town, and a place to find brigands and poisons, weapons, and slaves. A haven for pirates and kidnappers and traitors. It was said that a dozen disinherited branches of royal families lived there, waiting for the day they could return home with highly paid mercenaries and reclaim the thrones their ancestors had lost through villainy or foolishness.

The slavers most likely to have snatched up the battered survivors of shipwrecks made their headquarters in the trading town. The rumors couldn't agree on how many foreign ships had been dashed on the rockiest parts of the coast near the dividing line between Nedaia and the
~~~~~

brutal lands where it was every rich and powerful man for himself. Two ships, five, even eight. The conflicting stories had led Steffyn to doubt there was any truth in the tales, until the rumors and gossip yielded some consistent details: maidens with silver hair and flutes that glowed and changed color when they were played, healed, and even set drenched wood on fire.

Sholeh tried not to be peeved with Steffyn, when he finally told her all the stories and bits of information he and his men had been gathering and following for the last two moons. She understood that he had been trying to protect her from disappointment and false hopes. Would she want to know the tales he had been investigating if they turned out to be lies? Especially if they turned out to be lies spread to lure her into danger? Only the tales of wolves who guarded the healer maiden kept some of the powerful men in the nearby towns from trying to capture her now.

Kratos brought some good news. The slavers had a large, fortified estate on the southern edge of Ayesmosely. In wolf-shape, Kratos had infiltrated the estate at night. After five nights of spying, he found the foreign captives, kept separate from the general population of slaves taken for labor or breeding or entertainment. He couldn't get into the buildings in the center of the compound but had come close enough to listen to the captives talk. He had heard them speak of Verdidan and sing one of the worship songs Sholeh had taught her students. He couldn't get close enough to discern scents, male from female, but he could assure Sholeh they were healthy, their quarters clean.

She told herself it was enough for now to know both her cousins were alive. They couldn't be considered safe until they were out of the hands of the slavers.

Yet despite the imagined horrors of a slave compound, Sholeh felt a bubbling sensation she supposed was joy, and hope. Anticipation. She had found the descendants of the lost guardians. How could she despair, even now?

"What are we going to do now?" she asked Steffyn, after Kratos delivered his news, they thanked him, and he went to rest after his long journey.

"Our first law is to make it easy for the world to forget that the Kreefa exist." He crumbled the last bit of bread from the meal they had shared with Kratos and tossed it into the fire. "I will miss this place. A sanctuary of peace and ... beauty." His smile went crooked, and he looked around the clearing holding her hut. Sholeh suspected he did so to avoid meeting her gaze.

"So ... you are saying we cannot go directly to this Ayesmosely to free my cousins and brothers and our people?" She wasn't surprised by this. It made perfect sense. "A direct attack would harm the reputation of the Black Wolves, and even if you had enough gold or jewels or other property to trade to buy their freedom, it wouldn't be wise to let the world know you had so much."

"And the rumors would only be fed and grow wider. Especially if you are seen with us. We must discourage people wondering about the Black Wolves, until they are brave enough to watch us, follow us. No one knows our homeland. We have intermediaries in four countries who contact us by regular courier, with offers from those who would hire us to fight their wars or protect their families or estates. When we go home to visit and rest, we disperse to be difficult to follow. If anyone were to know that the Black Wolves come from the quiet households on the slopes of Mount Aerno, they could try to hold our families hostage, to force us to serve them. No matter how vigilant our sentries, someone, someday, would learn our secret. We would be worshiped as gods or reviled as wicked enchanters or offspring of dark spirits, and eventually hunted down. There are tales of those who came to hunt us down, generations ago. To punish us for the crimes of our bloodlines."

"Yes, the vengeance hunters." She reached to catch hold of his hand. "I am sorry they found you."

"Who says they did?" His smile thinned and he twisted his hand in her grip so he held her hand in return. "I promise you, Sholeh-child, on my mother's blood, we will free your kin and your people."

"But you must never risk the safety of your own people to do so."

"We will find a way."

"Yes. We will. I have as much a duty to guard the safety of the Kreefa as you do, if the legends and prophecies spoken to your people and mine are ultimately the same plan before Verdidan."

~~~~~

Much as she disliked the idea, after the things Annis had told her, Sholeh went to visit her farm, and intended to go into the village after that. She couldn't sit still in the quiet of her hut while Steffyn and the leaders of the Black Wolves made their plans. Besides, if they were going to leave the land around Gytheion, she would need clothes more suited for travel.

Annis and her children weren't at home. The slaves working in the courtyard, one weaving and the other pounding grain, told Sholeh her friend had gone into the village. She thanked them and left and laughed quietly at herself because of the intensity of her relief. Now that the subject of Sholeh sleeping with all the leaders of the Black Wolves had been broached, Annis would likely spill questions every time they met.

The sooner she left Gytheion, the better, Sholeh decided.

Forgive me, Verdidan. Here I am fretting about silly lies that truly mean nothing when I should be rejoicing over the hope of finding my family and helping to free them soon.
~~~~~

Sholeh told herself firmly to stop worrying about those tales, as she trudged down the packed dirt path to the village. Deciding not to worry and actually ceasing to worry, or to think about it, were two entirely different actions. It was as if another person hovered at the back of her mind, whispering words of fear. Some of them, she couldn't ignore.

If enough people believe that I sleep with any man who can provide protection, and I use my body to buy friends and allies, then who will believe I said no when a man forced me?

Sholeh was grateful when she heard a woman calling her name, just after the path curved around a cluster of olive trees growing up through the ruins of a stone house. No matter how silly the gossip she might hear, it would help her keep her mind off her new worries. Then a few steps later, the woman approaching her grew close enough to make out her features. Callia gestured for Sholeh to turn around. She spread her arms and made pushing motions, as if she were herding her flock of geese across the courtyard.

Sholeh respected Callia, who most certainly was not a gossip or flighty, so she turned around and went back the way she came. When the path diverged, she took the branching that led to Callia's home, and she kept her steps slow. Just a dozen steps more, and Callia had caught up with her. Sholeh linked her arm with the older woman, who was out of breath and flushed, perspiration sticking loose strands of hair to her face.

"Thank you, child," Callia murmured, and patted Sholeh's hand. "So wise, keeping your head covered. Tug your shawl a little higher, though?"

Sholeh obeyed. They were silent, moving as swiftly as the elderly woman's tottering steps would allow. She didn't miss the times Callia turned to look behind them, toward the village. She thought she was even more relieved than Callia, when they stepped through the gates of the household, into the courtyard, and she could guide the older woman down to the nearest bench.

Chapter Thirteen

The table in the center of the courtyard had cups and plates, and an amphora of dark purple, sweet-smelling wine. Sholeh dipped up cold water from the well in the corner of the courtyard and mixed it with the wine, keeping the wine proportion stronger than usual, and pressed the pottery cup into Callia's hands. The woman took a few more quick breaths and thanked her with a nod.

"Such a good, kind soul you are. It simply isn't fair." She held up one hand, stopping Sholeh from asking what she meant, and raised the cup to her mouth with the other. Her color looked a little better when she had taken a few sips and lowered the cup to rest on her thigh.

"There is danger in the village? For me?" Sholeh went down on one knee in front of Callia, studying the woman's face, fearful she hadn't entirely recovered from the rapid pace and what could be a bad fright.

"You have heard of Vollen, king of Arkady?" Callia tugged her shawl down off her head and wiped at her sweaty face with the edge of it.

"Arkady controls four cities almost as large as it, and all the estates and farms beholden to them. Vollen is said to be just arrogant enough to stand up to the priests of most of the gods, and powerful enough to get away with it."

She could almost hear Steffyn's voice in her memory, as he taught her about the city-states and kings and alliances that made Nedaia such a tangle to navigate. Alliances and feuds changed almost without warning, making it precarious for merchants to make their rounds. Sometimes minor towns and nobles who would gladly be friends were required to patrol their mutual borders because the more powerful nobles and kings they were beholden to were arguing.

"One of his emissaries, Aies, is here." Callia gestured with her chin in the direction of the village. "Looking for you."

Sholeh held still, when her first reaction was to ask "Why?" and her second was to jump to her feet and flee back to the safety of her forest. Both were foolish. If her growing suspicion was true, Steffyn would know if she let her fear rule, and he would come to her. But would that be wise? Flight would only attract attention if the hunter was nearby.

"How do you know he wants me?" she said instead.

"He sits in the marketplace and tosses coppers in the air, and catches them, with a smile that warns anyone who takes one will lose a hand. He promises Vollen's gratitude to those who will lead him to the healer maiden who came from the sea, who commands wolves." Callia took another sip and her eyes narrowed. "He has sent to the brothel for the girls who regularly service the mercenaries."

"Why?" This made no sense. "He wants something from the Black Wolves, as well as from me, but what?"

The simple answer was to warn Steffyn so he could confront the emissary with the Black Wolves around him. No matter how powerful Vollen might be, no matter what influence he had over the local kings, only a fool would threaten or attack the mercenaries in full strength.

Callia summoned one of her sons, to run to the camp of the Black Wolves and tell Steffyn. Though he was a grown man with two children of his own, he blanched when his mother asked him to take the forest path to travel more swiftly, rather than going around the forest. Sholeh nearly snapped at him for being afraid. Yet this was another layer of protection for her, and for the Black Wolves, if the locals were afraid of the forest. If only Steffyn could read the language of the Isle of the Moon, she could simply send a note to him to explain.

She and Steffyn had planned for her to spend the winter teaching him to read and write. Winter seemed too far away now. How could she give him proof she was safe, and that the message did come from her?

Sholeh asked for parchment, ink and pen, but the household had none of those things. When Callia's sons did tallies for household accounts, they recorded on wax tablets. Orders were sent on small wax tablets with the family signet ring pressed into the wax, and simple markers for numbers. Sholeh drew a crescent moon in the center of the tablet Callia loaned her, then wrapped around it the bracelet Steffyn had given her. It was of green beads woven into a band of thin cords, as thick as her thumb. Since she never took it off, her scent would be strong in it.

With that accomplished, there was nothing to do but wait for the young man to return. However, visiting with Callia and her family was never a hardship. Sholeh offered to create some healing infusions, in thanks for the warning and hospitality. She kept busy throughout the morning and into the afternoon, but as the sun slid upward and then down the sky again, she couldn't hold off the worries. What was taking Steffyn so long?

Nedden came for her just a short time after Callia began preparations for the evening meal. Sholeh thanked her friend and let him hurry her away. She caught glimpses of movement in the growing shadows and guessed several of the Black Wolves in wolf-shape guarded them. Nedden walked with one hand resting on the hilt of his sword. He didn't speak once the gates of the household closed behind them, and Sholeh knew better than to distract him.

The tension vibrating through the air between them lost its edge the moment they stepped into the forest. She dared to rest her hand on his forearm and waited until he exhaled loudly and his shoulders relaxed visibly.

"Did something happen?"

"Emissary Aies came to speak with Steffyn and the rest of our leaders." He sighed and finally let go of the hilt, to clasp her hand resting on his other arm.

"What does he want? Callia told me he was asking for the harlots who serve your men."

"Among many other things. I'm sure he would be delighted if all of them were with child."

"Why?" Sholeh stumbled, her knees trying to fold. "He knows?"

"There is no knowing what that groveling schemer and his king know, or only hope." He shook his head.

Then he told her what Aies had said, during the short meeting Steffyn had granted him. Sholeh wished she could find some amusement in Nedden's skill in mimicry. His disdain for King Vollen's man was clear.

Vollen, according, to Aies, had great admiration for the Black Wolves. Their reputation made them highly valued and feared, especially by those kings they refused to serve. The king of Arkady offered them a great honor, a chance to become legends and rivals of the gods themselves.

"That sounds like the beginning of a cautionary tale," she said.

"We were warned by the simple fact that Aies and his men were all drenched in rich spices, so we couldn't read their scent and know when they were afraid, when they lied, when they mocked us."

"Do you think they know about your wolf nature?" Sholeh whispered. Even in the safe sanctuary of the forest, she knew better than to say such things where enemies could hear.

"He claims to know we come from Aerno."

"How?" She clutched at his arm, hard enough Nedden flinched. "Were you betrayed?"

"Our intermediaries? Steffyn has sent men to see how they fare."

He went on to relate the rest of Aies's declaration, using too many flowery, fancy words to be trusted. Supposedly, King Vollen knew about the wolves that ran with the mercenaries, guarding their flanks. He knew they possessed magic, gained by living on the slopes of Mount Aerno, welcomed by the gods. Vollen believed the Black Wolves had taken their name because they had been given magic enough to allow them to turn into wolves at need.

"That is why he seeks the harlots our men use to cool the Fever."

"I don't understand." She flinched as one of the wolves running as their escort stepped from the shadows and darted ahead of them down the forest path.

"He wants soldiers with the ability to become wolves. He wants an army of man-wolves."

"To rule Nedaia?"

"To challenge the gods."

"The man is mad."

"He offered us the use of his concubines, to father man-wolves on them."

Sholeh couldn't find words to respond. She didn't know how she felt, other than a horrid feeling of illness, and as if the ground would vanish from beneath her feet.

Steffyn and his subordinates had denied everything Aies stated as facts. Several laughed when he repeated himself. Their laughter seemed to shake him, but Nedden feared Aies was one of those men who refused to admit when he had made a mistake, or that he was wrong in any way. Such men had to punish others for his mistakes.

"Or it isn't that he refuses to admit he is mistaken, but he is terrified for his life if he fails," Sholeh offered.

"Such desperation creates danger."

"What are you going to do?"

"If we were far away from people who knew us, outside the laws of hospitality ... Even then, we fight so hard to tame our wolf-nature by being more honorable and civilized than the most learned philosophers and poets." Nedden chuckled, but the sound was sour, as if he felt sick. "So much of what he says is pure threat, wrapped in arrogance, and depends on our swords being blunted by our sense of honor."

"What are you going to do? How will you justify attacking them?"

"They will step too far. We must trick them into stepping too far." His smile thinned, and sparks touched his eyes for a moment. "My uncles always taught us that we should treat visitors as peaceful seekers of friendship and leave it to them to strike the first blow and bear the curse for breaking hospitality. Doesn't mean we can't be ready for a bit of treachery, and defend ourselves before it comes," he added, with a wink.

"How?"

She flinched when Nedden wrapped his arm tight around her waist and pulled her back from the first touch of light as they approached the clearing holding her hut. He nearly lifted her off her feet.

"Aies wants you as well. He boasted to us that slavers were bringing him two maidens with the power of the gods, and you will be the third. Vollen claims that women with the power to control wild beasts, the power of life and death in their hands, were sent to him from the gods to acknowledge his worthiness to rule all Nedaia, and someday the world."

"Foolish gods, to praise him, when he plans to overthrow them."

"More proof that Vollen is a madman, and the people of Arkady are either fools or terrified to disagree with him."

"Two maidens? Has he already bought my cousins?" She flinched when Nedden raised a hand to put over her mouth, and she softened her voice in obedience. "Are you going to follow him to the meeting place?"

"If we have our way, he will never go to that meeting, and he will not give your cousins to his filthy king." Nedden took a deep breath. "Can you be brave, little one?" He let go of her arm and nodded toward her hut. "Can you be the rabbit in the snare?"

"Is he coming?"

"His men are already here."

She took a deep breath and reached for the knife with an incredibly long, thin blade Steffyn had given her two moons ago. She had adjusted the seam of her dress so the sheath of the knife slid into it, and hid the hilt.

"There are tales already, claiming you hold the power of life and death in your hands. To defend yourself ..."

"The strongest, most skilled healers can cause pain strong enough to cripple, or even stop the heart. I am still learning."

Killing with her knife would be easier than pulling the life out of a body. She had seen older healers stand over the ill for hours, guiding the strength and life and health and wholeness back into sufferers. Several of her teachers agreed that destruction was far easier than healing, just as anger was far easier than self-control and cruelty was easier than kindness. Sholeh supposed that in a time of great need and fear, she could kill with the healing power residing in her blood, but she didn't want to learn if it was possible.

"If Verdidan blesses us, you will have to do nothing but pretend to be a frightened little rabbit." Nedden patted her arm and grinned. "Pretend."

Sholeh slowly mirrored his grin. She liked what he implied: she wouldn't be frightened or a rabbit.

If she knew Steffyn and his men would be close at hand, how could she be afraid?

Could she pretend fear?

Nedden patted her arm once more, then nodded toward her hut, and took a step back, deeper into the shadows of the trees. Sholeh wished she could simply stay here, where she could see the hut and no one could see her. What good would that do them? To find out what King Vollen of Arkady knew, what he wanted, what he planned, they needed more information. She imagined that even though Steffyn didn't believe half of what Aies said, he couldn't violate the laws of hospitality and attack the man while he was in their camp. However, if Aies assaulted her, if he tried to kidnap her and take her to his king, they would be justified in not just punishing him, but ...

She was wasting time. The longer she waited, the darker the clearing when the enemy made their move. Sholeh smiled, knowing that darkness would not hinder the Kreefa in wolf-shape. They were watching and ready. Pressing her lips flat to kill her smile, she stepped out into the clearing.

What good would it do them to capture and perhaps torture Aies and his men if they refused to reveal the truth of their mission?

What could she do to help find out what they needed to know? More important than knowing what Vollen truly wanted from the Black Wolves, from the people living on Mount Aerno, from her kin now in the clutches of slavers and from her ... Sholeh needed to know where the slavers would meet Aies. How could she find that out? Certainly, Aies was the kind of man who would withhold information just to be nasty. Could he be nasty enough he would choose to die before he gave her crucial information?

Sholeh stumbled, startled by a new idea. Her quartz flute had been tuned to her mind and spirit, to be used in healing. Sometimes, as her teachers had told her many times, healing had to start in the mind and in the heart before any good could be done to the body. What could she do with the music she had learned to play?

Combined with a strong brew of potent herbs, perhaps?

Later, she nearly laughed, realizing how gnawing on that problem in her mind helped her play the part Nedden asked of her. By the time Sholeh entered her hut, she was focused on the puzzle. She forgot about the hidden watchers as she went through her baskets of dried herbs and berries and roots, considering what would combine well, what would counteract the active qualities of other ingredients in the potion, and what combinations could turn poisonous. She laid out her tools on the low table set up outside, made by Perys, one of her students: mortar and pestle, knives, bowls of stone and wood and pottery, cups holding the ingredients she had chosen, jugs of oil, wine, vinegar, honey. She paused to look around her home, seeing it anew under this threat. Since she had come under their protection, the Black Wolves had made many repairs to this ruin, turning it into a real home, filling it with the tools she needed as a healer. She hated the thought of leaving it behind when she set off for Mount Aerno. Yet now, Vollen's interest made that journey even more necessary.

She stirred up the banked embers in the fire pit and tossed on tinder and a few pieces of wood, then picked up two jugs to go to the spring.

She sensed something. A vibration that wasn't quite in the air, wasn't quite in the soil, wasn't quite a scent. A change she couldn't identify. If the forest wasn't so quiet around her, she would have thought someone had whispered her name. In warning.

The forest was too quiet for this time of the day, slipping softly into evening. Sholeh hesitated as she approached the slight turn in the forest path leading back from the spring to her hut. The water slopped a little in both jugs. She was ready when she stepped into her clearing and saw the tall man standing at the far end of her table. He wore a tunic in a shade of purple-red that only the nobles who stood closest to the throne were allowed to wear. She had laughed when Steffyn and Nedden had taught her about the rules of colors assigned to different levels of society. Sholeh thought it was ridiculous, but she was grateful for such customs now. She was sure this man, with his elegant clothes, so clean, standing with his hands clasped behind his back, was Aies. Even before he opened his mouth. When he raised his gaze from the contents of her table, he tipped his head back, raising his nose in the air. His eyes flicked from side to side, then up and down, visibly assessing her. His mouth flattened, then turned down a little at the corners.

He was disappointed in what he saw.

Good. If he dismissed her so easily, he would be easier to conquer. She would play unsuspecting. She would play young and silly.

Sholeh had had the displeasure of dealing with people like Aies who visited Isle of the Moon. They always stepped on shore with the belief they were superior, even though they came in search of help, either healing or guidance or even prophetic visions. They assumed that the youths who greeted them, barefoot in their simple tunics and trousers, were the lowest of the low. They treated them as such. When they learned the royal status of those they had treated rudely, they were either terrified or acted as if they had been unfairly trapped. None ever apologized, and she doubted they had learned from their arrogance and assumptions. Could she deal with Aies as she had learned to handle those troublesome visitors?

"Everyone knows they cannot come to me here. The wolves will be here soon to drive you away. It is best if you leave before dark falls." She set the water jugs down on the raised platform by the fire pit. "If you are looking for healing, I can meet you in the marketplace in the morning."

"You claim to be the healer woman?" Aies snorted. "You are just a peasant girl. I was told the healer carries herself as a goddess."

"There are no gods but Verdidan, All-Maker."

"I don't care about this barbarian god you speak of."

Sholeh muffled a bubble of laughter rising in her throat. Who was he to talk of barbarians? If he served Vollen of Arkady, he likely participated in the same brutality and licentious living as his master. She shuddered, remembering Vollen's offer to give his concubines to the man-wolves.

"You would be wise to leave now, before full dark falls."

"Are you the healer, the foreign woman who came from the sea?"

She turned her back to him and let her shawl slide down off her hair. Another shudder cut through her when Aies inhaled at the sight of her white hair.

"Yes, I have heard of you. The maiden with the power of life and death in her hands, who came from the sea, and walks with wolves. I look forward to meeting your guardians."

"That is foolish." She stepped to the far side of the table to keep it between them and focused on the ingredients she had laid out. Which potion would be ready the soonest? One took longer brewing to come to full strength, but it was gentler on those who swallowed it. The second would be ready quickly but it was harsh and could tear through a man's innards like a raging fire. Her hands shook twice as she chose the second. She didn't like Aies.

"Are the stories true?" He stayed on his side of the table. "Do you claim, as the other white-haired women do, that you come from a land beyond the edge of the world?"

Sholeh glanced up once at him. His lips glistened wetly, licking them in anticipation. He nauseated her. "You would be wise to leave now, before the wolves come."

"I welcome them!" He spread his arms and his voice sounded rich with repressed laughter.

She bowed her head over her task. The sooner the dry ingredients were prepared and mixed with the wine and set in the larger pot of hot water to steep, the safer she would feel.

"Can you bring the dead back to life, through song and the touch of your hands?" Aies waited and she wished she had the power to block his voice from her ears.

His big, clenched fists crashed down on the edge of the table. Sholeh went still. She nearly laughed at how everything leaped up several fingers' widths and came back down in the original spot.

"Speak!"

"You would be wise to leave before the wolves come."

Chapter Fourteen

"Why have they not come yet?" He leaned down as if to brace himself on the table, but he was tall and the table's surface was low, and he caught himself before he made a ridiculous picture.

"Mercy. And justice."

She knew she had read him correctly. He was like far too many arrogant emissaries. Such people only wanted knowledge, not wisdom.

"There is no justice but what my master decrees." Aies chuckled. "He does not believe in mercy, because it is weakness."

"Mercy. You have been warned and given time to leave and preserve your life. Justice. You will be punished and pay for your crimes." She finished chopping the deewa root and put it into the mortar, to grind into a paste.

"Crimes? I have committed no crimes. I obey my master, and that is the measure of right and wrong in Arkady."

"You are not in Arkady."

"All of this land will someday belong to Arkady." He stepped back. The stones at the edge of the paved area crunched under his sandals. "Just as you will belong to him."

She shook her head and focused on her work. She wasn't ashamed to admit she hoped he was one of those who would be miserably sick in the guts after taking the potion she made now.

"After all the fighting, all the searching, all the priests who argued that their gods had decreed you belonged to them, and yet none could find you but me. It is decreed by a power higher than fate."

Words burned on her tongue, but she focused on her task and kept grinding.

"Do you claim not to know about the battles?" He chuckled, a gritty kind of sound. "Great battles between the premier temples, to find and capture and then keep possession of those three women with moonlight hair. My king has been amused by the running to and fro, the expenditure of soldiers and ships and poison and gold, in the effort to steal the women from each other's temples. Each other's gods. They have done more damage to each other, and to the gods they serve, than he had hoped to do by overthrowing the gods someday."

"There is no god but Verdidan." She scooped the paste out of the mortar and slid it into the bowl holding wine.

Aies caught hold of the hand reaching for the next ingredient. He squeezed hard and yanked so she nearly fell across the table.

An image came to her mind and a bubble of laughter burst from her. He paused, startled, just long enough for her to lunge forward and bite his wrist. Aies shrieked like a fishmonger and flailed, shaking her off. He hit her across the nose. She flung herself backward, landing hard on her bottom. His shriek turned into a snarl of curses. He stomped around the table, hand raised, poised to strike again.

Nedden in wolf-shape leaped from the growing shadows and put himself between Sholeh and Aies. He crouched down, growling. In the back of her mind, Sholeh heard his distinctive rumbling laughter.

He was enjoying this.

Aies went pale, like a dead body that had washed up on shore. He pointed at the silver-gray wolf, but his gaze followed Sholeh as she got back to her feet.

"Which one is this?" He bared his teeth in silent laughter when she stayed silent. "Your slave? Bodyguard? Lover? Have they taught you the magic of shifting shape? My king will be most pleased when I bring him you and your slaves." He raised his hand. Movement among the trees revealed the hiding places of his men. "Tell the beast to submit."

"Tell him yourself." She eyed him a moment, then stepped around him, to return to her table and resume making the potion.

"You will obey me, woman, or there won't be enough of your beauty left to please my king. When he is unhappy, everyone is unhappy."

"Vollen is not my king. I care not." She focused on her hands, willing them to be steady, as she picked up the other ingredients and added them, one by one, to the bowl. One herb she crumbled into dust, another she left in large chunks, another she twisted, stripping the leaves off the stems and tearing them before tossing into the bowl.

"You will care."

She sensed the hand he raised before she glimpsed movement from the corner of her eye. Sholeh bent low, scooping up the bowl, at the same moment Nedden growled and leaped. Aies went down, shrieking, with the wolf's jaws clamped on his wrist.

Black-armored men leaped from their hiding places. Wolves and men in brass and leather armor jumped out of the trees and bushes above and behind them, with swords and spears and knives flashing.

Sholeh turned her back to the brief, fierce battle and concentrated on placing the bowl in the brass pan filled with water, to sit on the fire and steep. She was going to need that potion sooner than she had anticipated. Her hands shook a little when her task was accomplished. She was glad to retreat to her hut, sit on her pallet of blankets, and wait.

Steffyn came for her when all was silent outside again. He crept halfway through her doorway and watched her, his gaze sweeping over her again and again until she wanted to scream that yes, she was fine.

A hiccup of laughter slipped out of her tight throat. She feared if she sat there any longer, the next sound she made would be tears.

"I need to check my potion," she said, and rubbed once at each eye with the heel of her hand.

Steffyn opened his mouth, closed it, took a deep breath, then scooted backward out of the doorway. He was waiting, a hand out to steady her, when she emerged a few seconds later. She let him help her to her feet.

The clearing around her hut showed no signs of struggle. Someone had even cleaned up the herbs she had spilled. Steffyn followed her to the fire. His nose wrinkled up as she bent over to sniff the steeping potion, then dipped her littlest finger in to check the heat and taste.

"There is something not right about that brew."

"Oh, that is where you are wrong. It will be ready when we need it." She caught her breath. "Did you leave any of them alive?"

"Those who surrendered, yes. Those who kept fighting no matter how we ordered them to give up ..." He shrugged.

"Only two choices, death or surrender. No escape allowed." She nodded and finally looked him in the eyes now. "Were any of your men injured?"

"Scratches."

"I'm sorry."

"No, I am sorry." He caught hold of her hand. "I knew he would come after you, when I wouldn't give him what he wanted. I let his arrogance trap him and condemn him. He will not report to his master."

"But you fear that will do no good, if Vollen knows about you, if he knows your families are on Aerno, if he has proof that you are the man-wolves." When he nodded, his expression turning bleak and hard, she turned her hand in his grip, to grip his hand in return. "I can help."

Aies had twenty soldiers. He had left ten in the village, including a healer who was examining all the harlots, looking for any who might be with child. Of the ten who had come with Aies to capture Sholeh, only four remained alive, including Aies. He had ordered the Black Wolves to yield to him because Vollen claimed their service. Disobedience now would levy greater punishment on them in the future. He didn't cease his orders and curses until two wolves knocked him flat and sat on his chest. Then he shrieked terror until a soldier clubbed him into silence.

"The stink of his fear was the worst part," Nedden explained, as he led Sholeh to another clearing where the prisoners had been taken. "We had to stop him thinking and feeling, to clear the air. Our ears were grateful, though."

By this time, she had explained the intent of the potion, to pull the truth from Aies, guided by music from her quartz flute. Steffyn had clutched her shoulders and stared into her eyes, his shaken smile growing broader and steadier. His sub-commanders blurted questions and expressed their amazement or complimented her cleverness. Sholeh wondered if Steffyn might have tried to kiss her, if they had been alone.

Perys and three men stayed with her, to deal with the prisoners when the potion was ready to be used. They were needed to force Aies to drink. After that, they had to wait until the potion made him pliable for questioning. By then, Steffyn and the rest of the Black Wolves should have returned from the village. They had to deal with the rest of Aies's men.

Sholeh thought perhaps if she weren't so angry, so afraid, she might have felt a little sorry for Aies and his men. The holy writings of Verdidan decreed pity for the foolish ones who through their own evil endeavors harmed themselves.

Maybe when she had some rest and knew her cousins and brothers and the other survivors of the shipwrecks were safe, she would find the strength to do what was right and would please Verdidan. For now, though, she hoped Aies's men in the village arrogantly fought the Black Wolves. What kind of fools were so careless around men who could turn into wolves at will? Aies and his men had made no effort to stay hidden from wolf senses when they surrounded her hut. They had been ridiculously easy to find and follow, according to Perys and others.

"Perhaps they made the mistake of others who guessed our secret in generations past," Nedden said, when she voiced her thoughts. "They think our man half dulls the senses of the wolf half, and the wolf half limits the intelligence of the man half and makes us merely stupid beasts. They were careless."

"Or maybe Aies didn't tell them what they were up against," Perys offered.

"Ah, yes, of course." The older man nodded, his expression shifting to a grim smile. "Either Vollen does not trust his soldiers, or Aies acts on his own initiative. He has not told his master what he believes, either to gain an advantage, or because he fears punishment if he is proven wrong."

They had to force Aies to drink. Nedden held his head while Sholeh pried back the man's fleshy lips and put the mouth of the pottery jug against his teeth. Nedden held his nose until he was forced to open his mouth to gulp air. He choked and tried to spit out the potion. He vomited up the dose, and they had to start all over again.

Before she and Nedden could ask any questions, Aies started babbling, spilling every arrogant, confused thought in his head. Knowing the terror she would be feeling if she couldn't control either her thoughts or her tongue, Sholeh pitied him now.

Nedden was only partially right, they discovered. Aies had kept his ideas entirely to himself so he would be the only one rewarded when he brought Vollen his prize. He spoke with his scouts and spies in private, so his soldiers wouldn't learn anything.

Aies ordered them to release him, then cursed his men for making such a mess of the simple capture. After all, their prey had been just a silly girl. All women were good for was entertaining men and giving them sons. He chuckled and declared Vollen would certainly share Sholeh with him. He would teach her how to be properly useful and serve men. When he described her first lesson, Perys swung hard with a closed fist, breaking Aies's nose and several teeth, which he spat out with a mouthful of blood.

The potion blurred the mind but did little to ease pain.

Before Aies stopped spitting and clearing his mouth of blood, his stomach rebelled, and he spewed more potion. They had to start all over. He was just wobbly enough in his wits that this time he cooperated.

Steffyn and his men returned then. Their mission had been simpler than they thought when they braced for battle.

Aies and his commanders had forgotten they were only visitors in this portion of Nedaia. Many villagers had finally been angered beyond their fear. The village men protested when the Arkady soldiers took the harlots prisoner. They outnumbered the soldiers four to one, and their anger helped them triumph. When the Black Wolves reached the village, Steffyn found himself in the odd position of trying to save some Arkady soldiers for questioning. He only rescued three out of the ten, and they were all in bad shape.

Aies cursed his men as useless and worked himself into a drunken, sloppy fury. Steffyn took advantage of the disgust Aies's men displayed toward him, and gave them a choice: answer his questions, or be poisoned by the potion that was destroying their leader's mind.

Then he asked Sholeh to play her flute, while he questioned the remaining soldiers. Her need to focus on the tune made it hard to hear what the men answered. Aies kept interrupting, first commanding them to keep silent, then mocking them for their fears, then promising dire punishment for betraying him.

Sholeh gathered enough bits and pieces to understand that Vollen had sent several teams of hunters to different lands in search of the man-wolves. He wanted to control the magic that allowed men to turn into wolves or gave the minds of men to wolves. He would destroy everyone who possessed it, so only he and his warriors knew the secret. With that power, he intended to depose the gods, tear down Mount Aerno, and turn it into a flat plain.

Aies had the idea to breed a race of warriors on Vollen's concubines. When he heard about the temples seeking the foreign healers, he changed the mission of his team, to win a position at Vollen's right hand by bringing them to Arkady. He followed some tales to Gytheion, and learned the mercenary band, the Black Wolves, protected Sholeh. When he heard that wolves walked tamely with her, he had formed his own conclusions.

"Thank Verdidan. The All-Maker has indeed been protecting us," Nedden said, when he and Steffyn and several other leaders gathered around the fire very late that night, to discuss what they had learned. "He was only guessing that we made our home on Aerno."

"What worries me," Nicantor, another elder warrior added, "is that others could make the same unlucky guess someday. We have been careless."

"We have sat in one place too long and allowed people to become familiar with us." Steffyn flinched when Sholeh reached to take the pottery cup from his hand. With a crooked smile and a searching glance at her face, he let her take it. She refilled it with sweetened, warmed, spiced wine, gave it back to him, and continued around the circle, serving the rest of the men as they talked. "No, Sholeh-child. You are wrong."

"In what way?" She shivered a little, with the sensation she could hear his voice, whispering, but not exactly what he said.

"You think this is your fault."

"It is." She finished refilling Perys's cup, then straightened and cradled the jug of wine against her chest. "You have lingered here in Gytheion longer than necessary. You have walked in daylight in wolf-shape, many of you, to guard me as I went about healing and selling herbs and potions. When you leave and wolves are no longer seen, other will make the same conclusion, and they will pursue you."

"They will only conclude that the wolves followed you, when you and they vanish." Nicantor smiled as he bowed to her. "Did you think we would leave you here?"

"It might be wise."

"How are we fulfilling our heritage as guardians, if we don't guard you when we go to free your kin?" Steffyn said.

They had gained crucial information from Aies before he collapsed in a tangle of spasming limbs and madness. The slavers were waiting in their compound near Ayesmosley for him to arrive with the agreed-upon price for the foreign healer women and their companions.

The Black Wolves needed to cross out of Nedaia, surround the compound, and free the captives before news reached the slavers that Aies and his soldiers were dead.

"Or before someone else offers them a higher price," Nicantor said. "Slavers go back on their word as easily as breathing, for a high enough price."

~~~~~
~~~~~

The Black Wolves buried the dead Arkady soldiers in the forest. That was easier than burning them. Leaving their bodies to be devoured by wild beasts would attract too much attention, generate too much activity.

Steffyn chose to keep the few surviving Arkady soldiers prisoners, to gain more information about King Vollen and his plan to supplant the gods. That turned out to be a wise choice, when a courier arrived from Arkady. The rider arrived at the house Aies and his men had been using while a dozen Black Wolves were there with two prisoners to remove all their gear. The courier delivered his message packet, left immediately, and seemed none the wiser.

Vollen had learned of a woman, called the Blood Queen, who commanded man-wolves in the icy north, beyond the Shatras Mountains, which stood like a wall against the persistent ice and snow. The courier had brought orders for Aies to leave off his hunt in Nedaia, and head north to find the woman. He was to offer the Blood Queen marriage and a seat beside Vollen on his throne, if she would bring her man-wolf warriors to Nedaia. If she wouldn't accept the offer, Aies was to capture her and learn the secret of her mastery over the man-wolves by any means necessary.

Just after midnight, the entire company of the Black Wolves headed north. Mounted warriors, men who preferred to travel in wolf-shape, and four wagons of weapons and armor and supplies. Steffyn waited until they had left the sentry lights of Gytheion far behind them before sharing the courier's message with Sholeh. She rode in the lead wagon, and he stayed beside her.

"That confirms what we learned from Aies," she said, after considering the news for several moments.

"Yes, but creates more problems for us."

"Is this Blood Queen another Kreefa, do you think?"

He looked away, his face stark in the moonlight and shadows. "I pray she is not, and yet the alternatives are almost worse. We have heard tales for a few years now about the Blood Queen. They are so contradictory, sometimes fantastic and other times vile. We don't know what to believe and what to discount as wish-tales sent south to frighten away travelers. The people who live north of the mountains are a different breed altogether. A hundred city-states, fiercely independent, and yet united against the kingdoms south of the mountains. They say they believe in one god above all gods. A tribe of men called the Purifiers travel through all those northern mountains, wielding ultimate authority over life and death, enforcing the laws of this high god. He is cruel and demanding, with no mercy. Half the stories say the Blood Queen is allied with the Purifiers. The other half names her as their mortal enemy. The man-wolves either hunt them or are hunted by them in turn."

"If she is a Kreefa, she has taken the laws and customs of the households and twisted them, do you think? Become a despot instead of a guiding and nurturing mother?"

"Or she does what she must to survive among people who have set out to destroy her." He shrugged and turned from the road ahead of them to meet her gaze.

"Why are you … afraid?" she ended on a whisper. Again, that sensation had come that she heard Steffyn whispering to her.

"Laws." Another shrug. "Prophecies. The loss of my soul, if I truly have one." He shook his head, then tried to smile.

"If she is Kreefa, doesn't she deserve to be warned what Vollen intends? Don't other Kreefa deserve to be warned? They have the right to come to Isle of the Moon also and find healing."

"If they are Kreefa, yes, but … there are things I haven't taught you yet, about our history and our laws and the hunters who came seeking our blood, to pay for our ancestors' crimes. Please, let it wait?"

She ached from the pain and hints of fears she glimpsed in his eyes, and from that echoing sensation in her chest, as if she shared what burdened him. If she didn't know better, she would think that they were sharing thoughts and feelings. Such oneness only came after years of harmony and intimacy, sharing of body and work and worship and constant communion. Her parents had that unity, and so did her aunts and uncles and a sprinkling of others in the leadership of Isle of the Moon.

His words sparked a new train of thought, and she searched her memories until her head ached, trying to remember something having to do with the guardians. Sholeh had learned years ago that when she tried to remember something and it stayed firmly hidden out of her reach in her memories, the best tactic was to give up, to focus her mind on other things. The memory or idea that eluded her would seep to the front of her thoughts and become clear if she didn't pursue it. Just like a puppy her brothers had loved, that fled them until they gave up trying to capture it.

Chapter Fifteen

Sholeh focused on learning to read the language of Nedaia. Nedden became her tutor and taught her about the histories of the many city-states, the political alliances and battles that rewrote the boundaries.

On the fourth day since leaving Gytheion, a long tale of how an honor hunt resulted in two royal houses destroying each other sparked a memory from her lessons. She was grateful for an hour or two when, for safety's sake, she sat out of sight among the bundles and crates in a wagon, dozing in the stifling air under a groundcloth. She needed that quiet time to assemble the bits of lessons into a whole picture. She related it to Steffyn when they stopped by a stream that evening, to eat their dinner, refill their water skins and rest until moonrise, before resuming their journey.

"I told you how some believe the guardians, your ancestors, left Isle of the Moon because of conflict?" She had settled on her folded cloak on a mossy stretch of ground beside the stream.

Steffyn sat beside her. Perys stood somewhere behind them as he always did. Nicantor and Neddan were on the other side of the stream, which was thin enough to cross with just a running step. The other sub-commanders of the Black Wolves sat around them. It had become habit to share meals and thoughts during their short rests in the journey.

"My brother might know more details than I do. I pray Verdidan we find him, even if he is a captive of slavers right now," she added, her voice dropping to a whisper.

For the first time, something like fear touched her at the thought of what she would find when they penetrated the slavers' compound in search of her cousins and brothers and the surviving crews.

"We have always trained soldiers on Isle of the Moon, because of our treasures of learning and history, jewels and gold and crafting, healing knowledge, and the water of life. Then there is always the need to defend ourselves against those who would destroy us, simply because we are dedicated to serving Verdidan. Biss needs to destroy us, to wipe away all memory of our existence, if he wishes his rebellion to succeed."

"Yes, you have proven you are skilled in fighting, able to defend yourself," Perys said. "Why bring this up now?"

"I think … this is something you need to know so that we can gain more understanding on both sides," Sholeh said slowly, trying to watch Steffyn without seeming to watch him. "One tale of the lost guardians says that two generations after they fled Isle of the Moon, or were cast out, a branch of the Singer's family believed they were called to become vengeance hunters. They argued with the Singer and those who led in worship and scholarship. Some believe they were sent away as discipline, others believe they were sent with permission but not blessing, to bring justice to the guardians. To bring them back in repentance for either abandoning their post or for whatever crime originally drove them away."

She paused to take a deep breath, and her gaze locked with Steffyn's. "Or ... to bring them punishment, to purify them from their crime. Either they spilled blood, or blood was spilled because they were not there to guard the island as they had vowed to do." She spread her hands in helplessness. "There are so many tales, not even half of them could be true. There have been years of conflict, of tragedy, when we were few in number and weak. Enemies realized we were vulnerable and came to try to take over the island, to control the healing plants and water of life. Records were destroyed, the archives entirely emptied. The Painted Hall, where our memories are recorded in images, has been gutted by fire several times. We only have pieces of memories, tales, speculations. For this reason, we have tried to record the holy words and teachings of Verdidan in as immutable a fashion as possible. The archivists are dedicated to ensuring that each copy is exactly the same as the original, in every detail." She shook her head. "But the story of the vengeance hunters concerns me."

"What I said to you, about those who hunted us," Steffyn said, before she could turn to look at him again. He glanced around the gathered leaders of the band, just a few seconds in locked gazes with each one, until he returned to Sholeh. To her surprise, he smiled. Wearily, touched with sadness, and what she feared might even be shame. "I didn't want to have to relate this to you, but ..." He shrugged, and mirrored her gesture of helplessness, hands up, resting on his thighs. "We are ... forbidden. By prophecies, by experience, by fear perhaps. Forbidden to venture past those northern mountains, like a wall thrust down into the bedrock. On pain of losing our questionable souls."

"We have as many tales to explain this law as you seem to have about the turmoil after the guardians left the island," Nicantor offered. "We have been discussing if we should reveal this to you. Maybe we were ashamed. Maybe we didn't want you to think you had made a mistake, and we were not descendants of your guardians after all."

"The vengeance hunters found you?" she guessed aloud.

"Perhaps." He bowed his head to Steffyn, who gestured back to him. Sholeh guessed the telling of the tale had been handed off to Nicantor, when he took a deep breath and continued a moment later. "We are taught not to go over the mountains. Those who have doubted the command, who have tried to find a different interpretation, turning command into mere warning, who have ventured north, have never returned. Stories have come to us from traders, telling of a woman ..." He took another deep breath and focused on his hand, holding the remains of the bread and cheese from his dinner. "A woman who sounds much like this Blood Queen Vollen now seeks. A woman who commands wolves who speak with the voices of men. Many who disobeyed the command claimed they had a duty to go to the woman and bring her back among the Kreefa, for the good of her soul, if not to persuade her to change her ways, so she can be safe. So she does not attract the attention of men like Vollen."

"How long have these tales been told?" She looked around the circle.

"Generations," Neddan said. "Either this woman who commands the wolves is very long-lived, even immortal, or she passes her power down to her daughter, and her daughter after her. Is it possible that the water of life is not limited to just Isle of the Moon?"

"I do not think the water of life grants immortality," she said slowly. "We use it in healing, for holy ceremonies, but ..." Her thoughts turned to the sea holders. How long did the women of her family line need to live in that shape before they didn't care to speak with people any longer, and they stayed in the depths of the sea, and perhaps even lived forever?

"What matters," Nicantor said after a brief pause, "is that the woman came to her power after a great conflict, when hunters came among our ancestors. People with powers and knowledge. With music that touched minds. They claimed they had come from the crescent moon, to purify us. They took the warriors and scouts and the adventurers and went over the mountains, after promising to lead our people back to the crescent moon and give our race healing and purification. None ever returned. The stories began a generation after that. Of the woman and a battle against people who destroyed the soul yet left the body alive and enslaved."

"Yes," she whispered, trying to meet the somber gazes of everyone, "that sounds like the vengeance hunters. Either they were trying to go overland, rather than by sea, to take some of the guardians home, or ..." She swallowed against a tightening of nausea in her throat. "Or this was punishment. Leading them where they were forbidden, to punish them for the crimes of their ancestors against ... my ancestors."

"The question," Steffyn said, "is what could be the source of the visions that led to the warnings not to go north. Do they come from Biss, to keep us from finding a way back to the crescent moon, or to keep us from finding purification and making recompense for the debt we owe? Or are the visions and warnings a gift from Verdidan, to save our lives?"

"Did the vengeance hunters ever return to the crescent moon?" Perys asked, after a few moments of somber, thoughtful silence.

"Not to anyone's knowledge," Sholeh said.

~~~~~

The next evening, they crossed the border from Nedaia into the wasteland where unsuccessful rebels and patricides and runaway slaves and slavers and malcontents found sanctuary, simply because no one cared to chase them there. The Black Wolves left their wagons on the Nedaian side of the border, with a few men to guard them, and most of their horses, keeping only enough to carry their armor. Most of them went in wolf-shape, and found plenty of cover in the rough landscape. Sholeh rode dressed as a boy, with her hair braided tight and covered with a hood. She had a splint on her left leg from ankle to hip. Being injured would render her not worth the effort to kidnap and steal, and most would consider her no threat to them, so she would essentially become invisible.

Depending on what they heard in the streets and marketplace of Ayesmosely, she might need to become visible again. The right amount of attention would draw curiosity and set tongues wagging, so they could learn more about the slaves waiting to be sold to Aies. Steffyn didn't want to risk drawing any attention to Sholeh. The plan was one of several options, and he was very clear that he would prefer any of the others.

Sholeh wanted to play her flute somewhere in public, perhaps a fountain square or near the marketplace. Some place where street performers would ply their trade in hopes of a coin tossed their way or an offer to earn money entertaining at a feast or festival. She thought she could carry off the disguise of a poor, injured boy in desperate need of a patron or benefactor. If she gained entrance to the home of someone powerful and well-connected, she might learn something valuable to the rescue effort.

Steffyn didn't like that idea, either, because it might require her to go alone.

They still had time to think of more plans, with a full day of slowly picking their way down the rough coastal road. Sholeh was grateful for the smooth gait of her mount and tried to ignore the discomfort of her immobilized leg. So many watchful eyes on the road meant she could never have a moment of relief from the disguise when they stopped to eat or rest. She imagined there had to be some discomfort for those who spent all the journey wolf-shape, scouting ahead, searching out the ravines and crags, locating the watchful enemies always alert to anyone who might try to enter Ayesmosely.

When she voiced her thoughts at the late afternoon stop, to take advantage of a well and a small shelter by the side of the road, she earned a few smiles from her companions. They assured her that going wolf-form was no hardship, although there was sometimes a risk of sinking so deeply into wolf-mind that they never wanted to return to their human form. Usually that was after some sort of tragedy or loss. Most often after
~~~~~

the loss of a mate. The loss of someone who had become joined with them in mind and heart could be so devastating, the pain was a kind of madness. The unity of mind and heart made up for the physical separation that most mated couples took as a matter of course, simply because they stayed in their mothers' households and didn't set up households of their own. Mated pairs who had survived long enough to have grandchildren were known to spend their silver years together, usually the man going to his mate's household. That was rare, though, because life was harsh on the slopes of Mount Aerno, and males rarely lived into silver-haired old age.

Sholeh found that prospect sad enough to put a weight in her chest. She couldn't comprehend a life without her husband in the same house every day, working together, sharing meals and joys and new thoughts. How could mated couples grow into that unity her parents enjoyed, if they only saw each other for the physical aspect of their marriage? She supposed the Kreefa didn't consider what they had to be marriage, since they didn't use words like husband and wife, just mate.

The aching made her restless, but she couldn't get up to walk and work through the tangled thoughts and put them into words. What she wouldn't give to be home on the island right this moment, free to run down to the archives and find a scroll or a bound collection of fables, or poetry, or to go to the music hall and listen to the musicians creating new songs. Something to distract herself, or a bit of wisdom to untangle her questions, or simply soothe the twisting inside her mind.

"Would it be all right if I played for a little while?" She could think of nothing else to occupy her mind and resist the achy restlessness.

"That might help all of us," Nicantor said, after everyone traded questioning glances.

For a moment, Sholeh could almost hate them, their ability to see clearly in the shadows and communicate with just a look, a twitch of their lips or noses or the skin around their eyes. She took a deep breath and let it out slowly, trying to flush the restlessness from her flesh, and dug in the pouch at her side. It hung on a wide strap that rested on her shoulder and crossed her chest, and held not just her flute, but her two knives, the most precious of the rare herbs she had harvested, and the packet of thin gold sheets inscribed with the holy words. She longed for the day they were in safe territory, and she could read again and teach others from the gold leaves once more.

A moment of thought, and she knew what she needed to play for her own peace of mind. The tune was a worship song, but it bounced along pleasantly so it was suitable for dancing. After all, dance was worship too. She smiled as memories spilled through her mind, from worship days and festivals that had always been full of smiles and a bubbling sense of completion and fullness. Her smile was wide enough it threatened her ability to play the flute.

She played three songs in a similar vein to the first, eyes closed, drifting on happy memories. Sholeh came back to the first song and played through it once before she sensed something had changed. She opened her eyes and immediately stopped playing. Nedden and two other men knelt close by in the shadows of the ramshackle shelter around the spring. Their eyes were wide, focused on her.

No, not on her. The flute.

"Is something wrong?"

"How do you—" Nedden gestured at her flute. "How did you do that?"

"Do what?"

"It changed colors," Steffyn said from the doorway, startling her.

Slowly, Sholeh lowered the flute and held it out at arm's length. Her hands shook just a little, or was that shaking sensation just the racing of her pulse? All she could see now was the shimmer of green light, a soft swirling in the core of the quartz.

"What colors?" she whispered, and her voice cracked.

"Sholeh?" Steffyn dropped to one knee next to her and his face creased in worry. He touched her face and his fingertips came away wet, glistening softly despite the shadows. "What's wrong?"

"What colors?"

"It went from green to blue to purple, then back to green," Neddan said. "What does that mean?"

"How does it do that?" Byris said.

"The flutes are made for us, tuned to us. When we play together, our colors merge. Change. Reflect each other." She pressed her hand over her mouth to muffle a sob. "When I play with Loree ... her flute, her light is purple."

"Could she ...?" Steffyn's eyes gleamed, bright with hope and the words he couldn't say.

"I need to be seen." She tugged at the cloth covering her hair. "They won't come out unless they know it's me."

"That might not be wise," Nedden said.

"Sometimes wise isn't smart." Steffyn scooted down Sholeh's side, to cut at the strips of cloth holding the splint to her leg.

She nearly cried with the lightness, the release of ache, the coolness when her leg was freed. Then she nearly laughed when she tried to bend her leg, to get up, and it stayed locked stiff and straight. Steffyn caught her under her arms and heaved her upright with one swift motion, then wrapped his arm tight around her, until she could make her knee bend and flex and she felt steady.

Sholeh didn't want to move away from him. She caught her breath at the realization that she could indeed hear and feel his heart beating in perfect rhythm with hers. Her hands shook as she raked them through her hair, tugging it free, ruthlessly, from her many braids. It felt tangled and matted, but she didn't care. What mattered was showing her white hair and stepping outside where anyone spying on them could see her.

Oh, please, blessed Verdidan, let them be close, drawn by the music and signaled by the light.

The afternoon light had started to silver into gloomy sunset on the coastal road, winding between two long spines of rock that cast it into shadow. Sholeh walked out into the open and tried to find the place where the light was strongest. It seemed to retreat before her faster than she could step. A tiny, choked bit of laughter escaped her when she imagined running and stumbling over the rough ground, chasing the light. Aunt Noor used to play with her cats that way, bouncing light off crystals to make rainbows dance around the room for her pets to chase.

Verdidan, guide me. Speak to me. Please, bring us back together. Give us success with this mission, this quest to protect our people and the stewardship placed on our bloodline.

The light faded out around her, like water draining through a sieve. Sholeh felt Steffyn's gaze on her. He had stayed back in the shelter without her having to ask him, as if they did indeed share thoughts. Now she was out in the open with shadows spilling across the ground from the sheer rock walls on either side of the road. Sounds she couldn't identify clearly came to her from the darkness. Where the scraping, sliding sounds feet coming toward her? Familiar footsteps, creeping closer in a game of ambush? How long had it been since she played the running and hiding and stalking game with her brothers and cousins? It felt like years, not just a handful of moons.

Enough.

For a moment, she thought Steffyn had spoken. No, she had felt and heard with her mind, not her ears. Sholeh stopped and turned to look back. Steffyn was small enough to cover with her hand held out, standing in the doorway of the shelter. What was wrong with her, to become so distracted and careless? Yes, she was hungry to find her kin, but that was no excuse to take foolish risks. She had been guided on the currents of fate to find the guardians. She had no right to risk herself, and risk failure.

In those few seconds she stood still and thought and scolded herself, the evening shadows deepened. Long streaks spilled across her path, so she could almost imagine deep crevices had opened in the ground ahead of her, blocking her return to the Black Wolves.

A shiver ran up her back, as if she had somehow gained the sensitive crest fur of the Kreefa. Sholeh felt and heard movement in the shadows and gaps in the rock face behind her. She took a deep breath and muffled the need to shout for Steffyn. She turned to run back to him. She would never let so much distance come between them ever again.

"Sholeh!" His voice shattered against the rock faces around her.

Air movement warned her, the scent of dirty skin and metallic-salty sweat. Hard arms wrapped around her. One around her waist, the other across her chest. She shrieked and raised her legs to swing up and kick back, and a huge, calloused hand slapped down over her mouth. Her captor ran, his steps long and jolting, up and over the rough landscape. Sholeh yanked one hand free and dug her fingernails into the arm around her waist. She twisted her head and sank her teeth into the hand over her mouth. A man grunted. Men shouted behind them, echoes ringing from every direction.

Wolves howled.

Sholeh! We're coming. Fight!

What did Steffyn think she was doing? She needed to laugh, but the arm tight around her waist squeezed the air from her lungs. She bit and clawed and swung her legs back and forth, up and down, trying to break the man's running pace.

They fell. The man shouted and released her. She hit the ground and he landed on her. They rolled and tumbled and suddenly there was light. Her head banged against flesh. Hard, dirty legs, she realized a moment later, as more hands grabbed her and hauled her to her feet and she blinked her watering eyes in bright torchlight. Her captor scrambled to his feet, shouting orders to prepare for battle.

She knew that voice in her soul.

Chapter Sixteen

"Indago!" Sholeh stumbled and would have fallen, if not for the hands gripping her elbows. The world spun around her as she stared at her oldest brother, at the men scrambling to light more torches and block the narrow, sloping passageway through the rock.

He bared his teeth in a fierce grin, a bright slash in the torchlight against his ebony skin. Wolf howls blared in challenge and his grin shattered as he turned to face the opening that they had fallen down just moments ago.

Sholeh looked around at the dirty, ragged men, so many faces that seemed slightly familiar. Faces from home? Sailors, she thought. She tipped her head back and let out a sob. Garyon held her.

"You're safe now," her third-oldest brother said, in a voice like his throat was filled with sand.

The wolves howled again. Closer. They were almost upon them.

What would happen when the Black Wolves burst in here, to rescue her, and her brothers and their followers attacked, to defend her, and the Black Wolves reacted as they were trained?

Steffyn, stop them! These are my brothers. Please, hear me!

She jerked her arms free of Garyon and stumbled, reaching for Indago.

"Stop! Don't fight." She laughed, and that got everyone's attention better than her shout. "I've found the guardians!"

The howls grew closer, then faded to the sounds of claws on stone. Indago turned, looking at her, then the opening into their shelter, then back to her, then at the opening, clearly still expecting attack to spill through at any moment. The howls died out. Sholeh flexed her fingers against the slight tingling in the air that she associated with the moment the Kreefa shifted shape. Whether magic or some kind of heat that came with the change, it didn't matter.

"Sholeh-child, are you safe?" Steffyn said, from the darkness beyond the opening out of the rock shelter.

"As safe as I can be with these two bullies." She caught her breath and choked on tearful laughter when Indago's glare turned to a grin and he held out his hand to her. "Please, come through." She wobbled a few steps as she moved up next to Indago. He wrapped his arm tight around her waist. Garyon joined them and rested a hand on her shoulder as

Steffyn stepped into the torchlight. "Steffyn, son of Nioba, commander of the Black Wolves, these are my brothers. Indago and Garyon Adastra-na-Ilward."

~~~~~

The shipwreck survivors had taken nearly two moons to find each other, following tales of foreigners and sightings of the messenger birds and rumors of moon-haired women with the power of the gods in their hands. The priests of Pallon and Agantes remained a nuisance, with their spies everywhere making it hard for Loree and Cleita to move freely. There was always someone willing to risk injury to kidnap them and hold them for the reward from either temple, despite the problems caused by the rivalry between the two gods' priests. The survivors found shelter in the wasteland, where there were no kings who obeyed the priests or feared the wrath their gods. Hunting teams went out to follow new rumors, hoping to find Sholeh and those still missing.

Indago and Garyon and Caron were among the best warriors on Isle of the Moon. Their fighting prowess gained them some allies, who brought them tales of the man-wolves roaming the lands north of the sheer heights of the Shatras Mountains.

Cleita and Caron took half the sailors and warriors north into the mountains more than a moon ago, to find the Blood Queen and the wolves who served her. Indago, Loree and Garyn had stayed behind, following the trickle of rumors to find Sholeh. An ally betrayed them to slavers. Loree was captured and more than a third of the remaining soldiers and sailors were killed. Less than half a moon ago, Garyon and Indago had intercepted a message from Aies, saying he had found another "moon maiden," and would be coming to them soon to buy the two women promised to him. When the slavers packed up to head to the meeting place, the islanders followed, in hopes of rescuing Sholeh and Loree in one blow. A group of mercenaries hired by the priests of Agantes had attacked half a day from the slavers' compound.

Loree took a fatal injury in the battle. She lingered for two days while the survivors hid in the ravines and tunnels honeycombing this shattered section of the mountains. Her death broke something in Garyon. He took to playing her quartz flute for hours at a time. The depth of their growing bond manifested in the light he generated. It also frightened Indago. How long could Garyon fall further into depression before following Loree into death? He bullied his younger brother into plotting their strategy to find Aies and free Sholeh. The hope of recovering their sister seemed to give him some healing.

"It is Verdidan's blessing that he was playing at the same time you did," Indago said. He grinned and nodded to Steffyn. "Granted, we thought our sister was a captive, and Aies was impatient and coming here
~~~~~

to claim his purchase, rather than waiting for the slavers to come to the arranged meeting place."

"Our spies have seen them preparing several women to pass off as your cousins," Wyllan said. "Bleaching their hair, rubbing dye into their skin. We were even taking wagers how long it would take the man to realize that he had been cheated."

"We were also wagering on how much a fuss he would make when he learned the truth, and if we should wait that long, to use it as a distraction when we swept in to save you." Indago caught hold of Sholeh's hand and pressed the back of it to his cheek, as he had done many times through the long hours of talking and sharing their stories.

Sholeh sat between her brothers, with Steffyn next to Indago. The hint of sadness in his eyes sent an answering throb through her chest. She couldn't understand why he should feel hurt when she was so happy. Yes, she was devastated to hear that Loree had died, and yet how could she be other than giddy with joy? Her brothers were alive. Cleita hadn't been captured. Vollen would not win. Yet, there was an ache. It came from Steffyn, not from Garyon, who sat so silently next to her and kept reaching to touch her hand, as if he still couldn't believe she was there.

"Now we must decide what to do," Indago continued. "Do we send more messengers to this Blood Queen? Do we wait for Cleita to complete her mission and bring the northern tribes to join us in the spring? This is your land, and you know the people far better than we could," he said, giving a nodding bow of respect to Steffyn.

"Or care to," Garyon muttered.

"We have no contact with this Blood Queen. If she is Kreefa, or a sorceress with power over animals," Steffyn said slowly, "we have no way of knowing. The stories about her have grown over the years, making us fear she is more than just a story told around winter fires."

"Why didn't you go to investigate?" Wyllan said.

"They are forbidden by prophecies," Sholeh hurried to say. "I think the vengeance hunters reached Nedaia and found the guardians. Their stories say some Kreefa went with people who promised them purification from the blood that was spilled and cursed them. They went north, disobeying the orders not to go beyond the mountains and … no one has heard from them since."

"Are our cousins in danger, do you think?" Indago said.

"Stories change and are twisted by time and fear, or when people use them for their own profit," Steffyn said. "I think perhaps we were told not to go beyond the mountains because our ancestors were ashamed. They were afraid their descendants would be punished for the blood they spilled. Or there is true danger in the north."

"Or someone knows going north is the way back home to the crescent moon, and healing, and they want to punish us by denying us that healing." Nedden shrugged. "So many stories contradict each other, so who can be sure?"

"Are there any keepers of lore among you? Among your families?" Indago asked.

"The Elders. The grandmothers." Steffyn nodded and looked around the circle of faces around the fire. "That is what we should do. We have found what we came for, answers and your kin. Now, we should take you to the households, to consult with the Elders. Each household has the freedom to choose its own course. You need to speak with the mothers of each household directly, to convince them to go with you. It could take all winter."

"It doesn't matter, does it?" Perys said. "Even if they agreed tomorrow, we wouldn't be able to find a ship willing to take us across the sea until spring."

"If you can find a ship willing to risk falling off the edge of the world," Sholeh added.

"No wonder the ships hereabouts are made for hugging the coast and not plying deeper waters." Wyllan grinned, clearly finding the idea amusing. Then his smile faded. "But what do we do to go home? If no one builds ships that can take us across the open water, what use is it to find a captain willing to take the risk?"

"We have to build our own ships," Garyon said. "None of the shipwrights went with Cleita's people. We should head for the coast and start building. I'm willing to risk the winter storms, crossing the sea."

"I'm not," Indago said. "We will speak with the Elders of the Kreefa and shelter with them over the winter, if they will have us. We will teach them about Isle of the Moon and learn everything they know about the tribes beyond the mountains. By spring, we should have a decision and a plan."

"What if Cleita and Caron and their people are in danger?" Sholeh asked.

"We have made too many mistakes because we lack knowledge about the land and people and customs." He gestured around the circle. "We have lost too many people. Yes, I am worried about our cousins, but what good can we do them if we rush north without any preparation? If they are in danger, we need to be armed with knowledge as well as weapons. And we have neither. Perhaps when we are ready, we can persuade our new allies to go with us." He nodded to Steffyn. "We put ourselves into your hands and will be grateful for any guidance you can give us."

~~~~~

The journey from the wasteland to the border of Nedaia took longer
~~~~~

than the journey north, because so many islanders were injured, half-starved, and weak. Perys took a few of the swiftest runners with him, to go ahead and bring the horses and wagons and warriors. Until they were safely over the border, there was always a chance that more slavers or some bandit band would attack them.

The journey went faster once everyone was mounted. Sholeh thought her brothers improved from simply having better weapons in their hands. She tried to get Garyon to play with her on Loree's flute, for morning and evening prayers, but he merely shook his head and retreated into the darkness beyond the campfire.

Everyone's spirits improved, even Garyon's, when their company crossed the land bridge where Nedaia was nearly cut into two land masses, east separated from west, and then rode north to Mount Aerno. Beyond the mountain, the tallest in Nedaia, the land sloped downward to rich plains that were the home of wandering tribes of horsemen, then a wide river that was said to take half a day to sail across, and then the even taller Shatras Mountains range, with walls of seemingly sheer stone that barred the way to a land covered in ice and snow two-thirds of the year. Sholeh thought her brothers' spirits improved because they traveled the same path that Cleita and Caron had taken, following the tales of the Blood Queen. She thought they both held out hope that their cousins had been slowed, and perhaps had even decided to turn back.

Steffyn told her that if she climbed high enough on Mount Aerno, she could stand and look northward, and see over the plains and river to the Shatras range, and the narrow slice of the only passage through the mountains. When that was blocked with ice and snow most of the year, the only way to the northern lands was to climb the mountains themselves.

Sholeh was surprised when Nedden told her a few of the truly ancient tales of the Kreefa, older than the prophecy and command not to go beyond the mountains. One of the oldest tales claimed there was a land bridge far in the north, extending west, to another continent. The people on the other side of that land bridge were said to be twice as brutal as the tribes who inhabited the northern mountains. Sholeh knew those stories were true, because Tylanok's throne was established in the far north.

She thought she would miss this time of riding for hours on end, with nothing to do but talk and learn about each other's world. Her brothers shared stories of the trouble they had with the people of Nedaia, simply because they claimed to come from a land beyond the horizon. Everyone on Nedaia knew there was nothing beyond the horizon except the sheer fall to the Underworld. Probably the other hunting parties from Isle of the Moon were encountering the same difficulties in the other lands they explored. No wonder people distrusted them and thought they were insane when they spoke of home, and their quest for the guardians. They found some amusement in speculating on the trouble faced by the explorers and merchants who sailed east across the sea from Isle of the Moon. Perhaps this explained why some did not sail east again, but focused their efforts on the lands to the west, north and south.

Perhaps that refusal to believe there was anything beyond the western horizon explained why invaders did not come to Isle of the Moon from the east. Only from the north. Sholeh wondered if it would be wrong to argue and convince people there were more lands beyond the horizon. When people believed in other lands, would that lead to invaders coming from the east? Tylanok intended to take over the whole world. If he failed in his southward drive of conquest, would he send his armies over the land bridge and invade the eastern continent instead?

Sholeh saved such thoughts for later. She wrote them down, grateful to have the journals that had been salvaged from the wreckage of Cleita's ship. Winter on Mount Aerno would give them much time for thinking and planning and preparing for every contingency. Plenty of time then to consider possibilities and responsibilities.

Steffyn impressed her brothers when he asked that the islanders ride paired with his warriors, to teach them the language of Isle of the Moon. He wanted them able to teach their mothers' households over the winter. When they had settled in for the winter and more important matters had been settled, he wanted to learn how to read the sacred writings, and for Sholeh and her brothers to teach all the households about Verdidan.

Sholeh was stunned at how pleased she felt when Steffyn made his request. She had simply assumed that because many Kreefa refused to believe in the gods of Nedaia, they would have no use or interest in other gods, especially a god who claimed to be the only true god. She shared with him some of her trepidation over taking on such a somber, vital task. Steffyn smiled and shook his head, and she again had that sensation of sharing what he was feeling. Amusement, a touch of embarrassment, some sadness, all mixed together.

"My fear is that you will lose your students, once we have returned to our households," he admitted.

They had stopped for the noon meal before crossing the last plain to reach Mount Aerno. They were close enough she could make out the curving wave of stone jutting out from the high peak. Two more days of riding would put them among the scattered households of the Kreefa. The long houses were widely scattered across the slopes, with walls enclosing each household; the main house where the women and children lived, the small outbuildings where the grown men lived, storehouses, and craft houses.

The members of the Black Wolves came from nearly every household or clan group among the Kreefa. That was good in some respects, and troublesome in others. Everyone would hear about the islanders' quest for the guardians and Steffyn's belief that their legends and prophecies meshed with the legends and prophecies of the Kreefa. Everyone would soon hear that Steffyn believed they should go with Sholeh and her people, to cross the sea and return to the service of Verdidan. While the households were free to make their own choices, the Kreefa rarely chose any course of action that all the other households did not agree to take. If some households decided to believe and make the journey to the other side of the world, and other households refused to accept that prophecy had been fulfilled, what could they do? Would those who wanted to leave persuade the rest to come with them despite their doubts, or would those who doubted hold back those who believed? Could they leave with only half the Kreefa, or even less?

"I fear that those who don't want to believe in the prophecies will forbid your students to continue their lessons," he added.

"The Elders hold that much power?" Sholeh was pleased that such loyalty and obedience was ingrained in the Kreefa, and chafed against it at the same time.

"Our mothers and grandmothers are the ones who protect us from our animal nature. The blood links give them the strength to help us, much as you helped my men, touching their souls and calming their bodies at the full moon. The only bond stronger than that between mother and child is the bond between mates. Again, because of blood. No matter how belligerent a man may be, he will think twice, three times, before standing against the wishes of the woman who can keep him from becoming a blood-drunk beast."

~~~~~

Steffyn's mother, Nioba, was head of her household. She stood on the top of the steps leading up to the door of the main house, waiting as Steffyn and Sholeh, her brothers, and four other Black Wolves who belonged to the household rode into the courtyard. The rest of the islanders had been divided up among the Black Wolves, four or five to each household.

Nioba's face held a calm that Sholeh recognized as coming from long years of struggle and experience and loss. Along the journey, Sholeh had learned about some of the crueler truths of what it meant to be Kreefa. The weak and undisciplined often died in their first Fever, unable to control their animal nature, running wild and drawing the attention and the furious fear of the people who lived in the valleys around Mount Aerno. If the Elders could not stop and contain them, sometimes they had to kill the ones running wild. Sometimes those sufferers escaped the restraints meant to protect them and were hunted and killed by the villagers.
~~~~~

In the last five or ten years, that bitter practice had become vital to the safety of the Kreefa. Tales trickled through Nedaia of man-wolves who savaged people in the heat of the full moon, and the torment that the survivors of those attacks endured when they transformed into man-wolves at the next full moon. Each story always ended in tragedy, with the sufferers gone mad, killing others, passing on the curse, increasing the fear until some people took their own lives if they were bitten or scratched by a dog, let alone a wolf. To avoid hunters scouring the slopes of Mount Aerno in search of the feared man-wolves, stopping even a whisper of the existence of the man-wolves was vital. Even if it meant killing one of their own.

Sholeh shuddered now, thinking of the sons and daughters and grandchildren Nioba had watched go out to face their first full moon as adults, who hadn't come home. Or worse, the ones she had been forced to hunt down and maim to control them, or even kill, to protect the Kreefa secret. If the people knew that those who lived on the slopes of the mountain of the gods were the wild beasts who terrified them at the full moon, they might attack in large numbers. The Kreefa might be destroyed as a people.

Or worse, the fearful and foolish might make them new gods. Sholeh thought of Steffyn's childhood friend, Racc, who wanted to be a god. He had been suspected of encouraging the young and uncontrolled to run wild, to stir up trouble, to force a war between Kreefa and ordinary Humans. Steffyn had warned her that his former friend would not be pleased that she had come to bring fulfilment of the prophecies and help them better control themselves. Racc would see service to Verdidan as slavery. He might cause trouble for her once he learned of her quest.

Chapter Seventeen

Now, though, facing Nioba and making a good first impression was vital. With her support, they could stand before the Elders, tell Sholeh's story, and propose their plan for leaving Nedaia and crossing the sea.

"Mother." Steffyn dismounted and went to one knee on the bottom step.

"Welcome home, my son." Nioba descended with a stately grace that couldn't quite disguise a limp.

Steffyn had told Sholeh stories of his mother in her younger days. She had been a respected huntress and fighter, both in Human form and wolf. She had been badly injured during an uprising when a group of rebellious males tried to change the Kreefa way of life and abolish the matriarchy that had kept them safe for centuries. At the time, their family had feared Nioba would lose her leg. Sholeh respected a woman so strong that she could recover from such a grave injury.

Steffyn was the youngest son by Nioba's first mate. He had died in the rebellion, when Steffyn was only three years old. Since then, Nioba had taken two other mates. She had three daughters and one son by the next man before he died, and then two daughters and two sons by her third mate, seven years her junior. That was a common practice, when the women lived so much longer than the men, who bore the brunt of defending their households and secrets. Usually twice as many sons were born than daughters, and Nioba had earned great admiration for the large number of daughters she had birthed. She was considered blessed, and her bloodline was considered strong.

"Greetings, strangers and guests in our household," Nioba said, after going through the ritual greeting. Steffyn kissed the backs of both her hands and she bent to kiss his forehead. Her serene expression flickered a moment, revealing wonder and some apprehension. "You are not of the Kreefa, and it is unusual that a son would bring a woman through our gates. By your coloring … your coloring is spoken of in prophecies that my son knows well." She turned to Steffyn.

"Mother, we have much to discuss, and all my men know the news brought by Sholeh and her brothers. The Elders will be gathering when word spreads through all the households." Steffyn stepped up to Sholeh's horse and reached up both hands to help her down. He introduced Sholeh and Indago and Garyon. "Mother, they come from across the sea, where their mother is ruler of the Isle of the Moon. A crescent moon."

Nioba's eyes widened and a slight gasp escaped her. The hand she held out to Sholeh, to draw her closer, only wavered once.

"Welcome, child of prophecy, Child of Moonlight," she murmured, as she clasped Sholeh's hand. "Be welcome into our household. We had ample warning and prepared a feast to welcome our warriors home. I believe we shall have even more reasons to celebrate before this night is done."

~~~~~

Three of Steffyn's nieces claimed the right to help Sholeh. They guided her to one of the small guest rooms, then brought hot water infused with aromatic, cleansing herbs to fill a bathing tub, for her to soak in and relieve the aches and bruises of travel by horseback. The girls first seemed to be shy, somewhat giggly, but the giggles quickly turned into questions. She didn't really mind them sitting on the other side of the screen, asking questions. First, they wanted to know about her brothers and the other islander men who had gone to other households. They were honest about their jealousy that she had been allowed to travel with Steffyn and the Black Wolves. She found it amusing how they worked backwards through her story, to the shipwreck and the attempts by the priests of Pallon to take her and her cousins into the temples. The questions flowed even faster when she talked about Isle of the Moon and her home and the sea holders and the prophecy that had sent them all hunting.

No doubt, the rest of the household would know most of her story before she joined the leaders of the family at the feasting table. The girls told her the younger ones would have a feast of their own, but outside, where their bad manners wouldn't insult their guests and the adults would be free to have serious conversation. They laughed when they said it, so Sholeh didn't think they were upset in their turn at being left out.

"Will you take our uncle as your mate?" the oldest of the three, Damitia, asked. They had taken away the tub to dump and she came back alone to help Sholeh braid her hair. "Lorin says Grandmother means to make you a daughter of our household, to present you before the Elders, but then you couldn't take Steffyn, because you would be his sister. I think Grandmother will tell him to take you as mate, and then since you don't have a mother or grandmother, she will take you into the household as a daughter, and there will be nothing wrong. It's been done before."

"When?" Bythani said from the doorway. She giggled when Sholeh turned to look at her. "Damitia is a scholar. She likes to read all the archives. Give her enough time, she'll find actual records where a woman left her mother's household and joined another."

"Were any of those women outsiders? Women who weren't Kreefa?"
~~~~~

Sholeh asked, just to have something to say to calm the sudden racing of her heart.

Steffyn—her mate? It wasn't that she didn't like the idea. She had been so focused on finding her brothers and cousins, then all the danger they faced from Aies, then the stories coming from beyond the mountains, she felt guilty when her thoughts traveled to something so personal. Was it selfish to let herself dream about a man as strong and brave and intelligent as Steffyn wanting to marry her? She had turned fifteen after the shipwreck. That was old enough to marry, but she had always thought she would wait until she was at least twenty, as her mother had done. There had always been so much training and preparation ahead of her, and she had simply accepted the idea of finishing her training and settling in whatever role she would play on Isle of the Moon before she allowed the expected suitors to court her. Did she have any right to waste time on dreams of pretty words and courtship gifts? Still, it was hard not to let her thoughts drift along those lines. Steffyn had called her his love, hadn't he?

The problem, though, lay in one word: mate. She expected marriage, but the Kreefa did not have the daily partnership that Sholeh had been raised to expect and want. Could she ever accept a man who would leave the raising of their children to her brothers? A man who would share her bed, who might touch her mind and heart as the years went on, but still could not be part of the largest portion of her life?

"No," Damitia said, after frowning in thought for several moments. She met Sholeh's gaze in the polished bronze sheet that served as a mirror. "We have never brought in an outsider as a mate, but you are different. You are the Child of Moonlight." Her voice softened to take on a tone of awe as she stroked Sholeh's long, thick, silver-white hair.

"I don't know that prophecy. Steffyn mentioned it, but never told it to me. Would you tell me?"

Nioba came to bring Sholeh to the feast before the girls could finish giggling and whispering, trying to decide who knew the prophecy best and who was brave enough to recite it. She sent her granddaughters scurrying away with a stern glance, but Sholeh saw the twitch of one corner of her mouth, and noted how the girls showed no fear. She suspected much was ritual, manners used for company.

"Later, I will have some of our better scholars recite the many prophecies," Nioba said as they walked from one wing of the main house to the other. "So much seems clear, now that you are here in the flesh. Yes, my son mentioned several prophecies that he believes you fulfill. I would like to hear your prophecy that sent you across the sea." A chuckle bubbled up soft in her throat. "I am very pleased that the world does not end nearly as quickly as so many believe, and there is another land in the place where the fearful say we will fall off into the Underworld."

"Some of the holy words say there is no ending to the world," Sholeh offered.

"How can that be?"

"The world is unending the same way a circle is unending, because no matter how many times you follow the line, there is no stopping point. The world, some of the oldest scholars among us say, is like a cherry or a child's ball, and if you are able to cross land and sea, you can keep crossing forever and ever, always returning to your starting point, and never fall off."

"What about those who are on the bottom of the cherry?" Nioba sounded thoughtful, rather than mocking.

"We stay on the world by Verdidan's grace, because no matter where we are on the cherry, it is the top. At least, to those who are at that place." Sholeh shrugged. "It is beyond me, but I know better than to doubt the holy words just because I don't understand them."

"Hmm, my son has brought home a very wise woman indeed." She smiled and gestured for them to pause at the open double doors before them. "Steffyn has told me of your prophecy. There are many similarities with ours, and I am already half-convinced. The trick shall be convincing the other household leaders and the Elders."

"What similarities?" Sholeh lowered her voice and was content to pause there. Nioba showed no inclination to go into the feasting hall, brightly lit by lamps on long arms sticking out from the walls.

"Many words are the same, even with the differences in our language. Prophecy speaks of a crescent moon surrounded by water. Perhaps your island. Also, there is mention of night and day, man and woman, life and death, bound together, two faces of one form. Healer is merged with hunter …" She gave a little shrug. "I have my ideas, but that is not for now. Child of night and child of day. We have time to study. For now, though, be welcome. You and your people bring us hope, and for that we honor you."

"I pray Verdidan that I will be worthy, and all hopes will be fulfilled," she murmured.

"Indeed, and the most important lesson you must teach us is to know Verdidan. Prophecy speaks of lost knowledge, lost wisdom, and lost treasure. Turning away from knowledge of the one true god could indeed be reason enough for our exile and our punishment and burning torment." She caught hold of Sholeh's hand, pressing it between hers. "You will heal us in many ways."

Sholeh realized quickly that while the guests had been bathed and entertained, Steffyn had been preparing and planning strategy with his mother and the elders of the household. There was no need to tell their stories, because the household leaders knew them already. All the discussion centered around refining understanding and asking questions to get more details. Before the honey cakes and sweet watered wine were brought in at the end of the feast, the adults of the household agreed. There were still some questions that could only be answered by the other households, and what would be discovered when a hunting party caught up with Cleita and Caron and their people.

Only a few of Steffyn's aunts and cousins, sisters and brothers showed the same concern he did for the Kreefa households who had left generations ago. Most chose to believe that the stories of the Blood Queen were nothing more than that. They were created to frighten people from traveling through the mountains, rather than relating the fate of those who had disobeyed the warnings and commands in prophecy. The general consensus was that those Kreefa who went into the mountains had soon perished. Perhaps hunted down when they lost control to the Fever and revealed their wolf nature. Perhaps intermarrying with ordinary Humans diluted the magic in their blood, so no more children were born with two bodies.

Many in Nioba's household passed over the question of hunting down the Lost Ones, as they were called. Sholeh was pleased that Nioba was not one of them. Still, that left the unspoken question of how many Kreefa Elders would want to search for the Lost Ones before crossing the sea to Isle of the Moon, and how many would advocate to leave them to their fate.

The most important question was how many other households would agree to uproot themselves from their ancestral homes and cross the sea, and how long it would take to convince the reluctant ones.

"You, my son, have learned the lessons of leadership even more thoroughly than your father," Nioba said, late that evening, in her private rooms.

The other elders of the household had retired to their rooms and the outbuildings. Several men had promised they would go that night to visit their mates in the households allied with Nioba's, to speak with them and obtain an idea of how their household leaders felt about Sholeh's quest. Nioba had invited Sholeh and her brothers to speak with her, Steffyn and Nedden.

"He would be very proud of you," she added.

Sholeh was surprised to see a glimmer of what could have been tears, just for a moment, before Nioba blinked rapidly and turned to pour for them from a pitcher of honeyed water.

"We neglected one important detail," Nedden said, with a sideways glance at Steffyn. "Some of us have already benefited from the teachings of Verdidan."

"In what way?" Nioba glanced back and forth between him and her son.

"Those who choose to serve and worship Verdidan experienced some cooling of the Fever," Steffyn said. "We were prepared for the usual battle, on the journey home, when the full moon rose while we were still in the field, and no harlots nearby to provide relief. Sholeh thought she could calm the most inflamed with the power of her mind, her mastery of herbs, and her flute ... but the numbers and intensity of the sufferers were less than we anticipated. Those who are seeking Verdidan have found healing for their bodies, even though we have not formally vowed our minds and souls to his service."

"Why did you not mention this?"

"The ones who are proud of the heat in their blood," Nedden answered when Steffyn hesitated and met Sholeh's gaze instead. "They weren't happy to find their former partners in trouble didn't feel the flames like before."

"Fools!" Nioba spat. Then she shook her head and laughed. The laughter ended quickly, on a sigh. "Oh, my son, yes, your father would be so proud. He hated the fire in his blood, even after we were mated and found such joy in each other. He always felt shame. He cried out often to the darkness and silence, begging for the Power that made the world to hear him and heal him, and bring healing to our children."

"The holy words say that those who seek Verdidan, even unknowing of his name, will find him and find healing," Sholeh offered. "Your mate called out to truth and found Verdidan when he stepped from this life to the next, I am sure."

"May it be so." This time the tears were more clearly evident. She reached out to clasp Sholeh's hand, while knuckling the wet glimmer from her eyes with the other hand. "But yes, I understand. Some will not welcome the healing for what they do not consider an illness."

"Mostly those who don't want to believe in the prophecies," Nedden offered, turning to Sholeh.

She had already guessed that. Yet despite all Steffyn and Nedden and the other leaders of the Black Wolves had taught her about the Kreefa, there was still much she didn't understand, all the nuances and finer details of their society. No doubt there were things she could not understand because of the differences between men and women. She was grateful her brothers were here, to provide understanding where she was unable because of her age and her gender.

Sholeh felt small and weary and chilled, in anticipation of all she had to learn and understand, if she would help bring the Kreefa, the guardians, back to Isle of the Moon.

~~~~

Sylva, Steffyn's oldest sister and Nioba's heir, took charge of Sholeh
~~~~

the next morning. While the Elders sent messages back and forth between the households, deciding where and when to meet to discuss Steffyn's news, she would take the household's guest to meet the head daughters of their allied households. Nedden and Steffyn took charge of Indago and Garyon, to do the same, with a meeting of all the Black Wolves and the islanders later in the day.

As the two walked, Sholeh finally began to grasp the immensity of Mount Aerno. Travel on foot, in daylight, gave a better perspective than riding up the slopes on horseback in twilight. Sholeh found some amusement in how easily Sylva made her rapid pace seem like a stroll as the "short walk" to the closest household turned into nearly half an hour of uphill walking. When she asked why they hadn't taken the horses, Sylva seemed confused, and then laughed.

"Horses are for soldiers. We walk everywhere." Another chuckle escaped her. "Granted, those of us who are able to run as wolves without losing our clothes usually travel that way. It is much faster."

"I think I envy you."

"No, I envy you." She reached as if she would stroke the long braid hanging down over Sholeh's shoulder. "The Child of Moonlight, indeed. I wonder if your children will have your hair as well."

"My children?" Sholeh stumbled slightly.

"My brother looks at you as he has never looked at a woman before. Or does it repel you, to think of mating with our kind?" She stopped for the first time since walking out through the gates of the main house.

"No, not at all—but I didn't think Steffyn—I know he is very careful of me, but… well, Nedden told me half-bloods are nearly forbidden."

"Because those half-bloods come from our men cooling the Fever with harlots," Sylva said, her mouth flattening. "We cannot risk one of our kind growing up among ordinary Humans, with no knowledge of their blood. It would be cruel. Even if the only sign of their Kreefa blood was the crest fur on their backs, that would be shame enough, mocked as different or even disfigured. Imagine burning in your first Fever and not understanding what is happening to you. Imagine finding your second body during that same Fever. The terror and pain." She wrapped her arms around herself, shuddering for a moment.

"The terror and fear of those around that half-blood," Sholeh whispered. "I have seen little of the rest of the world, but I can imagine that those who saw what happened, saw that child turn into a wolf and turn back, if he could turn back, with no knowledge … they would kill that child."

"Or call him a child of the gods and worship him. That cannot be allowed. Some legends say that taking worship that did not belong to us caused our kind to be cast out from the crescent moon, where we were safe and whole. We cannot allow that to happen."

"It will not happen. I promised Steffyn, and I promise you now." Sholeh reached to clasp her new friend's hand. "I will stay with the Kreefa for however long it takes, until all are willing to cross the sea to the Isle of the Moon, where you will be healed and find your home again. I promise, on my soul." She squeezed for emphasis. "I swear on my mother's blood."

To her surprise, Sylva laughed and then embraced her.

"My friend, as smart as my brother is, he has not taught you properly. Only men swear on their mothers' blood. You swear on your own blood, the blood shed when you give your body's purity to your mate. The blood that begins the binding of your souls and bodies into one," she added, her voice dropping to a whisper.

As they resumed walking, Sholeh wondered if a Kreefa who mated with an ordinary Human experienced the same depth of binding. If Steffyn took her as his mate, would their souls touch and become one? In healing him, she had brushed up against his mind and soul, and there was a sweetness to the experience that made her shiver when she relived it in her memory. She hadn't understood, because at the time she thought he was just a wolf. Those gifted by Verdidan, whether in prophecy or healing or other talents, were said to be able join their souls, and as a result find a stronger merging in the marriage bed. Could what the Kreefa knew be similar to what her parents shared, knowing each other's thoughts and feelings without even being in the same room?

For a moment she stumbled as those moments flashed through her thoughts. When she had seemed to see through Steffyn's eyes, to know what he was thinking, to hear his voice whispering in her mind. Had some binding begun when she and Steffyn exchanged blood, in healing and then after the battle to protect her from the brute who tried to rape her? Were they already bound together, irrevocably?

She hoped it could be so. The intensity of her wish, in that moment of understanding, took her breath away.

Chapter Eighteen

Sholeh had considered herself strong, but the days that followed showed her that she had lived a comparatively indolent life. She woke with the dawn and joined the daughters of the household in preparing the morning meal, rousing the children, tending to essential chores of cleanliness. The cleanliness habits of the Kreefa pleased her, and she wondered if it was because their senses were so much keener than ordinary humans. Or was this just another of the many small actions in a never-ending struggle against their animal nature?

As soon as the washing and food preparation for the day had been done, she set out with Sylva or another elder daughter to visit households up and down the mountainside. Sholeh would have laughed at herself if she could have found the breath, in those first dozen days of constantly moving. The thinner air at the higher levels and the distances between households pushed her and tested her endurance. She had longed to get out of the saddle, near the end of their journey to Mount Aerno, but those first days of traveling among the Kreefa households made her wish for the horse again. The Kreefa reserved horses for pulling carts or for warriors to ride. Everyone else walked. Those who could shift to wolf-shape and carry small items with them did so. She envied them.

Sholeh spent her visiting time giving the history of Isle of the Moon, the prophecies, the stories and theories about the guardians. When she finished making the rounds of the households, telling the grandmothers and mothers and heir-daughters her story, she repeated those same rounds, in the same order because of prestige rankings and to avoid insult, and answered questions. Then she spent several days at a time at each household, studying the archives that were the responsibility of the heir-daughters.

Fall descended on the slopes of Mount Aerno. She learned to read the weather, though never as accurately as her hosts with their wolf-senses, to plan her travel and what to bring with her when she went on her never-ending rounds of education. When the rains fell for longer periods of time and the days grew colder, she and her escort were ready to spend the night, if travel back to Nioba's household would be too treacherous in the rain and darkness that came a little sooner every day.

Sholeh was so busy with preparing her lessons and recording what she had learned and bit by bit translating the holy writings from the gold pages, so all the Kreefa could have Verdidan's words, she didn't realize her brothers weren't doing similar work. She was always tired at the end of each day of walking in rain and mud, her mind caught up in word puzzles and new details of Kreefa life that she had learned. She didn't notice that they said less and less. She thought their physical exhaustion was just like hers.

Then one morning she gathered up the translation work she had risen early to work on, eager to share with Nioba, and the tension running through the household struck Sholeh for the first time. She would have been afraid, except that as Sylva took her hand and led her from the core room of the household, with the stone-lined fire pits in the floor, she noticed everyone they passed was smiling.

Her brothers waited for her at the bottom of the steps at the front of the house, and they were smiling also. They stood on either side of a white mare decked with wreaths of green leaves and dried flowers. Sholeh caught her breath, as she realized all the men standing behind her brothers were islanders.

"What has happened?" She flinched as Nioba settled her cloak on her shoulders. "Where are we going?" Her heart banged against her breastbone. "Has there been news? Did the outriders find Cleita?"

"No, I am sorry, child." Nioba sighed and tugged up the hood. "We didn't mean to frighten you, but … this is a very special, rare day. I know several of my daughters and nieces have mentioned the possibility that I would take you as a daughter of my household. I have been discussing the idea with the Elders, since we have never taken anyone into our families who was not Kreefa."

"Are we leaving?" she whispered, looking again at the horse. There was no saddle, just a bridle, so she couldn't be going on a long journey. Besides, her brothers were now grinning so widely she thought she could see all their teeth, even from twenty steps away.

"There is precedent." Nioba tugged up her own hood and held out her hand. Sholeh gave hers into her grasp and followed her down the steps. "In times of prosperity and fertility, daughters leave their grandmothers' or aunts' households to establish their own. The Elders hold you in high regard, because of the gift you bring us, the hope given by prophecy. As such, we have agreed that you must have your own household, and not linger as a guest."

"Your students will come to you now," Indago said, as Nioba brought Sholeh to him. He grasped her around her waist, like he used to do when she was half her size, and lifted her onto the back of the horse. "We've finished your part of the house, and we'll be working on our part, especially the teaching rooms, once you're settled. We'll have our students and you'll have yours, and a meeting place for the Elders in the winter."

Sholeh muffled a chuckle, remembering some comments she had overheard, concern from the grandmothers she had spoken with, that the preliminary work wouldn't be finished before they were all housebound by winter. Some of the odd looks, the inexplicable smiles, the cryptic comments about "other preparations" and "changes" and "new precedents" made sense now. Including her brothers' exhaustion so many nights, their lack of news about the meetings they had been having and lessons they had been giving. They had been working on building the household's core on clear days and slogging through mud and rain to meet with the Kreefa men on the bad days.

Nioba refused to climb up and ride behind Sholeh, when invited. The older woman made it clear this was part of the ceremony of taking Sholeh to her new home and establishing her as head of her household. No one could share the honor. Sholeh was just grateful that the rain hadn't been falling very long, and the previous four days had been relatively dry, so everyone wasn't slogging through ankle-deep mud. Indago and Garyon walked on either side of the mare, each holding the bridle, and Nioba led the way. Garyon played a tune on the ten-reed pipes, and Indago led the islanders in singing a worship song. On the second verse, the daughters of Nioba's household, who were following, joined in. Sholeh was startled to realize the song had been translated into Nedaian, but she hadn't been the one to do it.

Even though Nioba's and Indago's words had made it clear that the household being given to her would also serve as a meeting place for the Elders of the Kreefa, Sholeh was stunned to see the size of the building. Especially since Indago had said it wasn't finished yet. It stood on a ridge that had been covered by trees less than a moon ago. The roots of the walls of the inner and outer courtyards were barely visible. She ached just imagining the quantity of stone that would have to be dug out and hauled up and down the slopes to build the walls high enough for privacy and defense.

"Verdidan, give me strength to be worthy, and to serve you as fully as my mother and her mother before her," she murmured.

Indago reached up to squeeze her hand around the reins. Nioba allowed them to pause on the ridge opposite the one where the new household sat, long enough to take in the sight and appreciate the massive amount of work that had been done. Then she spread her arms, gesturing for them all to follow, and led the way down the slope, into the narrow valley, where a small bridge had been built to accommodate the stream created by the fall rains.

When the procession had climbed the slope to the top of the ridge, nearly all the Elders were waiting, and the mothers and heir-daughters of every household. Steffyn and all the Black Wolves, resplendent in their armor, stood on either side of the gap where the gates would be hung someday. When the mare came to a stop in front of the gates, on the freshly laid path of pebbles and sand, the warriors drew their swords and raised them skyward in salute. Sholeh heard Steffyn whisper her name, his voice rich with something she couldn't grasp, but it brought tears to her eyes. She had heard his voice in her mind, not her ears.

Indago brought her down from the mare and Nioba took her by the hand to lead her through the gates. Each of the Elders came up in turn, to take her by the hand and lead her a dozen steps or so, to pass her to the next Elder, until she had walked around the outside of her household three times.

When she returned to the steps, Clyvis waited in front of the doors, leaning on two canes, visibly trembling. He was the oldest man among all the Kreefa, his hair white, his eyes filmed white and blind. When he lost his sight in a time of great turmoil and loss, and saved many lives decades ago, he had become the repository of all Kreefa memories, and the leader for those who clung to the hope of regaining the crescent moon. Sholeh had spent several pleasant afternoons talking with Clyvis, delighted and surprised to learn that the Kreefa did have teachings about one creator god. He had taught her everything the Kreefa remembered about the prophecies and made her tremble when he proclaimed her the Moonlight Child and Moonlight Healer.

Now, Clyvis straightened as much as his frail, trembling body allowed, and he raised his voice to proclaim a blessing on the new household and all who would enter its gates for the sake of learning. When he finished, the clouds parted as if cut with a blade, and sunlight streamed down. Most of those gathered let out shouts of surprise and pleasure. Indago and Garyon linked their arms with Sholeh and led her across the ridge to the opposite side. After a shallow drop, a wide meadow spread out, nearly flat, nearly large enough to accommodate all the Kreefa on Mount Aerno. This meadow was used for the gatherings of the households during times of celebration, at the solstice and equinox. What did the households expect from her, that they would build a home for her, give her a voice in the council as the head of a household, and put her home nearly on top of the gathering place?

"You are probably wise to be afraid," Steffyn murmured from behind her.

She turned, not startled, because she had sensed he was there, within arm's reach during the ceremony, and would stay close until she sent him away. If she was ever foolish enough to send him away.

"But I beg you, Sholeh-child, do not be afraid. I have learned enough about Verdidan to agree that the Creator gives the skills and strength and courage and wisdom to carry out the tasks he puts on your shoulders.

Those who are chosen for destiny are never unprepared."

"Unless they choose to go into battle without their armor?"

Sparks of amusement touched his eyes. She thought he was about to say something else. The next moment, Sylva and several other daughters of the household swept her away to dance, and then to feast, for as long as the weather stayed pleasant.

Every household contributed something to fill the needs of the new home; dishes and pots, utensils, blankets, grain, fruit, meat, rugs, cushions. The sailors had turned their skills in ship repair and other shipboard tasks to homemaking, and Sholeh was pleased to learn that some already had requests for furniture, for blacksmithing work. Others had skills they traded with the friends they had made and the hosts of the households where they had been staying, repairing tools, building looms, butchering the results of the hunt. The islanders were considered part of her household now, and they had established themselves solidly among the Kreefa with the skills of their hands, as well as the information they could give about Isle of the Moon and Verdidan's teachings.

By the time the first snows swirled down from the highest slopes of Aerno, the routine of the household was solid enough Sholeh didn't have to think about it. While she enjoyed baking and other tasks that were considered the province of the women, she didn't have to spend all her time doing them or doing them alone. Her students traded household work for their lessons in healing and reading and writing and the language of Isle of the Moon, or they brought bread, cloth, other food, and other supplies.

When the Elders came to use the long hall for their meetings, to discuss the proposed plan to move all the households over the sea, they brought food with them, and oil for the lamps and charcoal for the fire pits. Sometimes the weather forced them to stay overnight, and then Sholeh played hostess.

Not everyone agreed immediately with the plan to leave their ancestral homes, where they were accepted by the nearby inhabitants. Sholeh would have been alarmed if all the Elders and household leaders eagerly accepted the news she brought, and believed she was the fulfillment of prophecy. Nearly from the first day she and the islanders had arrived among the Kreefa, the Elders had been conferring and arguing and coming up with objections and alternate proposals and possible problems. How many ships would they need to cross the sea to Isle of the Moon? How long would the journey take if they tried to keep the ships together, for support? What if they couldn't find enough captains, or any captains, willing to believe that Sholeh and her people indeed did come from an island beyond the horizon, and the world didn't drop off into a never-ending waterfall? What if there were no ships large enough, sturdy enough, to handle the moons-long voyage?

Enough of the sailors were trained as shipwrights, to handle any necessary repair, they could build ships if they had to. That would delay the first crossing of the Kreefa by another year. This provided a partial answer to another question: not everyone was willing to go immediately. Sholeh agreed that the prophecy that had sent her and her cousins on their quest had not specified *all* the descendants of the lost guardians had to return, only that the daughters of Isle of the Moon were to go and bring them back. Any who would willingly come, she had to believe, would be enough for Verdidan's purposes.

She had to believe the All-Maker knew the future. Knew the barriers and questions and fears and objections the Kreefa would raise. How long it would take to overcome them, and how many would be willing to come, enough for the need, and in the right timing. No matter how quickly Tylanok conquered kingdoms and conscripted soldiers and ravaged the lands to feed his armies, he could only move so quickly in his southward march toward the sea and the peninsula that pointed to Isle of the Moon. Adastra and the island leaders had more than enough warning to prepare, to strengthen the defenders and weave defensive shields of prayers, and songs filled with magic and faith, to ward away Tylanok when he sent his ships across the water. The despot and conqueror would never set foot on the shores of the island.

Unless there was treachery. Unless someone yielded to fear, greed, jealousy, or anger, and offered Tylanok a way through the defenses. Unless someone took down the defenses from within.

Sholeh could believe in treachery just as easily as she could believe that Verdidan would use her for holy purposes, despite her youth and fears, weaknesses, and selfish dreams. When she considered who among the Kreefa stood against them most fiercely, Steffyn's childhood friend, Racc, always came to mind. He led a group of men who insisted that the prophecy and the long wait for fulfillment had weakened the Kreefa. They believed the Kreefa had been led to Mount Aerno to take the place of the false gods. Instead of gods who had only been seen and heard in legend, the Kreefa could give the people of Nedaia gods of flesh, who were fierce in war and able to lead them in conquest.

Racc had burst out in fury when he learned about the proposal Aies had brought to Steffyn, allegedly from King Vollen of Arkady. He had mocked Vollen's dream of making himself a god, but he was furious that Steffyn had refused the proposal. He considered it an opportunity to use Vollen as a steppingstone to gain riches and power and prove the Kreefa were gods in the making.

He gathered discontented men around him after that argument, until the tipping point came. Racc was no longer content to argue and mock and threaten. He and his followers marched on Sholeh's household, howling from human and wolf throats, demanding that the Moonlight Child come out and face them. The Black Wolves gathered just in time to block their way, in the valley below the household. Steffyn refused to let the men come any closer, until they stated their purpose and their demands.

Racc wanted the magic Sholeh possessed, in the flute and her healing training, in her healing touch. He wanted her to serve him and his followers, to turn her magic into weapons against anyone who would stand against them. The louder he raged, the quieter Steffyn's voice grew as he refused all Racc's demands. Until his childhood friend leaped, and shifted to wolf. His jaws closed on Steffyn's arm when they collided.

The Black Wolves killed five of Racc's followers in the battle that followed. He and his men were called to stand before the Elders, to face discipline. Rather than submit, they fled up the mountainside, in the face of an oncoming storm. The battle stirred up more questions and doubts about the plan to go to Isle of the Moon.

Sholeh felt as if all the progress she and Steffyn and their allies had made in the past moons had been wiped out, like sparks in rain. Some nights she curled up in her blankets and wept at the futility of repeating the work of settling fears and questions, persuading the Elders that Verdidan would be faithful and true and fulfill the prophecies given to their ancestors on both sides of the sea. She and her brothers and those who chose to believe fully in Verdidan's laws and wisdom and love had only the remains of the winter to persuade the gathered households of the Kreefa.

The winter passed too quickly. Several reluctant households were persuaded. A few who had at first welcomed the news, the fulfillment of the promised healing and restoration, grew doubtful and reluctant. That was expected.

Sholeh knew her brothers planned to leave with a small mixed troop of islanders and Kreefa hunters to seek news of Cleita and Caron, when the snows left the northern passes. She still wasn't ready for the day Indago gave her the news. She wasn't ready the morning she stood at the top of her household's steps and held her brothers' hands as they prayed for Verdidan's blessing on the journey and the hunt. She was proud of herself that she didn't cry, and she smiled for them.

When she went to bed that night, after a long day studying with her students, she found Loree's quartz flute resting next to hers, on the shelf beside her bed. Garyon had held onto it all these long moons, while he gave up words. For him to give up the last link with his sweetheart, to leave it with Sholeh for safekeeping, shattered something inside her.

Tears and a smothering aching sent her running out into the chilly spring night. Steffyn met her in wolf-shape at the bridge in the valley below her household. Sholeh wrapped her arms around him and hid her face in his thick fur, and let the tears gush, until she wore herself out with weeping. When she woke, the moon had fallen halfway to the horizon and she lay wrapped safely in Steffyn's cloak and his arms. They leaned against the support posts of the bridge and watched the moon continue its descent, and she found healing in simply being with him. He walked her to the base of the steps of her house, as sunrise spilled pink and lavender around the mountainside to her right.

"I know you have much to do today," she began.

"Yes. Ask anything of me." He caught hold of her hand for the first time in moons.

"You don't even know—"

"You want me to stay with you today. Yes."

"I'm not imagining it?"

"Being inside each other's thoughts, our hearts beating together?" Steffyn smiled, but an aching spark touched his eyes instead of humor. "It's very real."

"I always thought that I would—"

"I will wait."

"Wait for what?" Her voice cracked. "What was I about to say?"

"You always intended to wait until you were twenty, before you considered taking a mate."

"Did I tell you that?" She settled on the third step, and Steffyn went to one knee facing her. His mouth quirked up on only one side.

"In our dreams, perhaps. Sholeh-child—"

"I am not a child! Not after everything I have endured in the last year. Not with everything I feel. That you make me feel." She tugged her hand free of his and pressed it flat against his chest. Steffyn inhaled sharply at the touch but didn't pull away.

"I know you are not a child. I have never seen you as a child. But I made that name a wall to protect us both from foolishness. No."

"No what?" Something caught in her throat, and she thought it was laughter.

Chapter Nineteen

"You want to ask me if it is foolish to love." He pressed his hand over hers, over his heart.

"Steffyn ... do I ask your mother for permission to marry you? Do I even need to ask permission? If this isn't my imagination, as I have feared for so many moons, this thing between us ... then we are already bound together, heart and soul, and surely bound as one person in Verdidan's sight." She cupped his cheek with her free hand, and chuckled when she felt his pulse stagger. "Will we only give the doubters and naysayers more weapons against the plan, if we reveal our love? You do love me, don't you? You said you did, the night you saved my life, and surely you know now how I feel?"

"You are right." He sighed, and one side of his mouth quirked up. "While you are admired and your people are welcome among us, and we are grateful that you do not regard us as monsters or gods, there is still the fear—"

"Half-bloods," she whispered.

"Which is the greater crime? To birth children who might suffer even more in their first Fever, or to refuse to seal our union with children?"

"I would want—" Her face warmed and her lips trembled with a smile. Sholeh hadn't let herself think that far along the path of her longing for Steffyn. It had been enough to daydream about kisses and being held by him. To conceive his children seemed several lifetimes off in the distance. Yet now that the words had been spoken, she wanted those children, with a strength that was painful.

"Will many stand against us, do you think?" she said, instead of confessing what had just come into her mind. From the slight widening of his eyes, Steffyn knew or at least sensed what she had been thinking.

"I will discuss this with my mother. If she sides with us, I will ask her to approach other Elders and household mothers, until we know how many support us, how many will help us." He caught hold of her hand and lifted it off his chest and held it between both of his. "But perhaps we are moving too quickly. We need to ask for your brothers' blessing. Perhaps by the time we reach Isle of the Moon, your parents could have a husband or at least a suitor they approve of, chosen for you."

Sholeh wanted to say her mother would want her to be happy, first. Certainly she had the right to choose the life-mate who made her happy, after all she had done and would do, serving the Isle of the Moon?

Steffyn kissed her for the first time, on the palms of her hands and her forehead, before he left her to go inside, wash and dress and eat breakfast. He returned when her first students arrived and stayed in her sight all day in the courtyard. He never said a word to her, except to greet her when he arrived and to make his farewells when he left before the evening meal. Yet that was more than enough. All day, she felt his thoughts, his reactions when a student did well or someone made a funny error. His support and the images that slipped into her mind helped her to understand a little better some of the differences in their two worlds, when a student couldn't clearly explain a custom or perception to her.

"Sleep well, my love," she whispered, long after the moon rose. She stood alone on the highest point of her house, where she could look across the ridges and down the mountain slopes and see the torches in the courtyards of other households. Tiny spots of gold and warmth in the darkness of spring growth. Nioba's household was a clear line of sight from her home on the ridge.

She promised herself, she would approach Nioba soon. She knew so little about the details of Kreefa mating, as opposed to marriage as Isle of the Moon practiced it. Now was the time to learn. She muffled a chuckle when she realized she hoped that Indago and Garyon took some time finding Cleita and Caron's trail. She needed time to prepare, before her brothers returned.

~~~~~

Four days after her brothers had left, Sholeh went out to visit the nearest households with Sylva. She was training Steffyn's sister as a healer. Over the winter, she had detected some small stirring of healing gift, and both were pleased when continual testing and use proved to strengthen that gift. Taking healing to other households also helped to strengthen their commitment to go to Isle of the Moon.

During the walk between households, they discussed the details of the traveling party being assembled, to leave after the full moon. The plan was to cross to Gytheion, which had a harbor large enough and population large enough to be a trade hub. The port had the resources to support ship building, if that became necessary, and enough traffic of ships coming in and out that word could spread to captains up and down the coast of what Steffyn was looking for. They would respond to the respected captain of the Black Wolves, when they would ignore or be suspicious of strangers. Especially strangers led by a woman. Especially if tales were still being told of the healer women with the moonlight hair.

Wyllan and the trained shipwrights had stayed back when the hunters left to seek Cleita and her people. They would go with Steffyn and his men to Gytheion. When Indago and his team returned, they would go
~~~~~

west to the coast, to meet Steffyn. If all went well, soon they would be sending for the other households to come and take ship and make the first crossing of the sea.

Sholeh's head was so full of plans and anticipation, she nearly ignored the prickling in her shoulders and scalp, the sense of being watched by unfriendly eyes. She did pay attention, though, and signaled Sylva that she sensed something was wrong. Her friend silently signaled her agreement. The last five minutes of their walk to Theona's household were silent and tense, and she breathed easier when the sensation faded to nothing just before they walked through the household's gates.

~~~~~

"Do you feel it?" Sylva whispered when they had left the last household behind.

The day had been long. While it had been rewarding to meet with friends and share healing and feel useful, it had also been exhausting.

Sholeh nodded, and it took some effort on her part not to look over her shoulder. The prickling in her scalp had returned. Just because she hadn't sensed those unfriendly eyes watching them until now, that didn't mean someone hadn't been marking their travels that day. What if the disturbances that had drawn away members of the households to investigate, during three different stops, had been caused by the owner of those unfriendly eyes? Someone tried to get close enough to hear what they discussed? Or someone prepared to do worse than eavesdrop?

Sunset painted the sky with hints of purple and crimson and gold. Sholeh tried to calculate the route to Nioba's household, their final stop of the day, how long it would take them to get there, and if they would reach the gates before full dark had fallen.

"What should we do?" Sholeh said after a moment, as they kept walking down the winding animal trail.

Her sense of direction indicated they were perhaps half an hour of swift walking from their destination. However, there were a few spots where she would have to slow her pace. She wished Steffyn were with them, but he had gone down the mountain today to the nearest village where he could learn the latest news. The actions of the kings of Nedaia, the rumors of wars, the political upheavals and petty arguments. Anything that might threaten the safety of the Kreefa, especially as they prepared to uproot their lives and abandon their homes.

Sylva startled, turning to look to their left. Her nostrils flared. She glanced at Sholeh.

"I can run," Sholeh whispered. "Don't worry about me."

"Running is more dangerous. No, I smell death. Fresh. The blood is still hot."

Sylva would not be disturbed by the smell of a dead animal, so it had
~~~~~

to be a person. Sholeh almost offered to turn around and go back, to see if she could help as a healer, but Sylva had said she smelled death. She had been given ample proof time and again of the sensitivity of Kreefa noses.

Steffyn, are you near? Are you on your way home? Sholeh tried to form a clear picture in her mind of where she was. Could he hear her over such a long distance? She knew they shared feelings over short distances, mostly when they could see each other. Surely their bond had grown enough that he could hear her when she needed him?

"Keep walking. I will be swift." Sylva turned, stepping into a patch of shadow among the trees to their left. She vanished into the shadow, and Sholeh's fingers prickled with the shimmer of magic as she shifted shape.

Sholeh rubbed her fingers together. Was the momentary prickling in them stronger this time? She had sensed the residue of magic in the air before, when Steffyn and other Kreefa had shifted from one body to another. Still, those times had always been full of danger, the air thick with blood and fury. Was she growing more sensitive to this shifting?

"It's not the full moon," a man said, emerging from the blot of shadows where the trail turned to the right, a good dozen paces ahead of her, "so it is the power in you that I sense. Good. That pleases me."

Sholeh slowed her steps, unsure if stopping would be unwise. She couldn't make out any details while the shadows enfolded him, except that he was tall, with wide shoulders and thickly muscled legs. His bare feet, bare chest, open vest displaying a chest dark with hair, and his dark trousers that stopped just below his knees marked him as Kreefa.

"You would be wise to please me always," he said, a touch of growl in his voice when she refused to respond.

She bit back a retort that he had no authority to speak that way to her.

"Does the healer power always hum in you, like it does now?" He chuckled and took another step forward, revealing his pale skin and dark hair. "Or is that your fear?"

"I am a healer, yes." She raised her voice a little, hoping to catch Sylva's attention. If there was fear, her anger fought it down. She felt incredibly clear-headed. She stopped and spread her feet, to ensure her balance for whatever came next.

"Anger always adds spice." He chuckled. "But it's the scent of a virgin that draws me now." He grinned, a fierce baring of white teeth in the black matt of his beard. "Steffyn was wise to keep you away from me. And a fool, for not claiming you the moment he realized what you were."

Now she knew who he was. Racc. She hadn't been ashamed to hope that he and his band of malcontents had died in the winter snows.

"There is more to being mated than mating."

"No, it's not the full moon, but if you have half the power the others say, a goddess in her own right, then you will serve. You will serve quite well and be quite tasty. A bonus for me."

"I will not serve you." She pressed her arm against the long knife hidden in the seam of her dress. The trees and bushes growing along the rough trail were thick here. Wiser to stand and fight in this spot, rather than turn her back and try to race uphill, and pray she could outrun this brute before he threw her to the ground.

"That," he growled, stepping out of the shadows to reveal more details of his muscular torso and the fire in his deep-set eyes, "is what must change. Here and now. In the rest of the world, women serve men, the way it is meant to be. That is the weakness of the Kreefa. Our women rule us, make us weak." He took a long, slow, arrogant step up the trail toward her. Sholeh slid her foot backward, trying to hide the movement, knowing he wanted to make her afraid, wanted to make her run. "We are meant to be gods, and it starts here!"

He leaped, shifting to wolf, his grin rippling horribly as his face elongated into a snout and sharp teeth. Sholeh turned and fled, drawing her knife. Her scream caught in her throat, even as a quiet part of her mind noted that a scream was a waste of breath better served in fleeing.

Steffyn! Hear me!

Three steps. Four steps. Five.

Weight slammed into her back, throwing her to the ground. She screamed and turned, kicking before she hit the pebbly trail. The jolt nearly knocked the knife from her grip, but she held on and continued turning, slashing and kicking, trusting to her father's training to guide her hand.

Her feet hit fur and hard muscle and bone. Her knife caught on something. A snarl turned into a yelp. She smelled blood. Terror shot through her as the hot, sour, iron tang filled her nose. Sholeh punched and kicked and bucked, anything to get away from the dusty, musky stink of fur and the weight.

Please, don't let it touch me. Don't let the blood touch me.

Then she could breathe, the weight and heat gone. She continued rolling, slamming into a bush that gave slightly before pushing back against her. The spines of the branches and the sharp prickles of the leaves scratched at her face and arms as she scrambled to turn over, to get on her hands and knees, to find her enemy and brace for his next attack.

"So, she has teeth," Racc said, his voice a rich chuckle that made her stomach churn.

Aunt Rayeen had warned her about men who were aroused by blood and pain, and insisted when they were brought to justice that the women they abused enjoyed it as well.

Steffyn, my love, come to me!

Sholeh found him as she got to her knees. Now he stood several paces up the trail from her. His smile was wider, and she thought his teeth looked pointed. The sunset tinted his black hair with streaks of red. He clasped his left hand over his right shoulder, and dark, glistening smears streaked his arm. Good, she had wounded him. Not enough, but she had drawn first blood and that had to count for something.

"The Nedaians want gods. I will give them gods. I will be king of the gods, and you will give me sons to rule after me. Maybe you can even grant immortality."

Why did every madman with delusions of godhood want immortality? First Tylanok, now Racc.

He withdrew his hand from his wound. "First you will heal this."

Sholeh clenched her teeth to hold back all the foolish, energy-wasting, breath-wasting retorts that filled her mouth. For answer, she held out the knife, tight in her fist, poised to slash downward. The only healing she would give him was the freedom from pain and bleeding that came through death.

"So that's the way of it, is it?" He chuckled, the sound low and rich. "You think you can delay me until someone comes to rescue you? You little fool, has no one told you of our law? The law of blood?"

As he snarled "blood," he leaped, shifting to wolf. Sholeh threw herself uphill, toward him, and turned, slashing upward. He overshot her, but her move flung her onto her back on the ground. Before she could turn and regain her feet, he was on her, shifting to man as his weight and the force of the impact drove the breath from her. The energy of the shift tingled and itched against her skin, making her writhe under him.

Steffyn! Please, Verdidan —

"The law of blood," he growled, grinding his hips against hers, "binds you to me the moment I spill your virgin blood. Nothing but death can separate us, and I need you too much to let you die. But I can make you wish for death every day." He chuckled, one hand sliding up her arm to the wrist of her knife hand. He squeezed, threatening to snap the fragile bones.

A black shadow plowed into Racc, rolling him off her. Sholeh couldn't breathe as she struggled to her feet and away. She stumbled and kept scrambling up the hill. Two wolves fought, snarling and snapping and rolling in a tangle of legs and teeth. One black, the other dark brown with red tints.

"Steffyn ..." Sholeh slowed and turned to look back.

More wolves emerged from the shadows of the bushes and trees lining the trail. Dozens. She thought she recognized some of the wolves of the Black Wolves. They all watched, their expressions solemn, and she shuddered, expecting the fight to be to the death.

A hand on her arm wrung a scream from her, then Sylva drew her close and held her while she shuddered and finally remembered how to breathe.

~~~~~

"Half our nature is wolf, and we spend our lives fighting to save our souls from that nature," Nioba said, as Sholeh and Sylva stepped into the inner courtyard of her household a little less than an hour later.

She held out a cup that steamed faintly. It smelled of calming herbs, sweet and mild, mixed with watered wine. All Sholeh's senses seemed triply sensitive now. Nioba hurried down the steps and embraced Sholeh. Before anyone could say anything, she ordered Sholeh into the bathing room. Then she saw the smears of blood on her clothes. She trembled hard enough to threaten her balance, until she saw that no blood had touched her skin. Damitia and her sisters attended her again, bringing her plenty of cleansing herb paste and enough hot water to drown her, but this time there was no laughing and teasing.

"While there is some bonding that takes place through blood, it is most often through the blood-bonding ceremony," Nioba said, after Sholeh confessed her fear in between sips of the warmed wine. It had to be re-heated, after her bath. "Man and woman cut the heel of their right hand and offer their blood for their mate to taste. Racc could not have bound himself to you just by his blood touching your skin."

"But … I healed Steffyn, when he was in wolf shape. His leg was broken. His blood was on my hands, and I have proof we are bound. Nothing can wipe away that binding, and force me to join another, can it? Can they?" She shuddered and took a large mouthful of the wine to wash the surge of sourness from her mouth.

She and Sylva and Nioba were alone in the smaller courtyard, the air chill and ringing with the tension and anticipation that filled the household. For the moment, they were alone, and Sholeh was grateful, for the privacy and the open air, when everything inside her struggled as if she might smother.

"Only death can sever a blood bond," Nioba said, her tone soothing. She stroked Sholeh's wet hair off her forehead. "Indeed, we all have seen that proof. No one can deny what Verdidan has woven between you."

"He heard you call to him when he was nearly at the foot of the mountain. All the men with him heard him shout that Racc was attacking you, and they ran faster than the wind, following him straight to you," Sylva said. "Mother, this bonding between them … could it be part of the prophecy?"

"There are many prophecies," Nioba said, nodding, her eyes hooded with thoughtfulness.

The sliding panel into the courtyard slid aside with some force, and Steffyn stalked out of the house. His hair was wet and slicked to his head,
~~~~~

a few drops of water fell from his beard and his shirt hung open, revealing healing scratches all across his chest. He dropped to his knees in front of Sholeh and caught hold of her hands. She thought she would fall into his wide eyes. The fury in them softened with every heartbeat until she couldn't stand it. But she couldn't fling herself into his arms and hold him and dissolve in tears. Not in front of his mother and sister. Not even with the knowledge that they approved of her and Steffyn being together.

Instead, Sholeh tugged one hand free and pressed it to his chest, over the widest and darkest and hottest of the scratches. She felt echoes of his fading pain as she poured her healing strength into him.

My love, he whispered into her mind. He caught up her hand to press it to his lips when the healing finished. "Is it true?" Steffyn moved to sit beside her on the long, low, padded bench, and kept hold of her hands in both of his. "Moerna is dead?"

"Amree blames Sholeh," Sylva said. "Just before you came home, her messenger left. She will not let any of her household make the journey."

"There is little else she can do to punish us," Nioba said. "There are enough witnesses that Sholeh rejected Racc's attempt to force her. She cannot demand the blood price from her, or any of us. But she will punish everyone she can. Until she has died, and her nieces and grandnieces soften toward us ..." She shrugged.

"No," Sholeh said, her voice cracking. "Moerna?"

Moerna was the only granddaughter and heir of Amree, one of the most powerful household matriarchs. She was also Racc's mate and had been devastated and shamed when he fled after his rebellion failed. They had one child, a boy named Theon, for Racc's mother, Theona.

Moerna had been the greatest influence in persuading her grandmother to agree to take the journey to Isle of the Moon. Amree was a sour-faced, bitter woman who gave grudging hospitality and suffered a sour stomach. Sholeh always had the impression that the household was deliberately set farther away from all the other Kreefa households because of some long-lasting grudge.

Then a new thought came to her, and she stiffened and tightened her grip on Steffyn's hand. "Was she the blood, the death you smelled on the trail?"

Chapter Twenty

"No." Sylva shook herself and got up to pour more of the herbed wine for all of them. "Racc has proved his madness. That blood was some innocent villager, most likely killed just to draw me away and leave you alone. Thank Verdidan you are so skilled with the blade, and so fierce." She sighed as she handed a cup to Steffyn and turned to fill Nioba's cup. "She will need that fierceness, brother, to survive among us."

"Moerna told her grandmother last night that Racc came to her while she was scrubbing clothes at the stream, and ordered her to free him from their bond, so he could take you as his mate and breed ..." Nioba sighed and shook her head.

"Breed gods." Sholeh took several deep breaths to quell the queasiness in her stomach. "So he told me."

"She went out, against Amree's advice, to meet with Racc this morning and try to convince him to give up his foolish plans."

"I don't understand how the blood bond, the mating bond, can be broken so easily. The growing bond of spirit and mind cannot be broken except through death." She thought of Garyon, suffering still from Loree's death, and the two of them had barely begun to weave that bond together.

"That is why he killed her, I think," Steffyn said. "Racc has proved the depths of his madness. Moerna's death only added to his madness. They have been mated six years. They have a son. She carried their second child." His voice cracked. "Mother, how could he?"

Sholeh swallowed a sob, feeling his confusion and pain through their clasped hands, and hearing it in his voice. She remembered stories Steffyn had told her on the journey to Mount Aerno, the years when Racc had been his best friend. Hunting partners, making plans to explore beyond the boundaries of the known world. They had dreams of finding the Lost Ones, persuading them to return to the ancestral home of the Kreefa, and returning in glory.

Then he had told her of his growing disquiet when Racc insisted that the Kreefa were born to displace the absent gods of Mount Aerno. He wanted to rule, first Nedaia, then the world, through the strength of their wolf nature.

"Madness. Evil. Sickness in his soul." Nioba sounded so weary, Sholeh wanted to put her arms around the woman and ease her into healing sleep. She feared, however, there would be little healing and even less sleep for any of them for many days to come. "Fueled by his madness, the wound he made in his soul, he came after Sholeh. And now Amree blames her, blames our belief in the prophecies of the crescent moon. She is in such fury of pain, she paused in the midst of mourning for her granddaughter to send a messenger to me, to spill her poison. She will stand against us for many years to come. She will call on the loyalty the other households owe her, to stand against us. How can there be healing for us all, if only a few of us go?"

"No," Sholeh said. "I promised, no matter how long it takes, I will stay here with you and work until all the Kreefa are willing to go, and we will all go together to Isle of the Moon. My mother sent us all to search, no matter how long it takes, until we find the guardians and bring them home. I will not go home without you. Until then, my home is here."

~~~~~

Three days before the planned departure of Steffyn and the Black Wolves, to escort the shipwrights west to Gytheion, Racc and his followers stormed the households of their mates and carried off their sons. The fires and dead bodies they left behind delayed those who would have gone out on their trail as vengeance hunters. The rebel band didn't stay on Mount Aerno but headed west as swiftly as they could move. When their path merged with the traffic on the trade roads, the hunters lost their scent, and had to return home in defeat.

The original plan had been for Sholeh to travel with them to Gytheion, but Steffyn begged her to stay behind, to be safe. Racc and his followers could be waiting somewhere along the road, to ambush them. Sholeh listened to his concern for her that he didn't speak with words but from his heart to hers. Since most of her household had left, either going over the mountains or to the coast, she agreed to return to Nioba's household to live while Steffyn was away.

A courier returned with news sooner than Sholeh expected, and that worried her. An old proverb of Isle of the Moon said that bad news traveled swiftly, but good news waited until it had matured and ripened into sweetness. She didn't know if she was proven right when the courier stood before the council of Elders and household leaders and spoke the message from Steffyn.

All the western coast of Nedaia was in turmoil. The spring storms had only worsened the rough conditions of winter. Many harbors were flooded, the piers destroyed or submerged. Warehouses and trading halls had been wrecked in tidal waves or eroded by fierce waves and swept out to sea. Entire fleets and the merchants who depended on them had been destroyed. The numbers of trained, skilled sailors had been reduced to less than a third of what had been available when winter set in. Lands that depended on importing food by ship were facing starvation. Merchant
~~~~~

caravans of wagons, hauled by oxen or donkeys or horses were in great demand, and the high prices they charged were making them extremely unpopular. Those prices only went up when the incidents of attacks on caravans tripled. No one could agree if the attacks were in retaliation for those high prices, or simply because entire villages were desperate for food and trade goods they had always obtained by ship. The increase of attackers and their fierceness led to speculation that the pirates who preyed on traders and villages up and down the coast couldn't go to sea, so they had turned their hunting inland.

Wyllan and the islanders had settled south of Gytheion and set up a business to repair ships. They promised to watch the sea and send word when the waters finally grew friendly enough for travel. The Black Wolves had been deluged with pleas to guard warehouses and merchant caravans. Steffyn decided to stay on the coast, using the work as an excuse to travel as far north and south as he could go and find if there was any port or harbor or ship that had survived the devastation. So far, everyone agreed these were the worst spring storms in recorded memory.

The priests of Agantes lived in fear for their lives because the people blamed them for the devastation. One old priest had proclaimed that Agantes had wrecked the entire western coast in retaliation for neglect of his altars. Two days later, he had been thrown from the tower of the temple and drowned. As the people of the coast put their lives back together, they slowly came to agreement: the storms could only have come by means of evil magic. Someone or something had roiled the seas so that even halfway through the summer, many seasoned sailors were afraid to go out beyond the shelter of their harbors.

Sholeh wondered if it was possible that Tylanok had grown so drastically in power, gained the support of the dark spirits to the point that he could disturb the sea and reach all the way across it. The devastation on the west coast reached far inland, affecting weather and crops everywhere. She didn't share her speculation with anyone all during that long, wet, chilly summer of waiting. She supposed it was possible for Tylanok to do that, but she couldn't begin to calculate what that cost him, in terms of power. What did he gain by blocking the sea? Did he know Isle of the Moon had sent its daughters in search of the guardians? Did Tylanok have even greater reach than the council had believed? Or did traitors send information to their enemy?

She saved her thoughts to share with Clyvis and the oldest of the Elders, those most thoroughly versed in the lore and legends of the Kreefa. They agreed with her theories and couldn't find anything in the few written records or their collective memories to dispute or to support. Time would answer them, if and when they were ever able to cross the sea. So she waited to speak with Steffyn, when he finally returned to Mount

Aerno in the fall.

Garyon returned with Steffyn. He and Indago had separated soon after crossing into the mountains, to follow two strong trails of rumors. Indago went after the Blood Queen, while Garyon and his warriors followed tales of men who were savaged by wolves at the full moon, who were condemned to turn into wolves at the next full moon. This was a magic the Kreefa feared, because it turned the gift of two bodies into a sickness and a curse. The Kreefa with Garyon felt duty-bound to find those sufferers to either help or stop them.

Garyon's hunters found a number of unwilling man-wolves, who were kept prisoner during the full moon and suffered torments during the change. They were all victims of a wolf attack and could provide little help in tracking down the ones who had infected them, who might just turn out to be victims themselves. Garyon brought three as prisoners when he went to Gytheion, believing Sholeh would be there, and hoping she could find a cure for their torment. Perhaps with the help of the quartz flutes, she could unravel the weaving of the evil magic that imprisoned them.

By the time the Black Wolves headed for home and Mount Aerno in the fall, two of the three victims had died during the transformation. Garyon feared something had started to go wrong, to warp, during the shifting from man to wolf in one man, and from wolf to man in the other. The third man lived for two more moons, but he also died during the transformation, on the journey to Mount Aerno.

Along the way, Garyon and Steffyn searched for more stories of man-wolves who resulted from wolf bites. They followed many of those trails to the southern kingdoms. One of those kingdoms was Arkady, and they dared not cross the border there. Not if Vollen had found someone who could give him the power of transformation between man and wolf. Clearly there was something wrong with the magic because no one seemed to live very long after they had been infected. As Garyon said, when he explained their decision later, the worst thing they could do was give a full-blooded Kreefa into the hands of a sorcerer trying to steal the magic from their blood.

Despite the bitter news, there was sweetness in their reunion in the fall. Garyon had regained his voice. He had also become good friends with Steffyn, and had proven himself skilled as a warrior, to earn a place among the Black Wolves. More important, he approved when Steffyn revealed the bond between him and Sholeh. He approached Nioba during the welcoming feast, in front of a household of witnesses, to ask for her blessing on the mating between his sister and her son.

They delayed the celebration feast until the first snows threatened, in hopes that Indago would return. That delay allowed the Kreefa to come to some acceptance of the pairing and the attendant difficulties and necessary changes The fear of the half-blood children who might result was overcome in the hope that they would inherit their mother's healing gifts. The second change needed time to gain some acceptance, after Steffyn declared he would leave his mother's house to share his wife's household, following the customs of Isle of the Moon.

When spring came, Sholeh traveled with Steffyn and Garyon and the Black Wolves to Gytheion. Wyllan and his crew prospered as shipwrights because the sea remained so brutally rough and repairs were always needed. The spring storms had not calmed the water after the bitter cruelty of winter, and the winter past had been the worst anyone could remember. The merchants were adapting to having to haul their goods overland on the coast. Sailors who couldn't find ships to sail on learned other crafts, and many became hired guards for the merchant caravans.

Word reached Mount Aerno that Racc was seen in the palace of King Vollen of Arkady. No one could verify if the rest of his rebel followers were with him. There was much speculation in the council of the Elders over what he had done to earn the patronage of the king who was adding to his reputation of decadence and madness.

The third spring, Wyllan and the bravest and most skilled of his crew of sailors and shipwrights detected a slight calming in the seas, coming at the turn from winter to spring. They headed out in a ship they had spent the last two years building, designed for speed and agility and stability.

They returned after two moons, to much acclaim. Kings all along the coast clamored to hire them to build the same style of ships to start the long process of rebuilding their fleets. Wyllan sent for Sholeh. He didn't want to write down what he and his crew had seen. For the sake of speed, and because they feared spies from Arkady following them, Sholeh traveled on the swiftest horse Steffyn could find, while he and a dozen Black Wolves kept pace with her in wolf-shape. They traveled day and night to reach Gytheion.

"We were half a moon away from where we should have sighted the northern horn," Wyllan reported, in a meeting held indoors for privacy. He still looked exhausted from the trip. "There is a wall. I don't know what it is. It seethes and buzzes like it's made of thousands of biting insects. The closer we came to it, the louder it grew, and the thicker. When we drew back, it calmed enough we could see through it, but not clearly. Half the time we were out there, we were sailing up and down parallel to the barrier, trying to see through."

"But you did see through?" Sholeh rested her hand on the young man's arm. She caught her breath, remembering for a moment the lively young son of the captain, so eager for adventures, so proud to be given any task on the ship, and to escort her on that fateful trip to the market.

"We saw land, where there should be open sea." Wyllan frowned down into the cup of warmed spiced wine. He took a deep breath and raised his head to look around the table. "Volcanoes. Still spewing molten rock, spilling it down into the water so it hisses and steams and bubbles. Growing the land. Always moving east. And that wall of hissing blackness moves with it, as the land grows."

"Land ... grows," Sholeh echoed. She had the awful feeling she knew what was happening but didn't want to accept it.

"We sailed all up and down the length, to where the volcanoes and all that fresh, hot land is attached to the northern land, long before it forms the northern horn. And it goes all the way down to the southern horn. Lady ... it's enclosing the sea. Imprisoning the island, maybe?"

"Maybe," she whispered, and Steffyn gripped her hand hard, sharing his strength. "That is how he hopes to take Isle of the Moon. Perhaps. Grow land all around it. Pour more land in, until the water flows out? Until the sea holders are forced up into the air, and they must transform back to women, or die? Until all our protections are useless, because Tylanok will possess the land and there is no shore to defend."

"We will find a way," Steffyn promised her. "This is why you were sent to find the guardians. The Kreefa will battle Tylanok. I swear it."

"We have to get there, first," Wyllan said. He visibly fought to wipe the sour expression off his face. "I promise, Lady Sholeh, my men and I will go back with every moon to watch the growth of the wall, the growth of the land. Someday, that magic will fail and we will be able to get through. We will not fail you. We will not fail our home."

~~~~~

Garyon made the proposal that the Kreefa go north. While he had been hunting the stories of the man-wolves who created more man-wolves with a bite, he had heard more stories of a land-bridge that went west and connected with another continent. Most people laughed at the story, because they were so sure the world ended only a short distance beyond the horizon. Taking into consideration the fear of going into the mountains and the prohibition imposed by prophecy, he proposed going as far west as they could go, until they reached the coast. The mountains were said to end before they reached the coast. He proposed traveling up the coast to where the land curved west and find the land-bridge. They would have to go through territory held by Tylanok, but how could he be expecting them to go through land he had already conquered?

Many warriors liked his plan for its audacity and unpredictability. They insisted on spending the winter in preparation for the journey. The Elders were divided, unsure if they could trust mere stories to ensure they would not disobey prophecy to head north. What would they do if they got to the coast and the mountains went down into the water, so no matter where they went they could not avoid breaking that one prohibition?
~~~~~

Sholeh didn't concern herself with the constant arguing all through the fall and winter. She was glad when the preparations took most of the men out of the household for days at a time. They were consumed with meetings, conferring over maps, discussing who would go, and who could be spared from the patrols to protect the households from the imagined threat of Vollen.

She had discovered she was pregnant, shortly after returning from that trip to Gytheion. At first, she had thought she was simply exhausted from the rigors of the trip. Then as her body continued to change, she realized the truth. She and Steffyn kept the joyous news to themselves as long as they could. They were relieved when the winter storms closed in, limiting travel and swathing everyone in bulky clothing. Her scent changed as her pregnancy progressed, but she hid the precious secret from her students with the help of the smells that filled the house. Soon, however, the smells of sweaty men and metal on the forge and tanning leather disagreed with her constantly. She retreated to her rooms as often as she could.

The potions she used to sweeten the air and her slower pace fed rumors that Sholeh was ill. For courtesy, she was left alone for most of a moon, until her friends and students grew concerned. They stormed the household in a large group. Most of Nioba's household and many of the young women Sholeh's age burst into her workroom while she was at her most awkward, struggling to get to her feet, with her belly out, laughing with Steffyn. There could be no denying her state. The word spread up and down the mountainside. Garyon's reaction was the most comical of all. He was infuriated and terrified and ecstatic.

On a quiet spring night, in the dark hour between moonset and the first light of dawn, Sholeh gave birth to her son. Because of his black hair and dark skin and black eyes, Garyon asked them to name the boy Indago, for their missing brother.

As the first rays of dawn touched the household, Sholeh gave birth to her daughter, with white hair and crystalline gray eyes. They named her Ambrys, meaning light.

END

About the Author

On the road to publication, Michelle fell into fandom in college and has 40+ stories in various SF and fantasy universes. She has a bunch of useless degrees in theater, English, film/communication, and writing. Even worse, she has over 100 books and novellas with multiple small presses, in science fiction and fantasy, YA, suspense, women's fiction, and sub-genres of romance.

Her official launch into publishing came with winning first place in the Writers of the Future contest in 1990. She was a finalist in the EPIC Awards competition multiple times, winning with *Lorien* in 2006 and *The Meruk Episodes, I-V,* in 2010, and was a finalist in the Realm Awards competition, in conjunction with the Realm Makers convention.

Her training includes the Institute for Children's Literature; proofreading at an advertising agency; and working at a community newspaper. She is a tea snob and freelance edits for a living (MichelleLevigne@gmail.com for info/rates), but only enough to give her time to write. Her newest crime against the literary world is to be co-managing editor at Mt. Zion Ridge Press and launching the publishing co-op, Ye Olde Dragon Books. Be afraid … be very afraid.

And please check out her newest venture: Ye Olde Dragon's Library, the storytelling podcast. Each week, listeners are invited to join Michelle on her blog to ask questions and give feedback and suggestions. Interspersed between the chapters will be interviews with authors of fantastical fiction. Listen to the podcast on your favorite podcast app or listen on the website: www.YeOldeDragonBooks.com, and click on the Ye Olde Dragon's Library link. Then go to her blog to interact: www.MichelleLevigne.blogspot.com

www.Mlevigne.com
www.MichelleLevigne.blogspot.com
www.YeOldeDragonBooks.com
www.MtZionRidgePress.com

Look for Michelle's Goodreads groups:

Guardians of Neighborlee
Voyages of the AFV Defender

NEWSLETTER:
Want to learn about upcoming books, book launch parties, inside
information, and cover reveals?
Go to Michelle's website or blog to sign up.

Thanks for reading!
If you enjoyed this book, would you help Michelle by posting a
review on Goodreads?

Are you a member of Book Bub? If so, please follow Michelle on Book
Bub, and you'll get alerts when new books are coming out.

As a way of saying thanks, Michelle invites you to the Goodies page
on her website. It will change regularly, offering you a free short story,
a sample audiobook chapter, sneak peeks at new cover art, inside
information on discounts and new release dates, etc.

Please go to: Mlevigne.com/good-stuff.html

Also by Michelle L. Levigne

Guardians of the Time Stream: 4-book Steampunk series
The Match Girls: Humorous inspirational romance series starting with **A**
Match (Not) Made in Heaven
Sarai's Journey: A 2-book biblical fiction series
Tabor Heights: 18-book inspirational small town romance series.
Quarry Hall: 11-book women's fiction/suspense series
For Sale: Wedding Dress. Never Used: inspirational romance
Crooked Creek: Fun Fables About Critters and Kids: Children's short
stories.
Do Yourself a Favor: Tips and Quips on the Writing Life. A book of
writing advice.
To Eternity (and beyond): *Writing Spec Fic Good for Your Soul.* A book
defending speculative fiction.
Killing His Alter-Ego: contemporary romance/suspense, taking place in
fandom.
The Commonwealth Universe: SF series, 25 books and growing
The Hunt: 5-book YA fantasy series

Faxinor: Fantasy series, 4 books and growing
Wildvine: Fantasy series, 14 books when all released
Neighborlee: Humorous fantasy series
Zygradon: 5-book Arthurian fantasy series
AFV Defender: SF adventure series
Young Defenders: Middle Grade SF series, spin-off of *AFV Defender*
Magic to Spare: Fantasy series
Book & Mug Mysteries: cozy mystery series
Quest for the Crescent Moon: fantasy series
Steward's World: fantasy series reboot and expansion
The Enchanted Castle Archives: fantasy series